THE
ORION
PROTOCOL

THE
ORION
PROTOCOL

GARY TIGERMAN

WILLIAM MORROW

An Imprint of HarperCollins*Publishers*

HarperCollins books may be purchased for educational, business, or sales promotional use. For information please write: Special Markets Department, HarperCollins Publishers Inc., 10 East 53rd Street, New York, NY 10022.

FIRST EDITION

Designed by MMDesign 2000, Inc.

Printed on acid-free paper

Library of Congress Cataloging-in-Publication Data
Tigerman, Gary.
    The Orion Protocol / Gary Tigerman.— 1st ed.
      p. cm.
    ISBN 0-380-97670-6
    1. Life on other planets—Fiction. 2. Official secrets—Fiction.
    3. Mars (Planet)—Fiction. 4. Journalists—Fiction. I. Title.
PS3620.I48O7 2003
813'.6—dc21   2002044888

03   04   05   06   07   WBC/RRD   10   9   8   7   6   5   4   3   2   1

To my wife, Wendy, and our son, Gabe

ACKNOWLEDGMENTS

For unflagging perseverance, support, and invaluable "notes": Richard Dreyfuss, Judith James, Carl Borack, Greg Szimonisz, and Laurence Rosenthal. For editorial wisdom and heavy lifting: Michael Shohl, Jennifer Sawyer Fisher, and Stephen Power, with help from Kaitlin Blasdell and Krista Stroever. For ongoing guidance, stewardship, and advocacy: Matt Bialer and Cheryl Capitani at Trident Media Group. And for their timely encouragement and reality checks: Rebecca Bonar, Harley Jane Kozack, Jill Wright, and Julie Cobb. Special thanks to Christina Simelaro, Charlotte Cohen, and Leonard Cohen.

I would also like to acknowledge the late Brandon Tartikoff, without whose early enthusiasm this book is unlikely to have been written. And my father, Captain Orville G. Tigerman, an aviator with his own measure of the Right Stuff, whose passing reminded me that there is *world* enough, but not that much time.

THE
ORION
PROTOCOL

PROLOGUE

1973/Lunar Receiving Lab/Houston

The huge, thwopping Navy helicopter set down like a prehistoric bird and disgorged the astronauts onto the pad at the Lunar Receiving Lab in Houston, Texas. Shuffling toward the NASA research hospital in their bulky BIGs (Biological Isolation Garments), the returning Young Gods of Space passed network cameras and a roped-off press pool that applauded them every step of the way.

"Welcome back, gentlemen! Congratulations!"

"Commander Deaver! What was it like on the Moon?"

Hustled inside by escorting Marine guards and Navy nurses, they could only give a big thumbs-up and grinned telegenically before disappearing from media view.

Once inside the lab and proceeding through the hyperclean corridors, Commander Jake Deaver and Colonel Augie Blake joked with the personnel bunched up in doorways and affected game swaggers, unconsciously competing in the effort to disguise any signs of strain from their 600,000-mile round-trip to the Moon.

"Colonel Blake! Whoo-ya! Some landing up there!"

"Piece o' cake."

"Can o' corn."

Sleepless for much of the ten-day voyage, the two-man crew of *Apollo 18* had splashed down in the Caribbean only hours before under marginal conditions requiring a retrieval/rescue in twelve-foot seas. Millions had watched the event *live,* holding their collective breaths as the helo from the USS *Hornet* labored to extract them from their bobbing and rolling spacecraft and then set them down safely on the carrier deck. But the odyssey wasn't over yet.

"Colonel Blake! You guys get wet out there or what!?"

"Hell, we're all ninety-eight percent water. At least the Commander is."

"Hoo-ya!"

Raucous cheers combined with sheer exhaustion-adrenaline buoyed them now as Jake Deaver and Augustus "Augie" Blake were led directly toward the quarantine unit.

"Augie-Doggie! You gonna let a Texas girl buy you a drink?"

"Later, darlin'. Gotta go kill us some cooties."

They banged through rubber-sealed double doors marked QUARAN-TINE and then stopped, standing patiently still as the antiviral team descended on them, ending their all-too-brief victory lap.

Protected by otherworldly clean-suits, the NASA doctors unceremoniously stripped off the bio-iso garments that had been delivered to Jake and Augie by rescue swimmers, and prepared the two men for decontamination. While everything from boots to underwear was being shucked, bagged, tagged, sealed up, and taken away to be analyzed and ultimately burned, Augie offered a deadpan running commentary.

"Ladies and gentlemen, I'd like to apologize in advance for how plain ungodly awful the Commander here smells right now."

Deaver acknowledged the team's laughter without looking at his pilot.

"In my own defense, I can only say that any urine-sample *je ne sais quoi* is probably left over from the Colonel's dead-stick landing and the rest is just honest American sweat."

Tested, poked, punctured, and prodded, none of it fazed them. They'd long since become inured to standing nude in a roomful of scientists of every gender.

But the next part was no joke. Sequestration in the "delousing" chamber, an ordeal involving radiation baths and noxious chemical scrubs, amounted to mankind's last line of defense against any friendly lunar microbes that might have hitchhiked their way back to Earth with the *Apollo 18* crew. Not a subject discussed much by NASA, any extraterrestrial virus had the potential to run through the human population like a massive biological terrorist attack. By comparison, the nineteenth-century ethnic cleansing atrocity that wiped out the Cherokee in Oklahoma (courtesy of smallpox-contaminated Army blankets) would rank as a bad flu season on the scale of human suffering. Classified worst-case scenarios involving alien pathogens projected millions to tens of millions dead or dying before medical science would have time to develop an effective response.

However, at the height of the Cold War and the Space Race, potentially catastrophic biohazards had been weighed against the unthinkable prospect of getting beaten to the Moon by the Soviets and judged an acceptable risk. Still, precautions had to be taken.

So, Jake and Augie's lean fit bodies were aggressively irradiated, purged, and punished to a degree commensurate with terminal cancer treatment until cautiously declared bug-free.

The buck-naked Buck Rogers were then zipped into sterilized jumpsuits fashioned like feetie pajamas and taken by another Marine escort to an unmarked white door with a stainless steel handle and a lock on the outside.

Taking up sentry positions, the surgically masked Marine corporals delivered crisp salutes and stood at ease, their hands sweating inside sterile latex gloves. Deaver and Blake looked at each other, returned the salutes and stepped inside the room.

What was said behind those closed doors at the Lunar Receiving Lab in Houston in 1973 would not be divulged in NASA-sanctioned media interviews or mentioned in any astronaut biographies, authorized or otherwise. The classified, psych-med debriefing notes of the Navy psychiatrist in attendance would remain an Official State Secret well into the twenty-first century.

▼

Within days of *Apollo 18*'s return, NASA and the U.S. government would cancel the remaining missions of the Apollo program, citing budget concerns and lack of public interest. In addition, it was announced that ambitious plans for sending American astronauts to Mars by 1984 would also be scrapped.

Thus the wonder and triumph of mankind's boots-on-the-ground exploration of the solar system began and ended with the Apollo program.

And no human being has ventured more than a few hundred miles from home ever since.

PART

I

I dreamt that I was walking with my
left side folded-over. *And I knew somehow that if I could*
just unfold it, *I would then be whole and complete*
and my destiny could be fulfilled.

—Descartes

1

January 27/Oval Office/the White House

"Two months ago, if anybody had said we were gonna catch this in the first hundred days, I'd have thought they were high."

The fifty-eight-year-old former senator from Colorado and newly elected President of the United States stared out the much-photographed bay window of the Oval Office and into the cut-back winter Rose Garden.

"What was it Truman said?"

On the desktop, the blade end of his letter opener, engraved with the presidential seal, tapped out a rhythmic figure from the *William Tell* Overture known to Americans who came of age in front of three black-and-white channels of network TV as the theme from *The Lone Ranger*.

"Truman, sir?"

From a clubby wing chair, R. Cabot "Bob" Winston, the President's national security adviser, recognized the galloping little perididdle and made a private note to include it in his memoirs: one of those little human details people liked to read about from a historic moment.

"When they told him about Fat Boy." The President clanked the blade into a decorated soup can/pencil holder his youngest daughter once made him for Father's Day. "Damn it, I know this."

"Ah, January of forty-five. In this room." Winston sat up minutely straighter, unconsciously signaling the sense of occasion he felt when past presidents were invoked within these walls.

The new President rocked in his leather chair.

"With Harriman and his whole sleek Ivy League crowd telling poor Harry-the-Haberdasher he had to nuke the Japanese."

"Or not," Winston said, in a small bow to the Office.

"Oh, I think Einstein's group was the only 'or not.'" The President's dry tone glinted off the darker edge of a sense of humor familiar to his campaign staff. "Jesus, what the hell did he say?"

Winston searched his own mental archives.

A buttoned-down Skull & Bones veteran of executive-branch politics, he had experienced an extraordinary tenure, having served at high levels in the NSA and on the National Security Council in both Bush administrations. His carryover appointment was both an olive branch across the aisle and a gesture of confidence toward Intelligence: a community beleaguered by scandal, Cold War excesses, and spectacular failures, now resurrected and seeking redemption through its mission against global terrorism.

Winston, their point man, produced an answer.

"Yes. Wasn't it, 'How much time do I have?'"

"No, 'How much time do I *get?*'" the President said, in Harry Truman's flat twang, savoring the Midwest inflection. "How much time do I *get?*"

Winston nodded, composed and ramrod straight.

Younger White House staffers had observed that he seemed to wear alertness like a mask, as if some hard-bitten mentor from the halls of spookdom had once cautioned him that blinking one's eyes was a sign of weakness. And, though word was passed down that the President regarded R. Cabot Winston as a symbol of national unity, many still referred to him in-house as "Robo-Bob." It was cruel, but fair.

"Well, I guess that's my question, too, Bob."

"We're a few days out from final testing, sir."

"Days." The President's surprise was eloquent enough.

Winston offered a thin-lipped smile. "With a caveat which I will explain."

As if triggering a pair of explosive bolts, the national security adviser loudly snapped open the bombproof briefcase handcuffed to his left wrist. He then produced a file stamped PROJECT ORION/POTUS/EYES

ONLY and laid it flat on the Oval Office desk. POTUS used reading glasses to inspect it as Winston explained.

"This is the executive order authorizing continuing funding of space shield research and testing. The record enclosed represents decades of development and half a trillion dollars invested, give or take, each phase of publicly funded R & D supplemented with discretionary monies by presidential EO. The line for your initials has been flagged."

Noting all the previous presidents' initials displayed in succession, the new Commander in Chief handled the documents like rare historical artifacts prepared for display at the Smithsonian. But he'd have bet his campaign debt that *this* record would never see the light of day.

"I guess Star Wars didn't just fade away when the Wall came down," he said, leafing through the pages.

"Fortunately not, sir."

Classified above top secret, the file in the President's hands charted the progress of Project Orion from its Cold War roots as part of Reagan's Strategic Defense Initiative, a.k.a. Star Wars, to its post-911 incarnation as a space-based laser weapons system adroitly repositioned as a shield against rogue terrorist ICBMs.

"Ups the ante from a few missiles on the ground in Alaska, doesn't it?"

"The photon laser leapfrogs all other missile defense technology, sir."

The President nodded, his apprehensions intact: space-based weapons more than violated America's post-ABM strategic defense agreements with Russia. And September 11 no longer provided a free pass for whatever the U.S. wanted in the name of national security.

"So, what's the damned caveat, Bob?"

Winston presented the facts unadorned, like a nice neat hanging.

"There's a hard window for deployment, sir. We have twenty-one days."

"That's ridiculous. We're still looking for the johns around here."

"I understand, sir. But geomechanically, if we don't deploy Orion within three weeks, NASA says we'll have to wait a full year before we can try it again, which would be extremely problematic in terms of realpolitik."

For all the speeches at the UN pledging antiterror solidarity, unilateral deployment of uncodified American superweapons would be like throwing a flash grenade into the 3-D chess game of international relations.

The wariness in the President's demeanor edged toward anger.

"Why wasn't the transition team brought up to speed on this two months ago?"

"Need-to-know, sir," Winston recited the intelligence mantra. "New staff have not been vetted above top secret yet. And frankly, proof of design data was not as hard as it needed to be."

"Christ." The President scowled, brooding behind the desk built for FDR.

Winston squirmed almost imperceptibly before launching into the sell.

"Mr. President, it is not the ideal circumstance. But I'm not exactly the Lone Ranger on this. Langley, Defense Intelligence, the Joint Chiefs, the FBI, key flag officers and National Security Council members, the feeling is very much across-the-board that we *need* this. And in any case, I'm afraid keeping our progress on Orion under wraps for another twelve months is less than realistic."

The President indicated the Orion file.

"Hell, it's been under wraps for thirty years . . ."

"True enough, sir, but at this point, with major visible assets necessarily in place and so many partners, secrecy is extremely problematic. However, looking at Russia vis-à-vis NATO, plus the new oil and security agreements, *now* is probably the best possible opportunity—"

"So, use it or lose it." The President said, not sounding happy about it. Up on his feet now, he began prowling the blue carpet emblazoned with the same seal engraved on his letter opener. "Fuck the EU and Moscow and Beijing and Congress, too. Field it now and finesse it later. Is that what you're saying?"

Winston's unbullied cool reflected his experience on the receiving end of presidential wrath.

"Mr. President, all we're saying is carpe diem. Place U.S. security interests foremost. The world acknowledges our legitimate right to self-defense and our motives are transparent, whatever diplomatic challenge that may present. I don't mean to underestimate whatever State's objections may be."

"Oh, you can be sure Secretary Wyman will object. You'll be able to hear her objections in Maryland and Virginia."

Beth Wyman, the forty-five-year-old former California senator and newly minted Secretary of State, had been a formidable candidate during the presidential primaries and a vocal campaigner against the militarization of space. Her decision to withdraw from the race and throw her support, along with California's huge cache of electoral votes, to the party's ultimate nominee had been shrewdly timed. And assurances about the President's go-slow position on national missile defense, not to mention the cabinet spot, had been hers for the asking.

"I have every confidence in the Secretary's ability, sir."

The President saw how Winston's formal body language had an almost Boy Scout quality that was not an affectation. He noticed this along with the messenger-killing anger he could hear in his own voice, and consciously dialed it back a few clicks.

"Shit," he said, stretching his long torso and adopting a more confiding tone. "Just tell me, Bob. Is this thing going to work?"

Winston relaxed a fraction.

"Yes, sir. I also believe that deployment of the space shield could become the most enduring legacy of your presidency."

If the Commander in Chief thought it a little early in his administration to be invoking the L-word, Winston ignored any hint that he might be presuming.

"Project Orion is an American technology triumph, sir. In one stroke, we can assure that America remains the strongest nation on Earth and the guarantor of world peace for the rest of the twenty-first century. It will be a defining achievement in leadership. People will start to feel safe again. And if we can successfully bring the developed world together under America's enhanced security umbrella these first four years, sir, I'm absolutely confident the second four years will take care of itself."

The President thought it was a nice, if hyperbolic, little speech. Although Winston had said "America" three times in one paragraph.

Feeling his morning appointments boxcarring in the outer office, he suppressed a bleak rebuttal concerning the flip side of Winston's rosy scenario. Such bold, unilateral defense posturing could just as easily lead to geopolitical disaster: fueling firestorms of anti-U.S. reaction and international paranoia, inspiring more low-tech terror campaigns against the Great Satan and earning him an ignominious one-term presidency.

Still, doing nothing was not an option.

"All right," he said, initialing the line marked POTUS on the executive order. "I want any and all options vis-à-vis Project Orion preserved during this twenty-one-day window, whatever that entails."

"Yes, sir."

The President could see Winston's natural mental acuity accelerate a few dozen megahertz, as if a pent-up tactical force of available clock speed had been given a call to arms.

"However, I'm authorizing final testing only, within the bounds of our current international agreements." He handed over the signed authority. "Deployment will be taken up separately after we see where we are. And tell the FBI to expedite those staff clearances, for Christ's sake. I need my people."

"Yes, sir." Winston's face stiffened. The President read it as either a stomach cramp or suppressed disappointment. He cut to the chase.

"You knew I wasn't just going to cowboy-up and green-light this thing. That's not what the People are paying me for."

His adviser smiled his patented thin smile, without showing any teeth.

"I knew we had to begin the conversation, sir. I'm sorry that events are giving it more urgency than either of us would have liked."

Slipping the Project Orion file inside the Kevlar-lined case manacled to his wrist, Winston moved with almost mechanical precision. His long-limbed new boss leaned forward, resting his forearms on the desk.

"Bob, I very much appreciated your willingness to stay on board. And I want a diversity of opinions around here, not a bunch of bobbing heads."

"I serve at the pleasure of the President."

Winston pronounced the phrase with all due deference. Yet something seemed vaguely withheld. Something the President did not fail to register before gifting Winston with his most level gaze.

"What I mean to say is, however it worked around here before, this is my watch. And I need to know everything there is to know that might possibly bear on a decision like this. Everything."

The security adviser blinked: he had not anticipated this, not completely. But any emotional reaction he had to being semiblindsided was smoothly submerged. He stood up.

"Mr. President, I'll have a brief on your desk by end of day."

His face, posture, and handshake: each one now presented a crisp and perfectly unreadable blend of corporate and military can-do spirit. Winston then turned smartly on his heel and headed for the Masonic trompe l'oeil door.

▼

In the brief moment alone, before Mrs. Travis, the President's longtime secretary, could leap to the task of getting him back on schedule, the inner radar screen of the most powerful elected leader in the world raised a small intuitive alarum.

He found himself wondering if the carryover appointment of R. Cabot "Bob" Winston might not have been his first presidential mistake.

Then the intercom buzzed and he decided it was too soon to tell.

2

NASA Space Camp/Houston, Texas

"Now I'm gonna need a few volunteers."

Eager hands throughout the bleacher crowd of Space Camp kids shot up in the air as former Apollo 18 astronaut Augie Blake shielded his eyes from the overhead lights and peered out into the auditorium.

"Colonel Blake! Colonel Blake!"

The chorus of young voices called out to him as Augie quit the lectern and ambled down front swinging a shiny Halliburton briefcase. A hundred pairs of arms were straining to be chosen by the time he set the metal case down on a folding table and opened it up.

"Senior Director of Astronaut Recruitment and Training" is what it said on his NASA business card, but some days he felt like just another full-of-shit military-industrial lobbyist trading on past triumphs to hustle the space program for a living. And some days maybe he was. But not today.

Today, in his tailored NASA jumpsuit and baseball cap, he was Colonel Augie Blake, bona fide American Space Hero and the best living cheerleader for human exploration of the solar system on the face of the Earth. Today he was having fun.

"Okay, four people." Augie looked out among the open-faced ten- to twelve-year-olds, quickly choosing two girls and two boys. As the volunteers came up, he shook hands with each one, smiling into their upturned faces as he learned their names and handed each of them an object extracted from his foam-padded aluminum case.

"Tasha, Stacy, Erik, and Josh are going to bring around four different samples. You've probably already guessed what kind of rocks these are . . ."

"Moon rocks!"

A buzz of anticipation circled the room as Augie dispersed his new assistants, who carried the lunar rock samples like they were the Crown Jewels.

"These specimens were brought back from the Moon by Commander Jake Deaver and me in 1973 on the Apollo 18 mission."

He watched the wonder in their faces as the kids tentatively reached out to touch the Moon rocks.

"Touching is okay! Go on ahead."

Augie glanced at his watch. This was not the only stop on his itinerary. He had a group of movie execs expecting a VIP tour through the Johnson Space Center. And a rah-rah, closed-door speech after that for NASA employees only, followed by an interview with a gaggle of Chinese journalists at Houston/Hobby about the latest additions to the International Space Station and future science plans involving U.S. astronauts and China's "taiko-nauts." If he was lucky, he'd be heading back to Andrews Air Base and his home in Washington, D.C., by about midnight.

"Okay, now, you notice how worn and smooth these Moon rocks are? Sort of like the rocks you find by a river or by the ocean, right? But river rock is worn smooth by water erosion. Are there any rivers or oceans on the Moon?"

"No!" a volley of voices answered back.

"That's right. So, what else could make them smooth? What about wind erosion? Is there any wind on the Moon?"

"No!"

The space campers shouted it out, responding in unison now.

"Whoa. You guys know your stuff, don't you? So, no air, no atmosphere, no wind. In fact, you see that picture back there?" He turned and pointed upstage.

On a screen behind him, a famous photo had been projected showing Colonel Augie Blake and Commander Jake Deaver standing proudly on the lunar surface, with an American flag between them and a tiny blue image of Earth reflected in each of their shiny gold visors.

"See how that flag is sticking out, like a breeze is blowing it? Well, we had a real problem with a little folding aluminum-bar dealie that was supposed to hold the top part up. I mean, just getting that dumb flag to work was one pain in the butt, let me tell you."

Augie got the cheap laugh he expected: "He said *butt!*"

"However, what makes these rocks smooth is something called cosmic rain. Tiny little grains of dust called micrometeorites are constantly raining down on the Moon from space at thousands of miles an hour, and this cosmic rain slowly wears down all the hills and rocks until everything is smooth as beach glass. All right, let's give a hand to our volunteers."

Collecting the rocks as the kids applauded, Augie could feel that they were more at ease with him, more comfortable with the larger-than-life face in front of them, which they had recognized from video documentaries here at camp and from history books at school.

He was familiar with people's initial awkwardness around him. It was part of the mixed bag of being an American space hero: respect, celebration, opportunity, and social access, excruciatingly wrapped-to-go with painful public scrutiny, inhumanly high expectations, and fierce collegial jealousies, all finally amplifying an already larger-than-life into a rock and roll of alcoholism, substance abuse, and divorce.

Wholesome now, even inspiring in the spotlight on this Space Camp stage, Colonel Augie Blake, the Last Man to Walk on the Moon, had been no exception. Lurching through his own fifteen-rounds-with-fame hell and its suburbs, he had survived; single, sober, and more often than not glad to be alive.

Out of the corner of his eye, he saw his blue-blazered NASA driver giving him the ten-minute high sign from the nearest exit. He grinned noncommittally and turned back to his audience.

"Now, I did promise your counselors not to keep y'all too long."

"No! No!"

The room erupted, shouting him down with a fired-up dose of unalloyed energy and enthusiasm which Augie thought of as his reward for every other Space Agency dog-and-pony show he had to slog through. And he was in no hurry for it to be over.

"Okay, two more questions. What's your name?"

He pointed at a tall twelve-year-old girl with braces on her teeth and a NASA-logo'd T-shirt.

"Melissa."

"Go ahead, Melissa."

"Um, Colonel Blake, I was wondering. Are we really going to send astronauts to Mars, and if we are, how soon?"

"Great question. Yes, about the time you hit grad school we should be interviewing for the first Mars mission. In fact, we have an astronaut training facility at the South Pole because the environment in the Antarctic is the closest thing on Earth to what it's like on Mars. Would you go to Mars, Melissa?"

"Yes!" she said, blushing at her own intensity of feeling.

"All right! Anybody else want to go?"

Everybody, counselors included, raised their arms and cheered.

"Well, I guess we won't be short on candidates. One more question." Augie nodded to a stocky twelve-year-old boy showing a downy hint of what would soon enough become a mustache. "Yes, go ahead. What's your name?"

"Fernando."

"Yes, Fernando."

"I just wanted to know uh, since you were on the Moon and every-thing, did you see any, like, UFOs or anything up there?"

Fernando sat down amid a wave of giggles, some of the space campers rolling their eyes as if it was so not cool. But Augie maintained eye con-tact with the boy and handled it as a straightforward question.

"Well, Fernando, I have to say no, I didn't see any extraterrestrials on the Moon. I wish I had."

There was a light laugh as Augie then addressed the larger group.

"That doesn't mean we might not have space-faring neighbors some-where out there. Maybe some that are much older and far more techno-logically developed than we are. In fact, the odds are looking pretty good that we are not alone in space."

Augie heard the hush of their curiosity, both about what he was say-ing and at the sense of gravity with which he was saying it.

"Think about it this way. Thanks to the Hubble Telescope, among other instruments, we now know there are sunlike stars throughout the Milky Way galaxy where we live. And across the universe there are bil-lions of galaxies each filled with billions of stars. Now, if only one out of a million stars had planets like Earth, and only one out of every million of those Earth-like planets had intelligent life, that would still mean there are thousands of planets out there populated by intelligent beings like ourselves, just waiting to be known."

The Apollo alumnus paused to let that sink in and then continued.

"The fact of this presents us, as a species, with a tremendous chal-lenge. First, exploring our own neighborhood, our own solar system; taking up the search for life in whatever form we may find it on the other worlds nearest to Earth. And then, using everything we have learned from traveling in space and surviving in inhospitable places like the Moon and Mars, taking that knowledge and going further. Because ultimately, I think we as human beings have an even greater destiny to fulfill. I believe it's our magnificent destiny that we take our place among all the other intelligent species in the universe which God has created. To know and to be known. 'To add our light to the sum of light.' And to do that, we must reach for the stars."

Augie was interrupted by applause, but he raised a hand for quiet.

"This is going to be a long journey, over many generations; some-thing that is going to take time. Now I'd like everybody to please stand up and take a good look around you."

Waiting as they all stood up and looked self-consciously around, he could see their embarrassment at having the attention shifted to themselves.

"Do you know what I see when I look around this room? I'm seeing the astronomers, the pilots, the principal investigators, the engineers, the planetary geologists and biologists; the young men and women who will make up the space science teams of the first half of the twenty-first century."

The kids couldn't help but squirm, giggle a little, and whisper to one another. But Augie knew they were taking this to heart. The legendary Colonel Augie Blake was calling on them, asking them to join him in something big and exciting, something with unquestionable greatness to it.

"*You* are the generation who will make possible mankind's next giant leaps in an era that will be known as the true Golden Age of Space Exploration. *You* are the ones who will lead manned missions back to the Moon, and on to Mars. Even out to the moons of Jupiter, to Europa and beyond. And I have to say I envy you."

His eyes toured the pin-drop-silent room like the slow sweep of a lighthouse beam.

"Yes, I envy you. Mercury, Gemini, and Apollo did well, but you will do better. It will be you and those of your generation who will take part in a great adventure full of discoveries that will alter the course of human experience, bring us together, and peacefully change our world in the best way possible, forever."

Augie then stood at attention and gave them a smart salute, as if addressing the first graduating class of some glorious U.S. Space Academy of the future.

"Good luck," he said. "And Godspeed."

It was a wow finish, one that few in the cheering group would soon forget.

Catching Augie's eye, his NASA driver waved emphatically and held up a cell phone. Mouthing something unintelligible, she then charged out the side door.

But as Augie turned and began shaking hands with the camp counselors seated near the podium, a faint shadow crossed his face. Anyone noticing it might have thought he'd aged ten years in an instant and looked suddenly exhausted. It was not fatigue, however, but the effects of an irregular heartbeat, which he'd experienced before and which sometimes left him a little light-headed.

This episode, though, was more than just arrhythmia: he felt a long bad moment of pain shooting down his arms, and a blurring sense of displacement in time. With a kind of amused abstraction, Augie found himself wondering if he was dying.

And then, almost as quickly as it had happened, the worst was over and the pain passed. Swiping at the sheen of sweat now slicking his forehead, Augie took a look around, feeling just a little shaky.

Fuck, he thought, not sure if he'd said it out loud.

He could clearly see where he was: standing in the sun outside the Space Camp assembly building, signing autographs and shaking hands. He just couldn't remember quite how he got there.

Well, I'm not dead. If I was dead I'd be lying down.

Looking down at the plastic ballpoint pen in his hand, Augie noticed the whoosh of the NASA logo as if for the first time, sensing some profound multilevel meaning beyond the overt graphic symbology. It was an odd sensation, mixed with a certain overall self-consciousness that was rather curious.

But in spite of everything, he somehow seemed to be carrying on, interacting in a normal fashion with everyone around him.

"Hey! What's up? What's your name, darlin'?"

Augie chatted and joked, and watched himself perform at the same time; listening to his own voice as if it were on automatic pilot, feeling his own smile waxing and waning as he took the children's soft small hands into his own.

Then another unbidden sensation washed through him, like the apex of a wave, taking him to yet another subtle state of being where he could literally see himself from outside his body. Along with a heightened perception of sound, Augie began to experience a luminous color sense, as if everything and everyone around him were somehow lit from within.

But strange as it was, he felt no apprehension or anxiety. Only wonder.

If this *is me,* he thought, seeing himself signing a program, *and* this *is me watching myself, then who is it that's watching me watch myself?*

It's me, he answered his giddy tri-located self. *Out of my fucking mind.*

Then this experience, too, was over. And he was wholly and completely back inside his body, with the winter sun warming his face and a slight tremor in his left hand that hadn't been there before and caused the first stab of real fear.

Stroke?

He imagined his biannual NASA physical and seemed to remember reading that signs of stroke could still be detected months after they occurred. Being forced to retire was his worst nightmare. There was so much he still hadn't done and needed to accomplish.

If they catch it, they'll sit you down, son. But there's nothin' you can do about it. So, just let it go, let it go.

Augie willed his hand to be steady; and it seemed to work. He then found himself looking up into the eyes of a sun-bleached Space Camp mom thrusting a notepad in his direction, a pretty blonde with a trim athletic body and one got-to-be-illegal smile.

"Colonel Blake? Would y'all mind makin' that to Bonnie Jean?"

He recognized the Texas lilt riding Western-style in her voice and thought that smile was like a "Welcome Home" banner strung across his own front door.

"Would that be Houston I hear, ma'am?"

"First-word-heard," she said, beaming with honest pride over the historic first message transmitted from the Moon: "Houston, the Eagle has landed."

"Yes, ma'am, it surely was. Is that Bonnie with an *i-e*?"

And in his jaunty NASA baseball cap and top-gun mirrored shades, Colonel Augie Blake was now every inch his old self, laughing and teasing, taking pleasure in the familiar cadences of a down-home flirt.

With two quick beeps a white GM sedan emblazoned with the NASA logo pulled up to collect him. He waved his good-byes, slipped into the backseat, and was spirited away.

But not to his scheduled rah-rah at Johnson Space.

"Change of plans, Colonel," the driver in the blue blazer said, glancing back over her shoulder and making the turn marked for Putnam Air Force Base.

"McMurdo?"

"An evac crew's going in tonight, sir. Langley's got equipment at Putnam Field deadheading to San Pedro. They're holding it for you."

Augie knew about the deteriorating situation in Antarctica: he had astronaut candidates down there on Extreme Environment Training.

"Pass me that thing, would you, darlin'?" He indicated the cell phone lying on the front seat.

Dialing the area code for Washington, D.C., Augie found himself imagining all the ways that things could be going seriously south at the

Pole and felt an odd sense of release. Though concerned for his people down on the ice, if he had to choose between glad-handing journalists or jumping into a full-blown operational crisis, he'd take the crisis. It made him feel more alive.

"Where are we?" he said to whoever answered the phone, and then listened without comment. "Hell, yes. Tell them I'm filling my pockets with salt."

Augie hung up and stared straight ahead as the NASA driver gave him a puzzled look and then put the hammer down for Putnam Field.

She didn't know what the hell he meant about salt and wasn't about to ask. But in the rearview mirror she noticed that Colonel Blake seemed younger than he had been only minutes before: his head held slightly higher, his eyes clear and steady with what seemed an effortless and irreducible self-confidence. An echo of the Right Stuff.

3

Once through the Oval Office door and the President's busy anteroom, the national security adviser had headed directly for the antiquated White House cage elevator, his face as blank as a fresh plaster cast.

"Shit," Winston said, under his breath.

Beneath the impervious self-possession, he was upset. Not so much with the decision-making style of the new Occupant of the Oval Office, irritating as it was. No, what was bothering him was the President's subtly reproachful tone, especially when he had insisted on knowing "everything that might bear on this decision." He punched at the elevator button three or four times.

"Everything . . ."

Of course POTUS had been implying that the NSA, CIA, FBI, the Defense Intelligence Agency, and national security advisers like Winston might presume to keep some categories of "sensitive" information under wraps despite requests from their Commander in Chief. Which, historically, they had done and did do: it was practically part of the job description.

"Christ." Winston gave up on the balky elevator and took the stairs down to the parking garage.

Customarily, nothing stamped ABOVE TOP SECRET was ever divulged, even to the President of the United States, except on the strictest need-to-know basis. This policy had evolved for many reasons, chief among them to protect the republic and the office of the President by preserving the President's crucially important ability to credibly lie about what was known by his government and when it was known. And if a man doesn't know he's lying, he's more likely to be convincing.

Withholding information, cynical as it might seem, was also a prophylactic against the plain fact that some politicians were better public liars than others. At the highest levels of government, deniability was more than a term of art. The strategic preservation of one's own ignorance and/or the ignorance of superiors had become a basic survival skill. But it required at least tacit cooperation.

What is the correct course of action when faithfully executing a presidential order is a certain prescription for disaster?

Clanging down the interior metal stairs to the White House parking level, Winston imagined himself retired to an emeritus professorship, lecturing about his current dilemma to government students at Yale. Fact was, there were some things about defending the republic, not to mention political survival, that you could only learn by doing.

Once through the parking-level doors, he flashed his White House pass at a young white-gloved Marine who had already recognized him and began calling for his car.

As he waited, Winston became concerned that perhaps he was being maneuvered into an untenable position on purpose: if the new President was at all naive, his staffers certainly were not.

So, what the fuck is really going on, then?

Breathing the claustrophobic monoxide-heavy air of the underground garage, he tried to step back and see the big picture.

What was the President playing at? A realignment of executive-branch power? A hidden agenda he wasn't picking up on? Some kind of loyalty litmus? Or was this just yet another professional challenge in the finessing of conflicting vital interests in the environment of White House intrigue?

Winston wondered for a moment if this particular Occupant was simply oblivious to how conflicting interests between the intel community and the Office of the President were supposed to be handled.

No, no. It's a test, he decided. The partisans on the White House senior staff who had opposed Winston's carryover appointment would be looking to seize on any arguable failure and use it against him.

He mentally addressed his imaginary students again.

The question then is: Where does your duty lie if your Commander in

*Chief demands access to highly classified information, the undeniable
knowledge of which might well cripple his presidency and by extension the
republic you are sworn to defend? And is the answer different in time of
war than in a time of peace?*

At the moment, though, these were not academic questions. Whatever action he took, if Winston was perceived as withholding crucial
information from the President, the knives would certainly come out.
The hypocrisy was galling, of course, but politics ain't beanbag:
divulging *everything* about an above-top-secret project like Orion to a
new Occupant who barely had his legs yet would be almost a dereliction
of duty.

"Shit," he said, in a laconic voice loud enough to echo off the underground concrete pillars.

Then his sober black Lincoln LS was being brought up, the Marine
driver leaping out and holding the door open in one smooth athletic
move. Winston nodded, sliding in behind the leather-wrapped steering
wheel as the driver's-side door was shut with a vaultlike thud, the sound
of Ford Motors closing some ground on the Bavarians.

Using a handcuff key, he detached the hardened briefcase from his
wrist and locked the doors. Weathering the political wind shear he was
flying into would require pitch-perfect finesse and a Teflon vest.

With the President's directive to tell him everything relevant to the
decision about Project Orion cycling through his mind, Winston
strained to detect the smallest hint of linguistic wiggle room, but without success.

"Shit, shit, and shit."

This was a problem. He slid the brushed-aluminum gear selector into
drive and headed up to the guardhouse exit and Pennsylvania Avenue.

This was a serious problem.

4

January 28/PBS Studios/Washington, D.C.

Ensconced in a video editing suite at the Public Broadcasting building just off K Street, Angela Browning and veteran producer Miriam Kresky were busy cutting promos, eleven hours into yet another deadline-driven fourteen-hour day.

Angela, at thirty-five and very much at the top of her game, didn't think of herself as laboring on someone else's clock. As science reporter, on-camera host, and cocreator of PBS's Emmy Award–winning series *Science Horizon,* her work had pretty much become her life.

On a Trinitron monitor, a video sequence showing an iceberg the size of Rhode Island breaking off the Ross Ice Shelf in Antarctica was being played back on an Avid digital editing system. Timing the assembled edits, Angela snicked a chrome mechanical stopwatch and showed it to Miriam.

"Works for me."

"With bumpers and ten seconds for the affiliates . . ."

"Let's cut this puppy."

Miriam took over on the Avid keyboard. Angela stood up out of an off-black Herman Miller chair and shook out her tensed-up hands and fingers, cracking her neck vertebrae with chiropractic precision.

"Coffee?"

"Oh, yeah."

Among the media-savvy in Washington D.C., or "Hollywood for Ugly

People," as James Carville liked to call it, Angela Browning was a beauty, though probably only a "pretty brunette" by Left Coast standards.

BOSTON DEB WEDS WALL STREET HEIR might have been her fate had it not been for an eclectic array of high school passions: writing, acting, filmmaking, and, curiously, astronomy and physics. Armed with stellar SATs and a vivid aversion to social clichés, Angela had eschewed Cornell and Columbia for a neobohemian Vassar education. And that road less traveled had made all the difference.

▼

As the Krups machine in the tiny studio kitchen hissed itself awake, she shuffled over to her office, where a slumping mountain of letters and packages lay dumped on her desk.

"Oh, God."

All the mail in the Capitol was routinely sanitized by Titan electron beam machines, and at her mother's insistence, Angela still kept a Cipro prescription in her bag at all times. But fear of terrorist biotoxins was not the issue. She eyed the avalanche of snail mail: a critical mass had been achieved.

"Well, hell, Bullwinkle."

Adjusting the posture of the Beanie Bullwinkle doll propped atop her computer, she separated out two things immediately: a baby shower announcement that made her wonder if she was wasting her life for about 2.5 seconds until she opened the second letter, an invitation to a party at the former vice-presidential mansion to celebrate International Space Station Alpha.

"Whoa! Big bash at the Blair House . . ."

The minor perk of minicelebrity made her feel instantly better.

Working her way through the stacks, she came to a manila envelope with "ATT: Ms. Angela Browning" neatly typed on a white address label but no return address. The otherwise plain envelope had already been opened and inspected in the mail room.

Angela consulted her moose.

"Fan mail from some flounder?"

Inside she found one item: a CD-ROM in a clear plastic jewel case.

"Curiouser and curiouser . . ."

Held to the light, the unlabeled disk offered up nothing more than semipsychedelic rainbows refracting off its laser-etched grooves.

"Muy mysterioso."

The smell of dark-roast coffee began wafting its way to her work station, promising a second wind, but Angela ignored it. Loading in the CD, she let Norton Utilities scan for virus encounters of the digital kind until a single icon appeared labeled TOLAS.

The TOLAS file opened to reveal a high-res satellite image of the Cydonia region on Mars and its most infamous anomaly, the leonine-humanoid "Face."

"Oh, God." Angela rolled her eyes, but her attention was immediately drawn to a cluster of faceted objects near the Face: several four-sided and five-sided geometric shapes rising up out of the frozen Martian plain, monumental artifacts that looked for all the world like Egyptian pyramids.

"Aha." She grinned and shook the hair back out of her face, pretty sure where this had come from. "Those Goddard boys and their high-tech toys."

Angela keyed the speed dial on her phone.

"Hell-o, Goddard Flight. Richard Eklund, please. Thanks."

While on hold, she searched her e-mail for new messages about this from Goddard Space Flight Labs or from NASA researcher Richard Eklund but found nothing.

Angela had first met Eklund while prepping a *Science Horizon* show on NASA's late-'90's faster-smarter-cheaper robotic Mars program. Eccentric, brilliant, a confirmed workaholic, Eklund had quickly become her compass in navigating the labyrinth of Space Agency politics as well as an all-around go-to guy on all things Martian.

"Richard? Angela Browning. Are you guys smoking the drapes over there, or what?" She tried not to giggle, but not hard enough to succeed at it. "I mean the Mars CD." Angela glanced up at the pyramids on her screen. "The one with Little Egypt on it. Nudge-nudge, wink-wink?"

On the other end, Eklund sounded puzzled, but Angela wasn't buying.

"Come on, CGI Boy. Confession is good for the soul. I'm not saying it doesn't look good. It's too good! What? Nope, no note, nothing."

She reinspected the envelope to be sure and looked around in vain to see if something had fallen out on the floor.

"No note, no return address, *nada*. Just a file labeled TOLAS with a high-res photo of Cydonia, including some pretty kick-ass pyramids . . . yes, T-O-L-A-S."

She heard the NASA scientist laughing as he explained the acronym. Angela didn't think it was as funny as all that.

"Oh, Tricks of Light and Shadow. Great . . . so it's probably some geeksters at MIT or something, firing up a fatty and having too much fun."

She glared at the pyramids in the beautifully rendered Marscape, no doubt the beneficiary of state-of-the-art computer graphics. Eklund invited her to bring the disk out to Goddard Labs so they could check it out.

"Oh, I don't know." Angela glanced at her watch. "If I'm done before midnight. Leave me a pass, anyway, okay? Thanks."

▼

"Hokey smokes, Bullwinkle." Angela hung up the phone, studied the Pyramids-on-Mars for a long moment, then shut down her computer. She squeezed her Beanie moose doll and tucked the mystery CD into an overstuffed shoulder bag her chiropractor had warned her about. She then followed the coffee smell to the kitchen.

But the Mars photo still nagged at her.

So, if it's not from Goddard Space, then who sent it?

Angela thought about people she'd worked with, those who had access to sophisticated computer graphics hardware: cameramen, other producers, political consultants, people at video production houses. Mostly they just edited news stories or created campaign ads. Nothing like this.

No, no, it's just a sophomore prank.

"Beware of geeks bearing gifts." In the cramped office kitchen space Angela laughed, pulling together a tray and a pair of mugs. But pouring out two black coffees, she couldn't help feeling a little creeped out. It was not like she was being *stalked*, exactly. Or like she was in any personal danger. Still, it was weird.

TOLAS. Tricks of Light and Shadow.

Like it or not, her curious/critical mind, the reporter part of herself, had become fully engaged. And she knew she couldn't let it go until she had tracked down whatever she could about the who, what, where, when, and why behind this unsolicited disk. Sometimes being the relentless Angela Browning was no picnic.

Oh, God, you're not really going to drag your tired Vassar-girl ass all the way out to Goddard tonight? You're insane.

Balancing her tray, Angela slipped back into the editing bay, and set the coffees on the console.

"It's hot. You ready?"

"God bless you." Miriam moaned, rolled back from the keyboard, and doctored her cup with pink sweetener. "You got voice-over copy?"

Angela took out her notes. Without looking at the spectacular Antarctic glacier collapsing in freeze-frame on the Avid, she palmed her stopwatch and timed herself as she read.

" 'The Greenhouse Paradox: Is Global Warming Triggering a New Ice Age? Sunday, on *Science Horizon*.' 9.5 seconds."

"Triggering?" Miriam said, tasting her coffee.

Manufacturing? Creating? Leading to? Bringing on?

"Give me a minute."

Angela planted herself back into her high-tech chair. Reworking the copy, she thought about the mystery disk in her bag again and was sorry she'd straightened up her damned mail pile. It was going to be an even longer night than she'd imagined.

5

Auckland, New Zealand

On the LC-130 Hercules from San Pedro, California, through a refuel at Auckland, and then on toward McMurdo Station, Colonel Augie Blake had slept like the dead, his inveterate snoring drowned in the thrum of the great cargo plane's Pratt & Whitney engines.

Awake now, he remembered to take salt tabs and downed two with some bottled water from his flight bag.

He'd survived a palpable cardiovascular event back in Houston; he knew that. But Augie consciously pushed it aside, relegating the event and what it might mean to the dank mental storm cellar where most of Augie's personal bad news got stored. Especially things he'd decided he couldn't do that much about, in this lifetime. Of course, there was nothing he could do about this latest bit of bad news, at least not right now. Nothing except think about it.

And all thinking about it would accomplish would be to set him brooding over things like his father dying of heart disease when he was two years younger than Augie was now. So, he had chosen not to think about it.

His married sister, Emily Blake Warren, a veteran nurse-practitioner in D.C., had made that do-the-math point about their father last year when Augie had confessed to mild, recurring dizzy spells. She had lobbied hard at the time for a cardiologist she knew at Bethesda Naval Hospital in Maryland, but Augie balked.

What are they going to do? Fuck with my diet? Tell me to get more exer-

cise and take baby aspirin? Counsel me to retire if I want to live? Tell me
"work-related stress" is the bad actor here and stick that crap in my jacket
for the next review? Forget that noise, Nurse Warren.

Hell, retirement would probably kill me, he thought, gazing out the big
cargo plane's window. Maybe later he'd let his sister privately arrange an
MRI or a full-body CAT scan, or whatever. Then they could see what
was what.

Augie looked down into the preternatural dark at the Antarctic
Ocean, dotted with bergie bits twenty thousand feet below. Somewhere
down there, thanks to accelerating Earth changes, 400 million billion
tons of freshwater ice called the Ross Ice Shelf had just warmed up
enough to shear off from the continent and fall into the world's south-
ernmost sea.

What that might portend for ocean currents that drive the increas-
ingly erratic weather systems on the planet was a problem for supercomputers to model.

But within hours of the Ross collapse, satellite photos had picked up
something previously hidden under all that ice: an unprecedented scientific discovery now involving the National Science Foundation, U.S.
Defense Intelligence, and Special Operations forces.

Code-named "Dunsinane," it appeared to be the site of a prehistoric,
temperate-climate forest, frozen inside a glacier for over ten thousand
years.

A full lid was still down, vis-à-vis the media, because the situation on
the ground had become fluid, dangerous, and complex, and the U.S.
government was still struggling to get a handle on it.

For Augie, though, it was simple: the young men and women he had
handpicked for EET, Extreme Environment Training, at the South
Pole—*his people*—had suddenly been put in harm's way. And he was
coming to get them the hell out.

Leaning his chair back as far as it would go, he stretched his legs, feeling fine if a bit tired. And his prescription for that was simple, too: kick
back, drink bottled water, and sleep.

He pulled his NASA cap down over his eyes.

6

Goddard Space Flight Lab/Washington, D.C.

Entering Goddard Space Flight's waxy fluorescent-lit corridors required the usual security passes, though nothing like the fingerprint and retinal-scan lockdown at the CIA sister lab in Langley, Virginia. Langley fulfilled NASA contracts, too. But it operated in a different culture altogether, "haut spy" culture: a civilian/military hybrid long ago transgendered by the Cold War into something alien, virtually invisible, and much harder to kill.

The Goddard facility, by contrast, was a more freewheeling science-friendly environment and a haven for odd birds like Richard Eklund and his colleagues in the *Mars Underground*, an eclectic and wildly unofficial confederation of hard-core space fanatics "with a whole lot of fucking élan."

Frozen in time architecturally, the Goddard campus preserved the clean, modern design aesthetic of the late 1950's and a relatively businesslike attitude, from nine to five.

After six o'clock, though, once the presence of supervisors and administrators could no longer be keenly felt, the sprawling Space Flight Center transformed itself into a co-ed, quasi-Wozniakian Greek house with the greatest gear on Earth. And for those in the main domain of radically committed spaceheads, Goddard After-Hours was definitely *the shit*.

"Sincerity begins at sixty hours, commitment at one hundred," Eklund and his *Mars Underground* colleague John Fisher liked to say, leading by example. And with its red flag of Mars emblazoned on newsletters, bumper stickers, and buttons, the *Underground* had "cadres" at every NASA facility from Johnson Space in Texas to Cal-Tech and JPL in California.

Membership was earned by sweat equity, and whatever official government projects consumed them by day, the *Mars Underground* passionately invested nights and weekends free/gratis in one thing and one thing only: a manned mission to Mars.

Prohibitive space agency cost estimates running to some $100 billion for such a voyage was the principal obstacle; heavy lifting, a two-year journey, and its attendant cost of fuel being the largest expense.

So, each *Mars Underground*–affiliated scientist or engineer took up the challenge and struggled with his or her piece of the puzzle: plasma/fusion propulsion systems to shorten travel time, solar-powered oxygen-from-water electrolysis, zero-g greenhouses for grow-as-you-go roughage, and dozens more.

Researcher Richard Eklund's contribution to the effort was something called the Intelligence Hypothesis, and it was a cheap enough project to pursue. All it really required was off-peak time on the Goddard mainframe and unfettered access to NASA and JPL archives. And an open mind.

With war-related projects grabbing the big budget dollars and the great Soviet-American space rivalry long dead, the *Underground* knew it desperately needed a catalyst, something that might inspire and galvanize public opinion in favor of a return to the glory days of manned exploration of space.

More satellites finding frozen water that hinted at possible bacterial life were not going to cut it. Neither were more fossilized Martian microbes. They needed something that'd seize people's imagination and never let go, something worth spending tens of billions and risking American lives for.

Something like confirmed evidence of former intelligent life on Mars.

The Intelligence Hypothesis, as a legitimate line of scientific investigation, was, however, frowned on by NASA administrators. They labeled it speculation, and firmly distanced themselves from any such efforts, inside or outside the Space Agency. But from the Viking Mission in the '70's to the more recent *Mars Global Surveyor* and *Mars Odyssey* satellite data, many honest scientists believed there were too many intriguing enigmas on Mars to be dismissed.

Eklund and his colleague, planetary geologist John Fisher, had collected striking images from regions around the planet showing much more than just the controversial Face on Mars: there were monumental four- and five-sided pyramidal mounds, serpentine tubelike objects, even a field of what appeared to be identical-sized triangular monoliths.

And no credible models of natural forces like wind, water, volcanic, tectonic, or meteoritic action could be combined by NASA computers to account for them.

Yet when confronted with such evidence behind closed doors, Space Agency officials consistently demurred, characterizing the unexplainable anomalies as "tricks of light and shadow," too open to subjective interpretation to be of any scientific value.

Undaunted, however, Eklund and Fisher persevered, becoming more and more convinced of what they hoped the Intelligence Hypothesis would ultimately prove: that the fabled Red Planet was littered with artifacts, ancient ruins, and the degraded constructs of a once highly evolved civilization.

Which would be every reason on Earth for mankind to have to go see it and confirm it *in person,* and take the world along for the ride.

"Eat food, drink water."

Eklund dumped an armful of Goddard snack-room munchies onto the table in their workstation. Fisher didn't look up.

"In a sec."

Intent on a strip of *Mars Global Surveyor* imaging, John was lost in digital minutiae that'd blind a lace-making Belgian nun.

On-screen, a black-and-white *MGS* frame brought to their attention by Sir Arthur C. Clarke of *2001: A Space Odyssey* fame appeared to show an astonishing grove of trees over forty feet high and hundreds of meters across. NASA had dismissed it as probably frozen carbon dioxide somehow shaped like trees, perhaps by Mars's un-Earth-like magnetic field. As a geologist, John Fisher considered that a feeble theory at best and wholly unsatisfactory, but his tweaking of the highly organic-looking shapes still wasn't gleaning much.

"If we just had altimeter readings over a cycle of seasons . . ."

"It's on the request list." Eklund sipped tea and worked on a box of raisins.

"Yeah, right."

Given the deep, dark circles in permanent residency under Fisher's eyes, it did not require much to imagine cartoon wisps of smoke curling up from his ears as well. Eklund spoke to the back of his head.

"You've got a granola bar, black tea, and a green apple."

"Almost there."

Eklund generally refrained from clucking over the younger scientist's driven demeanor and grunge-garage personal style. Neither one of them really had a life. Eklund, a suspenders man and collector of vintage bow ties, just dressed more neatly and took a little better care of himself.

The intercom erupted with a piercing high-end crackle.

"Dr. Eklund, Ms. Angela Browning to see you."

"Uh, thanks. Send her on back." Eklund looked at his partner. "John. This is that thing I told you about."

"Fine, fine. I'm toast, anyway."

They could hear Angela's Niketowns squeaking down the hall toward them.

"One decent break. That's all I ask." Fisher hit a key, making the Martian trees disappear, and grabbed up a granola bar.

Eklund opened the door and found Angela already there, looking cheerfully wired and tired.

"What's up?" She grinned at him, hefting her shoulder bag.

"The gods are laughing."

"I wondered what that sound was."

Eklund waved Angela into their boho science confines. "You remember John Fisher?"

"Hey, how's it going?"

"Good . . ." John stood up with his mouth full, managing to appear starstruck, fiercely bright, and pretty much like he'd just vacated a sleeping bag all at the same time. Shaking hands, Angela thought he was actually kind of cute.

"So, whatcha got?" Eklund rolled a desk chair her way.

"You tell me," Angela said, and produced the unsolicited Mars CD.

7

The lights were still burning in the East Wing of the White House, which was not unusual, the burden of the Office having accelerated exponentially in the nation's third century, paralleling that of super-industrial human progress.

Typically scheduled until 11:30 P.M., and then up again at 6:30 A.M. and jogging by 7:00, the fit and youthful twenty-first-century President set a killing pace, even for his junior staff. Some kept up and some were mercifully platooned into two eight-hour shifts, the second shift having already said good night.

In the residential living room, furnished largely with family photographs and a few familiar pieces from back home, the new Commander in Chief had stretched himself out on a comfortably beat-up old eight-foot leather couch and was scowling down at the briefing paper in his left hand.

"Shit," he said, snapping to the next page.

The Seal of the Office blazed in blue and gold on his loose gray sweatshirt, and a pine-log fire hissed and popped off raucously like a miniature Chinese New Year in the brick fireplace, which had been rebuilt by Teddy Roosevelt.

"One page of hard-core hype and three pages of tortured crapola."

Reclining in a club chair a few feet away, White House counsel Sanford "Sandy" Sokoff yawned in agreement. He'd already reviewed the brief prepared by Bob Winston, the national security adviser, and found it an information-free exercise in arcane spy argot and self-important, euphemistic bureaucratese.

"Not exactly what you asked for." Sokoff nodded, recrossing his boots.

Sandy, a legendary campaign manager, arch fixer nonpareil, and self-styled "Texas Jew-boy," stared into the merry fire. His black Tony Lamas, worn partly to buy an extra inch of height, rested cowboy-style on the brass-handled distressed old chest that did duty as the presidential coffee table.

"What about the bullets on page four?" he said.

The President cursed quietly and read aloud, the bad taste in his mouth becoming progressively more audible.

" 'Protecting rapid-response theater communications, cleaning up dangerous space junk, blinding enemy satellites in time of war . . . ' "

"Yeah"—Sandy laughed—"that is quite a steaming pile. There's smarter ways to do all those things without spending a trillion dollars."

"Not to mention shit-canning international arms agreements. If we still give a shit about stuff like that."

"There is that."

"Our friend Bob." The President leveraged his long body up and consigned the briefing paper to the fire. "Maybe I made a mistake there, Sandy."

"Then again, 'if you want a friend in Washington' . . ." Sokoff thumbed a smudge off his butter-soft boots.

"Hell, I've *got* a dog. What I don't get is why the full-court press."

Sandy shrugged. Post-9/11, the traditionally enriching revolving door between Washington, the Pentagon, and the defense/aerospace industry was back, big time, and shielded from cynicism by the enduring national outrage and resolve.

"Maybe Bob is looking beyond public service."

"Maybe this is his idea of public service." The President watched Winston's top-secret briefing paper turn to ash in the fireplace.

Having had a good working view as a senator over the last twelve years, he was not naive about the nature of the executive branch of the U.S. government at the beginning of the twenty-first century. The constitutional pillar of democracy that his presidency was expected to embody was a multilayered labyrinth, with real power spreading far out and down from the Oval Office.

In fact, an extraordinary degree of decision making was done at many levels that, by custom or by covert design, flew beneath the radar of the incumbents at the White House. Over the years, scholars at prestigious private universities had published papers arguing that this quiet erosion of powers once concentrated in the Chief Executive had gotten out of hand.

The Iran-Contra scandal during the Reagan years and other lesser-known foreign-policy contretemps were held up as prime examples. But the status quo rattled on, untroubled by the critics and resistant to reform.

The newly elected President was aware of it and considered it a hydra-headed problem born in the alphabet soup of the U.S. Intelligence community, bad neighbors though they might be, which had enjoyed a steady rise to executive-branch power ever since JFK was murdered or terminated-with-extreme-prejudice, depending on which of the many stories you liked.

In any case, beneath the wings of the Johnson administration, its Great Society good intentions paved over by the Southeast Asian road to hell, civilian and military intel agencies and spy domains of every stripe had proliferated ad nauseam. By the end of what had become Nixon's war, this New Jerusalem of overlapping blood turfs had evolved into a deeply rooted executive-branch stronghold, well positioned to prosper regardless of which political party might be nominally elected to power.

By the time former CIA chief George Herbert Walker Bush ascended to the highest office in the land, some saw it as an almost embarrassing redundancy. Bush's presidency was practically emblematic of spookdom's neohegemony, a bald public enactment of what had been quietly going on behind the scenes for decades. Senior acronymic warriors with noble lineages back to the Secret Service, Sig Int, and the Last Good War may have had misgivings. But the limelight-shy spymasters needn't have worried. Once Bush's elevation was a fait accompli, the American people did not seem all that troubled that spies were now running the White House: they were our spies, weren't they?

However, while the newest Occupant of the Oval Office might have been skeptical about conspiracy theories, he could read a national security briefing paper and know when he was being worked.

"Well, fuck it, Sandy."

"What do you want me to do?" Sokoff sat up and took out a notepad.

"Consider yourself tasked, counselor."

"I figured."

Sandy took notes as the President ticked off a laundry list, neither of them prepared to guess yet what might come out in the wash.

"I want to know how and why Project Orion got started, all the parties involved, and what their interests are. What it really will and won't do. Cost to date in today's dollars, cost of deployment and readiness, and environmental impact. And I need an independent risk assessment that doesn't pull any goddamn punches, if possible."

Sokoff looked down at a list he'd been making.

"So far," he said, "I've got former secretaries of defense, Joint Chiefs, NSA heads, Naval Intelligence, DIA, CIA, and security advisers. But nobody is going to want to talk to me."

"Remind them that conversations with the private counsel of the President of the United States are covered by executive privilege."

"And when they stop laughing?"

The President laughed himself, stretching his arms up into the air, looking like he could almost touch the chandelier picked out by Jacqueline Kennedy and still polished weekly by housekeeping staff.

"If anybody needs face time, call me."

"Mr. President." Sokoff stood up, girding for battle. This was going to be delicate and difficult. He rubbed a freckled earlobe.

"D'you care if it gets back to Robo-Bob?"

"I hope it scares the Yale out of him."

The President relaxed his lanky frame back into the long leather-covered cushions, experiencing the pleasure of releasing himself, however temporarily, from the weight of a heavy burden.

And the equal, if not greater pleasure of seeing it bend the shoulders of a younger man.

8

Fiddling with the Goddard security guest pass clipped onto her jacket pocket, Angela looked over John Fisher's shoulder at the TOLAS Mars photo now loaded onto the mainframe.

The planetary geologist was working with the image, using shape-from-shading algorithms to pull out even more visual detail.

"Whoever did this is good."

Many of the satellite images of the Cydonia region, where the Face on Mars was found, were distorted by camera angles or sun angles or otherwise made useless for research because of low resolution, transmission glitches, or cloud cover. But not this one. This image was absolutely perfect.

"Jesus, every little rill and berm is so pristine. And this came from where?"

"Over the transom," Angela said. "How about the pyramids?"

"Too good. Much too good. We can crack this."

"Ya think?" Angela glanced at Eklund, but his expression was guarded.

"They can run, but they can't hide."

In their obsession with finding supporting data for the Intelligence Hypothesis, Eklund and Fisher routinely pored over every Mars satellite photo as it came in and every frame ever released of the Cydonia region in the NASA archives. But there had never been a capture like this; Eklund was certain it was not something they'd have missed.

"John? Check the mission code on this thing."

"Sure. This is so weird, though, it's like the dream capture of all time."

Angela enjoyed watching Fisher whack and slash at the keyboard. It was like a virtuoso piano recital.

"What's mission code?" she asked, leaning closer toward the screen.

"Each frame dumped from the satellite buffer carries code numbers to ID the origin for archiving."

Fisher enlarged the sequence and then stopped, staring at the monitor.

"Shit," he said.

"Shit what?" Angela stabbed two blunt-cut wings of dark hair behind her ears and out of her face. Eklund read off the code in an oddly official tone.

"F26/OP5/1/394MO."

"Shit diddly." John smacked angrily at the keyboard, enlarging the sequence on-screen. "Well, they knew what they were doing, no question about it. No telltale little insert edges, no outlines. Smart-ass little fucks . . . sorry."

"John's pissed because with all the real anomalies on the planet that we're trying to get taken seriously or at least looked at with an open mind, this kind of thing getting dumped on the media just makes it so much harder . . ."

"But it's a hoax, right?" Angela knew something was going on that she wasn't quite getting. Eklund sidestepped the question.

"Let's just go in on a pyramid until it falls apart."

"Absolutely."

Fisher scrolled up and zoomed in radically until the image broke up, hitting the faceted mounds on Mars with the digital kitchen sink.

"Damn. What we're looking for is evidence of tampering, little soft spots, little giveaways here and there where something on the original image was erased so the pyramid image could then be supered in."

"But it's not cooperating."

"No, ma'am." John fumed, exhausting his bag of tricks. "I'm seeing no apparent degradation, no visible tampering or erasure. Maximum pixel resolution, full gray scale, format is mission-correct. Fuck me."

He rolled back from the keyboard and flicked a sidelong look at

Eklund. Angela saw a world of unspoken information flash between them.

"All right. Will somebody please tell me what the problem is? Or do I have to kill one of you to make the other one talk?"

"Sorry. This is the problem, down here." Eklund scrolled back to the code sequence. "F26/OP5/1/394MO. . . . *F* means 'frame number.' *OP* is 'orbital pass'—"

"Wait, wait, wait." Angela refocused on the screen. "So, this was the twenty-sixth picture, taken on the fifth orbital pass . . ."

"And one-three-ninety-four is the date . . ."

" 'January third, 1994 . . .'"

"And *MO* identifies the mission for archiving: *Viking Orbiter* was *VO*; *Mars Global Surveyor* is *MGS* . . ."

But Angela had already worked it out.

"This is from *Mars Observer*."

No one spoke. In the quiet hum of the Goddard workstation, the words *Mars Observer* seemed to carry a kind of emotional weight, like invoking the name of a martyred saint. Angela looked from one scientist to the other.

"But that's not possible, right?"

John looked somber, as if grieving a personal loss. Eklund nodded.

"*Mars Observer* was launched in late ninety-one with Mars Orbital Insertion set for mid-ninety-three. Perfect launch, perfect wake-up, status was one hundred percent, right on schedule."

"And then it disappeared."

"Final midcourse corrections went right by the numbers, boom-boom-boom. Then, around forty-eight hours out . . ."

"Phhht! Gone. Two billion dollars and ten years of work."

"Do they know why?"

Eklund shrugged, keeping a neutral expression on his face.

"NASA says the radio was turned off by accident and they never regained contact. Point is, *Mars Observer* went dark in '93 and no imaging was ever sent back. Period. *Nada.* Zero."

Angela indicated the photo dated 1994 still being refreshed on-screen.

"So, this is a picture that can't exist."

John ejected the TOLAS disk and handed it to Angela.

"You might want to get a second opinion," Eklund said.

Angela thought about the other Mars satellites gone missing, *Mars Climate Orbiter* and *Mars Polar Lander*. Images from angry House hearings came to mind: an embarrassed Dan Goldin, former NASA administrator, on CNN and testifying about bungled metric fuel conversions, basic math failures messing up the satellite's telemetry. It hadn't made much sense at the time and didn't now.

Neither Eklund nor Fisher said anything.

Suddenly Angela's neck and shoulders ached and she felt dead on her feet, even in her comfortable running shoes. Her ankles hurt and her lower back was stiffening up and she wanted to just go home and lie down in a hot bath more than anything she could think of.

"Look, guys, I really appreciate your help, but I need to go away and think about all this. And I'm sure I don't have to say it, but . . ."

"Don't worry. It won't leave this room."

"Thanks."

Angela shouldered her bag, slipping the disk with its Tricks of Light and Shadow back into its original envelope. She would not have been entirely surprised if the Mars CD had emitted some portentous sci-fi hum and sweep, and then folded itself up and disappeared into a parallel dimension.

"One more thing. What you said before about *Mars Observer* and the radio? That's the cardinal sin, isn't it?"

Both men were impressed that she knew such minutia about the arcane art and science of satellite tracking. Eklund nodded.

"It's the cardinal sin."

"Never—turn—off—the—radio." John pronounced it like a catechism.

"That's what I thought."

Angela let herself out, dropping off her pass at security before trudging outside to the magnesium-lit parking lot and her red Jeep Grand Cherokee. Her brain was running on fumes. Angela could not have said exactly what she thought, how she felt right now, or what the hell she was going to do next. But she knew her life was about to change.

9

McMurdo Station/Antarctica

Across from Augie Blake, inside the cavernous fuselage of the LC-130 Hercules, Captain Wesley Bertrand looked out the window at a skyful of spectral auroras dancing in the polar dark and listened to his Spec Ops crew arguing in their jump seats.

"Wrong, you are so full of shit. Blake had the left seat. Do the math."

"Deaver had command."

"Doesn't matter who has command."

"You don't know jack, Dubczek."

"I know that the mission fails if the spacecraft does not make it safely home. I know that without the pilot, the spacecraft is a whole lot less likely to make it safely home. So, who goes first up the ladder, fool? The pilot, Augie-fucking-Blake. Which means Jake Deaver left the last boot print on the moon."

Bertrand got up and leaned over the seat backs, keeping his voice down.

"All right, everybody put up or shut up. Last boot on the moon. Twenty bucks says it was Colonel Blake. Come on, show me the money. I'm gonna go ask him."

Collecting bets, Bertrand looked at his watch and glanced over at Augie. Then, feeling the eyes of his Spec Ops team on him, he worked his way through strapped-down medical equipment and containers marked DANGEROUS and EXPLOSIVES to where the legendary astronaut was slumped, fast asleep.

"Colonel Blake."

Augie roused himself and peered groggily up at the young Air Force captain who was touching his shoulder and pointing out the cabin window.

"Thought you might like to see the show, sir."

Augie squinted out at the amazing electromagnetic Aurora Australius, its silent green and indigo waves rippling from horizon to horizon.

"Some show," he said. "Thanks. What's our ETA, uh, Captain . . . ?"

"Bertrand, sir. We're out about twenty-five minutes and change, Colonel. With your permission, sir?"

"Don't stand on ceremony, son."

Augie waved Bertrand into the empty seat facing him and then rummaged in a carry-on bag. Finding a plastic container with his salt tabs, he shook out two and chased them with bottled water. Radiation exposure, including the UV rads increasing yearly at the poles, caused rapid dehydration and salt depletion. He offered some to the captain.

"Thanks, I'm good, sir. I understand you're evacking some astronauts?"

"Taking them to quarantine in Auckland. You on a Shared Assets ticket?"

"Yes, sir. Shared Assets."

The Antarctic was technically off-limits to the military by UN treaty, but Bertrand was unsurprised that someone of Augie's stature would know about their presence. NASA, the aerospace giant Raytheon, and the Pentagon had recently begun combining forces on various projects, with as little fanfare as possible.

This so-called Shared Assets policy amounted to a Trojan horse, a move by the Defense Department toward reversal of the strict civilian status with which NASA had been endowed by charter back in 1959. President Eisenhower had held a wisely jaundiced view of the U.S. military controlling space activities and had insisted that NASA be established outside the Pentagon umbrella and accountable to the citizens.

But a lot can happen in forty-some years.

Long the Space Shuttle's primary client, the twenty-first-century Air Force, and its newly created Space Command Wing, routinely requisi-

tioned civilian NASA test-bed rockets and borrowed their top personnel to aid the military's own space program. In exchange, NASA got to
piggyback Earth Sciences projects onto the Pentagon's Low Earth Orbit
or LEO satellites, although all data collected was controlled by the military and was not to be made available to the public.

As it happened, it was global warming and the Shared Assets inter-
face that was bringing Augie Blake and Captain Bertrand to the South
Pole.

Augie eyed Bertrand's Spec Ops insignia.

"How much did they tell you?"

"All they said at Langley was, the National Science Foundation had
inserted a team to do some ice-core sampling and then started having
problems at the dig site. Some kind of weird bacteria or microbes . . ."

"At Dunsinane."

"Yes, sir. Op Dunsinane. Some kind of prehistoric virus in the core
samples they were bringing up. People on the team started getting sick.
So, they stopped coring and the hydraulics on the ice drill froze up."

"The nuclear-powered ice drill."

"Yes, sir. Sounds like quite a mess, sir."

Aside from a brief summertime outburst of hardy vegetation, the
dominant plant life tough enough to exist in the Antarctic is lichen. And
the closer you go to the pole, the more the only life capable of surviving
in such an extreme environment is microbial: tiny bacteria hibernating
under the surface of ice-covered rock. What a temperate climate forest
of trees was doing frozen in glacier ice at that latitude was mystery
enough. But the historic find held the potential of filling in huge gaps in
our planetary history, if not rewriting it altogether, and even of adding
new phylum and new species of plants, animals, and insects long lost to
the rolls of terrestrial life.

Unfortunately, after ten thousand years, modern Homo sapiens no
longer had any immunity to the hibernating bacteria now waking up at
Dunsinane.

The lumbering Hercules now began its approach and Augie felt the
off-peak fall of a roller-coaster ride as the guppy-bellied transport
dropped, shuddered, and then banked around low-wide-and-handsome,

the fat Pratt & Whitney props roaring and clawing for purchase in the hypercold air.

"McMurdo Station, gentlemen," Captain Bertrand called out to his crew, who responded with whoops and wrist-cracking high fives all around.

"Hoo-ya!"

"Who sled the dogs out?! Hoo-Hoo!"

The LC-130 dropped its flaps. Out the window an eerie nightscape was rushing up to meet them: a bulldozed ice airstrip scraped off the top of a glacier and lined and lit by burning barrels of diesel oil.

"Hoo-hoo-hoo!"

The pilot had obviously done this before, falling fast, setting down hard, and reversing the props furiously in a half-blind, screeching, gooney-bird skid.

"Hoo-ya!"

The chorus of pumped-up Spec Ops voices echoed across the cabin. Augie leaned closer to Bertrand.

"So, what exactly do they want you to do?"

"They want us to do what we do best," Bertrand said, with a good-ol'-boy shrug. "And then get the hell out of Dodge."

Augie nodded, smiling at the captain's man-of-action style as the plane slid to a halt and everybody started grabbing up their gear. Bertrand stood and glanced over at his crew.

"Uh, Colonel, would you be kind enough to settle a small wager?"

"Which side is your money on?"

"Oh, hell. Any schoolboy knows that Colonel Augustus Julian Blake, USMC, was the last man to walk on the Moon, sir."

"Your money is safe, Captain. And good luck."

The Hercules lowered its cargo ramp with a servo-driven whine and an explosive *bang*, sending a blast of subzero Antarctic air down their necks.

"An honor to meet you, sir," Bertrand said, saluting crisply and rejoining his men. Augie pulled up the fur-lined hood on his expedition parka.

"Jesus God Almighty."

Outside, a heavily bundled ground crew on snowmobiles had already swarmed in to chock the wheels and refuel the aircraft with the engines running.

He swiftly pulled on insulated gloves and began working his way cautiously down the metal rampway, grimacing into the shocking slap of polar wind.

"Fuck me."

Augie felt his eyeballs threatening to freeze. The dispatcher at San Pedro had said it would be about fifty below, making it minus ninety degrees Fahrenheit with the windchill factored in; the kind of cold that could slam through layers of arctic-rated gear like an amphetamine-crazed killer kicking in a cardboard door.

"Hey!"

Augie squinted and waved toward a snowmobile headlight emerging from the voracious dark that was McMurdo Station in February, then lost his balance on the icy ramp, grabbing a handrail with both hands.

"Colonel Blake!"

A hooded astronaut-trainee slid to a stop in a rooster tail of ice and quickly helped settle Augie on board the motorized sled.

"Let's do it!"

Augie braced himself and held on for the short run over to the electric lights and blessed warmth of the NASA compound's Quonset-style barracks. Peering back at the runway and its barrels of blazing fuel oil set alight every fifty feet, he could just make out Captain Bertrand overseeing the handling of pallets of aluminum containers, each stickered and stenciled with "Danger" symbols now illuminated by the oily fire.

He also saw the first contingent of scientists and engineers being evacuated as they struggled across the ice toward the cargo ramp. Most of them could make it under their own power, but some had been bundled up and were being carried to the plane on stretchers, like wounded soldiers rescued from a frozen battlefield.

In that moment, the flames of the runway fuel drums reminded him of torches flickering on the wall of Shakespeare's tragic Scottish castle.

"Until Birnham Wood come to Dunsinane . . ."

Augie recited the line from *Macbeth* and shut his eyes against the cold wind, the moisture of his own breath freezing instantly on his face.

Arriving at the metal-domed Quonsets, he was less concerned with the Bard of Avon than with assessing the damage in situ and getting his people out, safe and sound.

He would soon need to tell the media something as the evacuees arrived in New Zealand; a dramatic winter air rescue at the South Pole was certainly a newsworthy story. And what he told reporters would have to be only partially true and carefully crafted to explain why so many were "rotating out" of the science colony at once and why they were going into quarantine at an Auckland hospital. But first things first.

10

Goddard Space Flight Labs/Washington, D.C.

Behind the locked door of the Goddard workstation, what was either a brilliant fraud or the most important NASA satellite photograph in the history of space science was up again on Eklund's screen.

The mainframe computer had automatically saved Angela's TOLAS image. Not that it was going anywhere beyond this room. But they had to have it.

"We should dump it off the frame."

"Done," John said, copying to the hard drive.

The politics attached to verification of this Mars picture surged out in all directions in tsunami-style waves. Eklund noticed himself nervously clenching and unclenching his hands and then stuffed them into his pockets.

"The thing is . . ."

"We don't know if it's a fake or not," Fisher said flatly.

"I don't think we *can* know. Not one hundred percent . . ."

"Oh, man." John made a face. "If this thing is real, I don't even know what kind of scenario makes sense for why it exists at all. Plus, all by itself, it's still just a fucking frame on a photo strip. It's not scientific proof of anything."

"I have an idea," Eklund said, downing ginkgo tabs with his H_2O.

"Go." John propped black high-top tennies up on the computer table.

"How about bringing I-SAT to the party?"

"You mean the good stuff?"

"Just for us."

Eklund knew there was an ethical conflict. It was probably even a crime.

"You can say no."

During the day, John ran space-based analysis of the Pentagon's Space Command Satellite Intelligence Data, or I-SAT. Both what he did and how he did it were military secrets, and using classified Department of Defense software for unauthorized civilian purposes could be viewed as a punishable offense.

But after a moment's pause, Fisher's sneakers hit the deck with a rubbery slap and he twisted back to face the computer.

"No, no, good idea. Going fractal on this shit could be interesting. Something quantifiable." He gave Eklund a damn-the-torpedoes smile and attacked the keyboard. "All right. Let's let the Big Dog hunt."

Downloading the proprietary DOD program took only a few seconds for password recognition and soon the Cydonia desert Marscape was being rapidly overlaid with a 3-D numbered gridwork.

"Now it's a battlefield. And we're on a tall horse on high ground."

"Napoleon would be green." Eklund took over the keyboard.

"Okay, click on your targets." Fisher pointed at the cluster of pyramids. "We flag whatever we want the computer to analyze. Then do a quick pass. The fractal algorithms make it ignore, based on geometry, things like hills, boulders, or whatever. The I-SAT only brackets potential military targets, meaning anything it thinks are man-made."

"Things with geometry."

"When it comes to geology, Mother Nature doesn't do straight lines. Even on Mars."

"What kind of accuracy?"

"About eighty percent." John watched as Eklund marked up every geometrically shaped object on the Cydonia plain.

"I've seen it pick out five out of six tanks in the desert and then think an ammo dump is a big sand dune. But fuck it, the Bad Guys are still in deep shit. Imagine commanding this in a real-time fire fight."

Fisher rubbed his tired eyes and stretched his arms.

"Monitoring the whole theater ops from space and feeding all your targeting data to artillery, aircraft, a fucking fleet of missile ships and submarines . . ."

"Okay." Eklund indicated the overlay of *Xs*. John made final adjustments.

"Just making sure we're asking it the right question. Ready?"

"Go."

Fisher then stabbed a key and deciphered the instant data readout.

"Holy shit, Batman. We are target-rich."

Eklund exhaled, not realizing he had been holding his breath, as John jotted quick notes on a Post-it pad, checking the percentiles assigned to the Face, the pyramids, and dozens of other *Xs* flashing on the screen.

"These are high numbers for artificiality. Seriously high."

"So, the Pentagon's hottest I-SAT software, which we have never used, in analyzing this *Mars Observer* image, which we have never seen . . ."

Fisher gave Eklund a look.

"I-SAT says bomb the crap out of it," he said, and then made the TOLAS photo and the proprietary DOD gridwork disappear.

Eklund stared back at his colleague.

"Be careful what you wish for, right?"

11

"Tricks of Light and Shadow. That's cute."

It was late. Angela took honeyed Earl Grey tea with her elbows up on Miriam's beat-up old Provençal kitchen table as the two women pow-wowed around her producer/partner's iBook. The purported *Mars Observer* image glowed eerily on the active matrix screen.

"Trouble is," Miriam said, "it makes no sense, kiddo."

Awake and alert, though still looking vaguely dragged out of bed, she loosened the antique silk kimono she had thrown on when Angela called. Midnight crises were not that unusual. Guiding *Science Horizon* through a five-year odyssey to its current award-winning plateau, replete with A-list guests and classy sponsorships, Miriam had honed her skills as a producer. These included the ability to sleep on planes, nap on office futons, and rise with her game on, whatever fresh hell presented itself.

"First off, if *Mars Observer* had found extraterrestrial monuments on Mars, it would be the greatest scientific discovery of the century. Why wouldn't NASA plaster it all over the nightly goddamned news? They could write their own ticket for the space program. Slam dunk."

"I know." Angela sipped her tea.

"And number two, why the hell would NASA want to make its own two-billion-dollar satellite disappear? I think we need a second opinion."

"Maybe it didn't disappear, Miriam. That's the point," Angela said, rubbing her tired eyes.

"Aw, come on."

"Look, this whistle-blower, whoever he is, seems to be telling us two things: there are anomalies on Mars the government doesn't want the public to see, and NASA or the Pentagon is secretly using the *Mars Observer* satellite to study them. True or false, that's what I think he's trying to say."

Miriam looked at her partner, surprised at what she saw.

"Angie?"

"I didn't say I believed it." Angela sounded defensive. "I don't know what to believe. But you're right about authentication. Who can we get?"

"Christ. I don't know."

Miriam made a face as if that was one round of phone calls she didn't want to have to make. Angela raised her eyebrows.

"Hey, I'm agreeing with you. I'm saying let's at least get some heavyweight backup about what we're looking at here. Somebody with stature."

"Yeah, somebody who'll tell us it's a hoax so we can all get a good night's sleep." Miriam added hot water to the teapot. "Why do I suddenly feel like I don't have enough life insurance?"

"Hell, if this thing is not a hoax, I want bodyguards."

"Fine. But I get Kevin Costner."

"Fine." Angela laughed, gazing out toward the dimly lit living-room walls at a Matisse nude and some of Steiglitz's pictures of Georgia O'Keeffe posing with a huge and voluptuous calla lily. She loved how Miriam's apartment reflected the conviction that being at home should feel as much as possible like a bohemian summer idyll on Martha's Vineyard. But life, as the twenty-first century was getting up to speed, seemed determined to no longer be a picnic.

"Seriously, sweety darling." Miriam poured for both of them from a nice piece of chinoiserie. "Let's say it's all true, and somewhere out there, some Cosmic Deep Throat has the goods on this huge scandal: ARTIFACTS ON MARS; NASA HIJACKS SATELLITE; SCIENCE CRIME OF THE CENTURY. And this Deep Cosmo has picked *Science Horizon* out of a hat to help him blow the whistle. Who says we have to play his game?"

"Deep Cosmo." Angela giggled. "Yeah, fuck him. What if we don't choose to be the chosen? We can Just Say No."

"Yeah, really. We're not exactly the first place one imagines turning to for Pulitzer Prize muckraking journalism."

Angela looked stung.

"You know, hearing it phrased just that way? It makes me feel kind of like the Vanna White of science reporting."

"Angie, come on. I didn't mean . . . Hell, you know what I meant."

Miriam felt bad. Angela made no secret of the fact that, five years in, she was growing restless with the preaching-to-the-choir limitations of PBS and was eager for *Science Horizon* to seek new horizons of its own. And tackling a Pulitzer-worthy science story was exactly what might break them out.

"I'm not saying we can't do it, kiddo, I'm just saying it's not exactly the kind of thing we're really known for taking on."

But Angela was still upset.

"No, come on. What is it? We do our homework, our due diligence, et cetera, we deliver on this story like we have on every other story for five years, why can't we step up to prime time? Huh? You think PBS wouldn't back us? You think it's too controversial, too political, too Geraldo? What?"

Miriam felt stupid for triggering the argument, but the truth was, she was not yet convinced there *was* a story here. Much less one to go to the mattresses for.

"Angie, listen. As a producer, I'm concerned about getting it right, and so are you. Things like public perception of professionalism and the kind of respect that we have nurtured for *Science Horizon*. You know what the struggle has been. Not just as a woman journalist . . ."

"In the *science community*."

"Our lovely little Emmy Award notwithstanding, we go out on a limb making wild pronouncements that we can't prove? We lose credibility, we lose support, we lose access, we can lose sponsorship. We can lose everything, kiddo. Even if we're righteously right. But this thing came to you. So it's your call."

One thing Angela loved about Miriam: she pulled rank sometimes and they had had their conflicts over the years, but bottom line, there was complete mutual respect and appreciation, which meant a lot and had allowed them to weather a lot.

"Well, I just need to know, Miriam, if it's a fake or if it's for real," she said. "And whatever we have to do to determine that, I say we do it."

"Agreed."

"After that, I don't know. I'm too burnt to think."

Angela closed the clamshell of the iBook and retrieved her disk. Miriam gave her friend a hug and walked her to the door arm in arm.

"Then let's not think about it anymore, Miz Scarlett." She drawled it out as though they were two tendrilled belles of the Old South strolling out under the colonnade for a breath of breeze off the bayou. "We can think about it tomorrow."

"Yes, tomorrow," Angela said, picking up the faux fiddle-de-dee riff. "For tomorrow . . . is another day."

She then stomped downstairs in her Nikes and out into the street.

PART

II

We must guard against the acquisition of unwarranted influence by the military/industrial complex. The potential for the disastrous rise of misplaced power exists and will persist. We should take nothing for granted.

—Dwight D. Eisenhower, 1961

12

January 29/Dunsinane/Antarctica

The fact was, thousands of years of accumulated ice at both poles had begun melting into the sea. The ozone layer protecting the Earth from damaging UV radiation was breaking down so dramatically that a huge hole had formed above the Southern Hemisphere. This hole in the ozone now let in enough solar radiation that incidents of skin cancer were soaring throughout the region and school kids from Australia to Chile were no longer allowed outside on the playgrounds without wearing hats.

North American energy and car-building leaders howled that power plants and the internal combustion engine were not to blame, finding it easier to engineer the U.S. pull-out from the Kyoto Protocols than to develop nonpolluting vehicles and renewable clean fuels.

In any case, such highly paid lobbying and verbal obfuscation were moot as far as the Arctic Circle was concerned: for the first time in recorded human history there was open navigable water all across Santa's northernmost domain.

And whether the temperature was rising from industrial pollution or all the hot air sent aloft from attorneys, the situation at the South Pole, too, was degrading more rapidly than even Greenpeace and the Sierra Club had feared.

The bad news was, the Ross Ice Shelf had joined the massive Larsen B and Larsen C Shelves in cracking off from the continent and subsiding into the Antarctic Ocean about ten years sooner than the National Science Foundation's worst-case scenarios of the '90's had envisioned.

That there was good news at all from this was totally unexpected: a scientific treasure of inestimable value had been uncovered in the collapsing polar ice and picked up by one of NASA's Earth Sciences LEO satellites.

The find, code-named Dunsinane, was stunning: a frozen forest of temperate climate trees suddenly visible in the glacier like a portal in time, a pristine biosphere preserved for millennia and offering science nothing less than a firsthand look at the world of 10,000 B.C.E. Not to mention a first-rate mystery: How does a forest get to the South Pole? Within days, the National Science Foundation was galvanized into action.

All science done in Antarctica must be done according to rules enunciated in a United Nations agreement protecting the entire continent from exploitation and pollution: the Antarctic belongs to all mankind and is held in sacred trust. Thus, all junk, all refuse, including every ounce of human waste generated by the three thousand people in the science town of McMurdo, was flown out each spring in over forty-five lift sorties and recycled in California.

On the last airlift before all flights were shut down for the winter, foundation scientists quietly brought in a nuclear-powered ice drill designed to tunnel down through the glacier to the prehistoric forest waiting beneath the ice. After weeks of building out the dig site in the perpetual dark and testing the drill in various extremes of temperature and conditions, the excited waiting was over and they had begun tunneling carefully down to the trees.

But as it happened, there was something more contagious than the NSF excitement over their find. Within hours of retrieving the first core samples from Dunsinane, signs of severe viral infection began to appear at McMurdo.

The work was halted, the tunnel sealed over, and the dig site decontaminated, but it was too late: everyone exposed to the Dunsinane samples was quarantined, many developing high fevers and vomiting. The little science colony at the pole now realized that the ice samples held hibernating viruses that had been "switched on" by the relative warmth of the Quonset huts and were then released: twelve-thousand-year-old bacteria to which human beings were no longer immune.

By the time Bertrand arrived, thirty-five scientists and engineers were being extracted, including the McMurdo medical staff members who had treated the first sick ones and then fallen ill themselves. Augie Blake's astronaut trainees, wintering over, had not come into direct contact with the virus but were evacuated as a precaution. And all evacked personnel were sequestered for treatment in a military hospital in New Zealand.

▼

There had been no fatalities, but the worst was not necessarily over. After securing and cleansing the Dunsinane site, bundled-up Army engineers and National Science Foundation glaciologists now gathered to bring Captain Bertrand and his Spec Ops crew up to speed.

Bertrand peered at a dim, greenish video screen set up on a workbench in the main Quonset: the only remaining connection to the prehistoric forest down below was via the camera on their broken nuclear-powered drill.

"How far down is that?"

"About two thousand feet." The lead scientist pointed to a 3-D map.

The tiny reactor with its tank tracks and titanium bit had tunneled into the glacier efficiently enough. But weather at the South Pole is changeable in the extreme, with temp swings of as much as one hundred degrees in a six-hour period.

"How cold was it when you had to shut her down?"

"Yeah, that was the bitch. About minus eighty-five degrees, Fahrenheit," an engineer said. Approaching ninety below, running anything mechanical that required lubrication was to court failure. "The hydraulic fluid froze."

"That'd do it." Bertrand scratched at his jaw with a thermal glove. The rasping sound of his day-old beard was audible across the room. There was not exactly a vast array of options: restarting the drill and taking it out under its own power was out of the question. At least they were still getting video.

"How hot is it?"

"Celsius or rads?"

An Army engineer showed him the two readings.

"Jesus. We got us a little Chernobyl, gentlemen." Bertrand gestured toward his crew. Each man took a turn checking out the monitor, but they were all getting the picture: ground truth at ninety below was a sobering bitch.

"If you all will excuse us . . . ?"

Bertrand herded his guys together, away from the anxious civilians. It was his task to assess, make recommendations up the chain, and then ultimately implement whatever decision came back down.

While the Spec Ops team huddled, the heavily dressed foundation scientists stood around looking exhausted and depressed, arguing about how to handle the next press cycle.

The media had either been tipped off or somehow read the Web-traffic tea leaves and had gotten wind of the Antarctic evacuation. CNN, MSNBC, and the wire services were pressing McMurdo Station hourly for details. So far, the NSF had only put out a cryptic, one-page press release from McMurdo saying there was no "general evacuation," that a dozen people were being "normally rotated out," with the exception of a doctor who "needed an unexpected operation" and a few astronaut trainees who were simply "homesick" and taking advantage of the unscheduled air transport out.

But the numbers, like the story, didn't really add up. There were going to be questions about the military hospital in Auckland, demands for interviews with the personnel flown up there and others still remaining on-station. It was a mess. And until they had a solution in place, in progress, the situation totally "under control," they were terrified of involving the media.

"Captain?" the lead NSF scientist called across the hut. He hadn't slept much the last seventy-two hours and his voice sounded ragged and impatient.

Captain Bertrand turned away from his huddle and focused on the civilians. There was no magic wand to make this all go away. They all knew that, but he said it out loud anyway.

"Well, in and out and nobody gets hurt? We cut the goddamn drill loose, let it melt its way down as far away from people as it'll go, and then we seriously close that hole. But I suppose there is a good argument against that."

In his fur-lined hood, the lead scientist looked bleak. When he spoke, angry little puffs of condensed air formed in front of his face like clouds.

"We're standing over the first and only pristine prehistoric biosphere on the planet. To contaminate it with radioactive machinery would be a criminal act, not to mention the grossest possible violation of the UN no-footprint rules. American science would be disgraced, banished, and we'd all be out of our jobs."

"That's pretty much what I was thinking."

Captain Wesley Bertrand and everyone else knew that any real solution to this mess would be slow, nasty, dangerous, and seven-figure expensive with mega lift-tons of blame to go around. All the science folk and Army engineers could do was put in their two cents and wait until Bertrand's official recommendations set the process in motion. For the civilians, the scientists, this was not what they had worked so hard to be down here for. Not to preside over this huge messy disaster that could only blight their careers.

But Bertrand was here because, for him, disasters were kind of fun.

"All righty, then," he said, already dividing the operation into doable pieces, organizing, prioritizing, and saving the craziest, most risky "fun" for himself. "The way I see it, we're looking at mechanical retrieval of the drill; complete biohazard and radiation containment and cleanup; airlift and disposal of all contaminated water, ice, materials, and equipment. I see at least three lift sorties, maybe five, and we're gonna need hazard experts, radiation experts, one helluva winch that will still work at fifty below, plus a shitload of support from HAZMAT, the NRC, the Air Force. And is there someplace down here where my boys can get hot coffee and take a warm piss?"

Everyone in the freezing hut grinned and looked visibly relieved for a moment. The lead scientist did the honors, heading toward the insulated doors.

"This way, gentlemen."

Hundreds of what-if and if-then concerns began beating their wings inside each person's brain as the group shuffled out in their boots and bulky clothes. That the crisis would be resolved seemed a bit more certain. Bertrand certainly inspired confidence.

Whether the unexplored ancient biosphere in suspension beneath them would have to remain unexplored was harder to determine. At least for the paleobiologists and glaciologists it was still too early and too painful to think about that.

13

Old Executive Office Building/Washington, D.C.

Sandy Sokoff had had discreet meetings with military and intelligence people at the Pentagon, at CIA headquarters in Virginia, and at the vast NSA facility at Ft. Meade in Maryland.

Each intelligence officer or general officer questioned about Project Orion professed to have either no knowledge or very limited knowledge, operating within the limitations of institutional cutouts that prevented anyone from seeing the whole picture. And none of those Sandy interviewed were willing to speculate, at least not in front of the President's counsel. Many had seemed more intent on pumping *him* for information than on illuminating matters for the White House, which Sokoff found both curious and irritating.

Nevertheless, certain impressions were evolving, specifically that both inside and outside government, support for the building out of a vastly expensive space-based weapons system was wide, deep, and not justified by any military or terrorist threat that made any sense whatsoever.

It was a truism that the easiest way for a terrorist to deliver a nuclear bomb to any city in America was to hide it in a shipment of dope. And against this basic street reality, as far as Sandy was concerned, all the ICBM-killing Star Wars crap in the world didn't mean squat.

So, why the big push for Orion, if it was just some leftover big-ticket, pre-9/11 China-containment boondoggle in Republican geopolitical drag?

Sitting in his office in the Old Executive Office Building with the clock ticking, Sokoff stared at his list of spies, former spies, and close-mouthed generals. He then consulted his computer address book, made an impulsive phone call, and booked himself on the earliest morning flight to Atlanta.

14

January 30/Atlanta, Georgia

The next day, at a dead-end lot in one of Atlanta's sprawling suburbs, he stood and watched as former President Jimmy Carter banged away at the frame of a two-story house with a claw-head hammer, hanging Sheetrock for Habitats for Humanity.

The young intern who had met Sokoff at the airport said something to Carter, who just nodded and then finished knocking home the last nail before belting the hammer and wiping his hands on his overalls.

Turning toward him, Carter smiled and looked so fundamentally happy in that moment that Sandy felt a pang of remorse for bothering him.

But if "Jimmy," as he was called at the worksite, was feeling bothered, it did not show on his beaming octogenarian face. Motioning Sokoff toward a Dodge pickup parked out front, he stolidly led the way.

"Come on and step into my office."

Sandy followed, mindful of not getting mud on his boots as he crossed the unlandscaped yard. Climbing up into the cab of the 4 × 4, he slammed closed the passenger-side door.

"Mr. President, we appreciate this very much."

"My pleasure, Mr. Sokoff." Jimmy's eyes twinkled as they shook hands. "What can I do for you?"

"It's about Project Orion, sir."

Carter's cheerful demeanor faded slightly to a pensive smile as he turned over the truck engine and revved it a couple of times.

"Well, now. Are they about to test it?"

"A final test has been authorized, sir. The President asked me to provide some deep background before he takes any further action. But I've been encountering a lot of . . . well, reticence to discuss. I was hoping you might be able to help me not make a fool of myself."

The former Democratic President studied Sandy for a moment as if wondering what else he already knew and how frank he might be.

"Of course," he said, "but I think you better buckle up."

Carter grinned, adjusting his own seat belt, and then gunned the shiny Dodge truck out of the cul-de-sac and off to what Sokoff would later remember as the best beef brisket and hot links he'd had east of Louisiana and a top-fiver among the most extraordinary conversations he would never be allowed to share with his wife, Juana, back home in Austin.

It wasn't until three hours later, while he was waiting in the VIP lounge at the Atlanta hub, that a new plan began to suggest itself to the President's counsel about how to complete his task.

15

Little Cosmograd, Ukraine

Dr. Sergei Sergeivich Berenkov, senior scientist, kept a closer eye than usual on the data stream from the photon laser. He knew the crucial parameters of Project Orion by heart. He had, in fact, written them himself, but project managers always got so hysterical before a test.

Of course, this was not just another computer simulation. This was it.

Through the glass walls in front of him, American aerospace giant TRW's Orion laser cannon loomed in all of its forged-titanium glory. The danger inherent in firing the six-story-tall chemical/nuclear device was a given: they could all be incinerated in a blink, shadows burned into the ground. Not an atom or a particle identifiable as a project manager or a Sergei Berenkov would even be left to wonder what went wrong.

Berenkov shrugged off the risk with his usual fatalism.

So, why worry? he thought, pretending to concentrate ferociously on his computer screen.

Setting aside the chance for catastrophe, the principal fear in the Little Cosmograd lab outside the Ukrainian capital was about their "employment future" becoming an oxymoron. The plain fact was, if the Orion test worked they had a future. If it didn't, they probably didn't. A loudspeaker came to distorted life.

"Stations for pretest. We are calling pretest stations."

White-coated technicians hurried anxiously past Berenkov's workstation. He straightened the tie he was wearing for the occasion underneath the clean but shopworn lab coat that his wife, Ilyena, had laundered for him the night before. He owned only the one and she had a hard time getting it away from him long enough to wash it.

Delayed paychecks, stalled projects, physicists moonlighting as cab-drivers and waiters: to be a Russian scientist at the dawn of the twenty-first century was to be condemned to a not-so-genteel poverty. But at least the former dictatorship of the proletariat was also no longer a police state.

"Project managers, please report to the test director."

Exercising the newly acquired freedom of speech—"We are free to speak and they are free to ignore us"—Berenkov complained openly these days about the remnants of the former Yeltsin kleptocracy, the greedy oligarchs snapping up national resources at fire-sale prices, and the continuing abject neglect of Russian science. His colleagues would nod and ruefully agree with him about rampant corruption and Mafia entrepreneurs run amok. They listened to Berenkov's witheringly critical, often hilarious rants against the Duma leadership in Moscow, laughed at the painful truths, and then dubbed him with the nickname "Mr. Grumpy."

"Test programmers, take your stations for the duration of the test. Security, please clear the chamber."

Wishing desperately for a smoke, Mr. Grumpy stayed put at his station and sipped tepid tea instead, unconsciously avoiding the familiar chip in the ceramic cup as his eyes wandered to a dark blank space on the wall behind him.

A proud group photo had hung there, with many old friends and colleagues standing in front of a Titan-class rocket engine: Russia's part in a multinational space effort to study Mars in the '90's. Launching and then losing control of the plutonium-powered spacecraft with its hundreds of millions of dollars in international experiments had marked the nadir of the Russian space program.

Delivering their key contributions to the International Space Station years late and millions over budget had not redeemed Russian space science, either. So, to Berenkov and everyone else, it was obvious: the success of the Orion test was absolutely crucial.

"Recalibrate and reset your instruments for Primary Alpha."

He had already recalibrated, but he did it again. Listening to voices around him, he smiled: the murmured litany of the final checklist sounded like an Orthodox church full of penitents petitioning the God of Physics for mercy.

"Project Orion. Primary Alpha testing. Prepare for countdown."

Glancing up at the observation platform where former KGB politicos huddled nervously with U.S. military and aerospace VIPs, Berenkov also reflected on how, in the Church of Space Science, the parishioners made such strange bedfellows.

Soviet space weapons work countering the Americans' SDI, the so-called Star Wars program, had made him proud during the Gorbachev years. He'd felt as if he was "defending the Motherland" against President Ronald Reagan, that charismatic cowboy actor, and the reckless arms buildup of the West. By the time Reagan proposed sharing Star Wars technology with the Soviets in Helsinki, Gorbachev already knew the game was up: the Russians were too broke to go on.

Emerging from long years of post-perestroika depression, they were now in a new, more hopeful era, though with the U.S. aerospace industry largely funding the Russian side of joint laser defense research, it all seemed a bit surreal. Was he now defending the Motherland for TRW?

"Project Orion Primary Alpha testing in minus five minutes."

An alarm began to pulse and the tension around him rose perceptibly.

And so it begins, he thought. Berenkov saw the countdown numbers appear in a window on his new IBM PC, a nice thing: he didn't have to look up to follow the rolling count.

The new CPUs they all had now were a gratifying improvement, with Russian-language software and blazingly fast Pentium upgrades. Of course, in the old Soviet days they had gone into space on a slide rule and a stopwatch, a fact he brought up to his computer-mad younger colleagues at every opportunity.

"Elegant and sufficient to the day," he would say as they shook their heads and rolled their eyes. "Those days were truly heroic, a time of greatness."

"Primary Test Alpha. Initiation in minus ninety seconds."

The senior scientist glanced through the wall of tempered glass at the huge, imposing laser weapon. An insistent bell heralded the opening of automated sections of the lab's domed articulated roofing, irising wide to the night sky. Berenkov noticed that he seemed to be the only one interested in what might be a last look up at the stars.

"Primary Alpha Test. Initiation in minus sixty seconds."

With the verbal count under way, the entire facility became eerily quiet, heads bowed over each piece of the streaming status data in digital meditation.

"Minus . . . thirty . . . twenty-nine . . . twenty-eight . . . twenty-seven . . ."

Above them large monitors displayed various views from geosynchronous satellites and the U.S. Space Shuttle Atlantis. Cosmonauts manning cameras aboard the ISS Alpha could be heard locking down their videos and chatting.

"Minus ten . . . nine . . . eight . . . seven . . . six . . ."

Berenkov and the others around him now donned dark glasses, as the project director's voice came over the loudspeaker.

"Project Orion. Initiating Primary Alpha Test."

In an underground lead-lined core, a controlled nuclear explosion telegraphed a low rumble through the floor and then the fission flash of a hundred Hiroshimas was directed and transmuted through the multistory titanium weapon just fifty yards away.

If Berenkov had looked up, he would have seen how the entire airspace up and out through the open dome had now been replaced by a spectacular rod of laser light, one hundred feet in diameter and brighter than the sun.

How quiet it is, Berenkov thought, fighting the urge to steal a peek at the blinding energy column thrusting out into space, its giga-trillions of electrons per second streaming in lockstep alignment.

"Sixty percent and stable . . ."

But the senior scientist stayed riveted to the fluctuating readings on his monitor. Everything was remaining within parameters, but his eyes played tricks on him and he found himself hallucinating tiny alarming changes. It was excruciating.

"We are at seventy-five percent and stable . . ."

He began to hear excited yelps and cheers, which he presumed were coming from the Americans on the Atlantis and the cosmonauts and Chinese taiko-nauts on board Space Station Alpha.

So far, so good.

On the monitor, Berenkov could see how the laser looked from orbit; this magnificent beacon beaming out from the Earth, all the way out as far the eye could see into the solar system.

If some extraterrestrial beings were watching this event, what would they make of it? he wondered. An impressive human achievement? A bold statement of an emerging species arriving at a new threshold of knowledge? A wake-up call?

"We are at nominal target volume, ninety percent and stable . . ."

Each nanosecond seemed like an hour of doubt and fear, the smell of his own suppressed terror sweating through Berenkov's undershirt. If something went bad at this point it would likely happen far too fast to retrieve it. The Russian scientist realized that the last thing he ever saw in this lifetime might be a tiny little sine-wave spike on his nice new American PC.

"Sixty seconds at ninety percent and stable . . ."

But it was holding. Orion was holding.

Berenkov heard the exclamations of his colleagues as the reality of their achievement began to sink in.

"Two minutes at ninety percent and stable. Going to one hundred percent . . ."

If focused on the Moon, the Orion laser weapon would melt the surface silica into molten glass, burning a hole the size of a football field a half-mile deep. If it targeted the Clark Belt, where the world's key military and civilian satellites orbited, a nation's communications could be vaporized in half a heartbeat.

"We are at one hundred percent and holding."

Project Orion was working.

Berenkov thanked God, in whom he did not believe, and then shivered involuntarily as he imagined this same awesome power directed downward from space at the great cities of the Earth. The potential for holocaust that this would add to mankind's already planet-wasting nuclear and biological arsenals was suddenly palpable.

"*Project Orion. Preshutdown and counting ten—nine—eight—seven—six—five—four . . .*"

And then it was over.

The dazzling rod of light disappeared, leaving bars of after-colors swimming on everyone's retinas. Cheers of triumph and waves of applause erupted around the room. Berenkov blinked and took off his cheap sunglasses. Looking down at his hands, he found them slick with sweat. The hair on his arms and on the back of his neck was sticking up.

Well, he thought, *we lived. That was something.*

As loudspeaker voices chanted through the postshutdown procedures, a party atmosphere began to blossom. On the observation deck, the generals, politicians, and businessmen were popping open French champagne. Everywhere people hugged one another, crying and laughing in relief.

Orion was a success. A resounding success.

Berenkov blinked and then abandoned his workstation, his clipboard still clenched unconsciously in his hand. He could feel colleagues clapping him on the back, pressing little paper cups of export-quality vodka into his hand, but he waved them off.

"Sergei Sergeivich!"

"Aw, Mr. Grumpy. You must drink a toast!"

Pushing his way through the knots of celebration, Berenkov lurched out of the control room and down the empty linoleum-covered corridor.

The implications of his work, the potential nightmare of horrific *applications,* hadn't really hit him full force until this moment. His mind flashed to the '40's, to Fermi and Oppenheimer and all the elite minds weaponizing the physics of fission; what ambivalence they had felt even in a time of world war.

Orion had begun long before the end of the Cold War and had continued now for decades since the Wall had come down, and the Americans had become our partners and allies. So who, then, was the enemy? Who except we ourselves and our will to destroy one another? Who, now that we are in bed with the enemy, is the enemy?

Stumbling into the chill and ill-kept men's room, Dr. Sergei Sergeivich Berenkov was overwhelmed with dread and an inexpressible fear for the future. Losing his grip on the clipboard holding the day's test protocols, he heard it clatter to the floor.

We are all insane, he thought. *We are . . . insane.*

The Cyrillic letters spelling out PROJECT ORION fell facedown into a small unmopped puddle of water, but he didn't notice and would not have cared.

Mr. Grumpy was too busy at the washstand, throwing up.

16

"We are alive in a new Golden Age of Astronomy." Angela could hear her own prerecorded voice-over as she stepped up to a yellow tape mark on the floor of the PBS soundstage.

"In the Orion Nebula, thanks to the Hubble Telescope, mankind can now watch stars being born for the first time in history."

Behind her a large Sony monitor displayed an opening *Science Horizon* montage of spectacular space images gathered from a host of NASA instruments.

"And with this first look at a 'cosmic nursery' comes a new view of Creation as well. Not as something long finished and slowly dying, but as a glorious, evolving work-in-progress."

A stylist knocked down the shine on Angela's nose and forehead with a Victoria Vogue sponge. Behind the glass in the producer's booth, Miriam made eye contact and hit the talk-back button.

"Three minutes, kiddo."

Angela nodded. Standing in a tight pool of light, she closed her eyes and let go of everything she could do nothing more about today, particularly everything having to do with their would-be whistle-blower, Deep Cosmo.

During the day, calls to all the courier services used by both PBS and NASA had come up with zilch in tracking the package back to its source. Neither day-shift security nor the mail-room people had been any help, either. But this was just the beginning and she and Miriam had an overall battle plan.

A plan that they were initiating tonight.

Up in the producer's booth where Miriam called the shots for three cameras, the hard decisions in terms of the show had already been made, but the booth was where it all came together. It was also ground zero whenever things went to shit, as they were always threatening to do, though Miriam handled the pressure with an enviable smart-ass aplomb.

"When the going gets weird, the weird turn pro," she whispered breathily into the talk-back mike, cracking up Angela, the crew around her, and everyone wearing headsets on the soundstage floor. Broadcast production was en eccentric enterprise about which Hunter Thompson's smart remarks on the '60's New Journalism were often apropos.

"Two minutes, everybody."

Miriam buzzed the stage manager.

"Billy? Let's have places, please. Where's Eklund?"

"On his way. I called Goddard and they said he left an hour ago."

"Okay, if he's not here by break time we go to plan B." Miriam was already marking up her copy of the script with potential revisions.

"Uh, what plan B?"

"I'm workin' on it. Places."

On the monitors, Angela's recorded voice-over continued.

"In Upsilon Andromedae and scores of other places in our own galaxy we are also seeing the first thrilling proof of planets circling sunlike stars. Giordano Bruno, an Italian monk, was burned at the stake four hundred years ago for suggesting that the cosmos was home to thousands of Earths. Perhaps Father Bruno deserves an apology."

▼

Miriam looked up from her rewrites as Professor Stephen Weintraub and the famed Nobelist Dr. Paula Winnick were escorted from the backstage makeup room and settled into chairs on the raised platform of the set. As always, she thought the septuagenarian Dr. Winnick had a fascinating presence.

What an incredible woman, she thought.

Wearing a Chanel suit and radiating an effortless, exuberant intelligence, Winnick was by far the most publicly recognized name in American space science after Einstein and Carl Sagan. Now that she had outlived them both, her star in the Academy of Sciences and the media firmament was fixed and unrivaled.

Getting the high sign from the sound guy on the set, Miriam checked the clock, cursed the tardy Richard Eklund in absentia, and warned Angela.

"One minute. I'll count you in."

"Okay."

"Everybody. We are go in one. Ready?"

Holding up her hands like an orchestra conductor, she cued the camera, saw the red light come on, and spoke into her headset.

"Angie? Camera One. On ten . . ."

Using all ten fingers, Miriam orchestrated the visual cross-fade from STAR 51 PEG, forty light-years away, to Angela's live, studio close-up.

"All these dramatic firsts pose a profoundly new question. Not what if there is life out there, but what if life . . . is all around us?"

Angela paused, holding an enigmatic smile for dramatic effect, then crossed over to the *Science Horizon* set and her distinguished guests.

"Anyone interested in joining the discussion on-line, you can find these images and more, plus a new viewer bulletin board, at www.sciencehorizon.org/tolas—spelled T-O-L-A-S."

▼

At the meeting in Miriam's office at 10:00 A.M., the TOLAS bulletin board had been Angela's idea.

"I think we can assume Deep Cosmo is watching."

"So we use the show to send him a message, establish contact, let him know we got the package and we want to talk," Miriam said, swiveling in her chair. "It could also scare him the hell off."

"If he's not talking to us, he's as good as scared off already," Angela pointed out. "I think we're demonstrating good faith."

▼

But Miriam Kresky was not thinking about Deep Cosmo right now. She was too busy cuing visuals, calling cameras, and wondering how she could ever have thought that late-ass geek Eklund was attractive.

"What's the penalty for killing an astronomer, anyway?" She shot a look at the twentysomething mixer working the console faders.

"Billions and billions of years," he said in a perfect Carl Sagan cadence that almost made her fall off her chair.

▼

A half block away in an early-adopted General Motors EV-1, Eklund had long since given up on his malfunctioning cell phone and turned off both the a/c and the radio in a desperate effort to conserve electricity.

"Come on, let's go, let's go, let's go!"

Being jammed up in traffic and trapped in an electric car running out of charge was a uniquely agonizing purgatory for a techno-freak and avowed environmentalist. A warning light flashed on the dashboard: 5% OF CHARGE REMAINING/RANGE .5 MILES.

"Oh, no." He checked his watch and pounded the dash in frustration.

Honking the horn could drain the last trickle from his battery pack, so Eklund had been reduced to fiddling with his wilting hand-tied bow tie and yelling things out the car window.

"Yes! Yes! Just move over. Just move it a little bit . . . Yes!"

At last able to maneuver into the PBS parking structure, Eklund raced up the concrete ramp on his last remaining electrons. He felt abjectly stupid and embarrassed for being so late. But as he jumped out of the car and ran flat out into the building, he reminded himself that nobody was going to kill him for screwing up the show and if he was lucky they'd still have time for at least part of his planned presentation.

Later he'd wish that they had just killed him.

▼

At Goddard, Eklund had given them a private glimpse of several archived NASA photos showing intriguing Martian anomalies, from tubelike structures to triangular monoliths. Angela and Miriam had been extremely impressed. And after being assured that all of the images were available for broadcast use and in the public domain, Angela had pitched him their idea.

"Okay, here's the deal. We want to provoke or inspire whoever sent that TOLAS disk I showed you into making contact with us and starting a dialogue. And to do that, we're going to produce a show about NASA's search for life in the solar system. And we'd like you to come on and make the case for the Intelligence Hypothesis on Mars."

"We've invited Paula Winnick," Miriam added, in the flat, matter-of-fact way she had acquired as a producer when invoking famous names. It was Eklund's turn to be impressed.

"Really."

"And we have confirmed Professor Stephen Weintraub."

"*Mars Observer* imaging team. Wow." Eklund sat up alertly, his mind shifting into a higher gear: this was pretty much raising the bar as high as it went.

"So, Richard, what do you think?"

While he took a moment to mull it over Miriam studied what Eklund was wearing.

Leather suspenders and a bow tie with little red rockets? She decided that a major part of him was still a twelve-year-old boy who loved the idea of space exploration more than anything, and she found his grown-up sense of style in expressing this both eccentric and rather charming.

"What about the TOLAS photo?" Eklund said.

"We're considering showing it to Weintraub. But not until after the show."

"We thought Stephen'd be a good person to authenticate."

Eklund blinked. An acknowledged NASA satellite imaging expert, Cornell Professor Stephen Weintraub, confirming the authenticity of TOLAS would carry significant weight in the science community.

"So?" Miriam smiled, wondering with a professional eye how the off-beat, speedy, but earnest scientist would come off on camera. Her grin balanced flirtation and dare in equal measure. Eklund found it impossible to resist.

"What do you want me to do?"

"It's what we don't want you to do," Angela said. "You absolutely cannot mention the TOLAS image, period."

"Understood."

"What we *do* want is for you to do just what you did today."

"You mean present the Mars anomalies I find hardest to explain away and then defend them against high-caliber, articulate skepticism."

Miriam added a note of fair warning.

"It could be fairly adversarial skepticism."

Eklund understood, but it was such a great opportunity. At the very least it would put the Intelligence Hypothesis out there and get a few million people thinking about how exciting a manned mission to Mars would be and what might be waiting there to be found.

Still, he was smart enough to know that the prospect of heavyweights like Dr. Paula Winnick poking holes in his hypothesis on PBS ought to give him pause.

"Yes, debating a Nobel laureate should be interesting."

"You can pass, Richard, if you don't feel ready. I know it's short notice," Angela said, meaning it. But Eklund smiled ruefully in Miriam's direction.

"No, no. They'll both probably eat my lunch. But what the hell."

▼

It proved a prescient, if cavalier, observation. In fact, once the taping of his segment of *Science Horizon* was over, he only hoped that nobody he had told about it would actually tune in to see what he considered his rattled defensive argumentation and unfortunate presentation.

The photos of intriguing objects captured by *Mars Global Surveyor* and *Mars Odyssey* may have wowed a few lay viewers, and he'd made some points. But all things considered, he felt he had largely screwed the pooch: the impressive and intimidating Drs. Weintraub and Winnick had sliced and diced him with an almost seamless politeness.

Angry at himself, Eklund passed on the postshow cocktail party despite entreaties from both Miriam and Angela, who clearly felt bad for him, which was also embarrassing.

Instead, he phoned the Triple A and went straight out to the parking structure with the minimum of good-byes: he still had a transportation problem.

"Zero-emissions piece of shit."

Eklund glared at his aging, red EV-1, blaming it for making his grid-lock lateness so stressful, throwing him off his game and now dragging out his already excruciating exit. Pacing in front of the shiny dead-in-the-water electric car, he tore at his bow tie.

"Fuck the ozone layer, you green-ass piece of shit."

He reconsidered the virtues of the ultralow-emissions hybrid vehi-cles from Honda and the Toyota and decided it was trade-in time. He wanted nothing this humiliating to happen to him again in this lifetime. But mostly Eklund just wanted to go home and get drunk.

Which, as soon as the Triple A truck showed up, is exactly what he did.

17

This guy Eklund is out of his mind, Winston thought.

An upwardly osculating staffer had taped *Science Horizon* and couriered a copy out to Bob Winston's all-white Federal-style home in the Maryland suburbs. He thought the national security adviser would find it amusing.

Scowling through Eklund's exposition of unexplained Mars anomalies as he washed down microwaved beef bourguignon with a Boodles gin martini, Winston was more appalled than amused.

"Scientifically," Eklund was saying, *"NASA doesn't seem to want to really look at these sorts of things, like the Face or these pyramid-shaped mounds . . ."*

"Who is this guy?" Winston wondered out loud.

"But if you take the time to look and see, you find that in terms of alignments with the sun, the cardinal points, or the equator, the more we compare the Face and these faceted mounds on Mars with structures on Earth like the Mayan pyramids or the Sphinx in Egypt, the more the data suggest intelligence was involved. Not just in their geometries, but in their placement."

"Unbelievable." Winston picked up the phone and then put it back.

"So, ancient pyramids on Mars, or tricks of light and shadow?"

Angela turned to her other guests for their reactions.

"Dr. Winnick, Professor?"

Winnick, the charismatic Nobelist, was the first to weigh in, and Winston saw her taking Eklund's measure: she could outpoint him in her sleep.

This will be interesting. He turned up the sound.

"Well, first I'd like to say that having a creative imagination is a fine thing, certainly," Winnick began. "But as evocative as these images might be, considering the thousands of big rocks on Mars, what are the odds that one might look a little like a human face, or a pyramid, or any number of things?"

"Richard? That's a fair question," Angela said. "What about the issue of 'projection'? Like seeing faces in the clouds . . ."

"Or finding a pumpkin that looks like your uncle Harry?" Eklund almost sneered.

"What a flaming idiot," Winston mumbled to himself, amused.

Eklund's case of attitude was coming off as arrogant, even insulting to his host, which was bad form, not to mention stupid.

"Well, you must allow that this is something we humans do," Winnick said, smoothly riding to Angela's rescue. "We look for patterns, we anthropomorphize. It's part of our nature, don't you know. But leaving that aside, what about Nature? Natural forces create lines of katabatic sand dunes and monumental shapes everywhere on Earth. Look at the magnificent buttes in the Southwest, cathedrals of rock thrust up by tectonic shifting, eroded and sculpted by water and wind over eons of time."

"Buttes and sand dunes." Eklund waved a hand at the video display. "Sand dunes on Earth do not show this kind of symmetry. Natural geography is fractal! Nature doesn't do straight lines and geometric shapes!"

Dr. Paula Winnick looked at him over her bifocals. But any impression of grandmotherliness was mistaken.

"I should think," she said, without raising her voice, "you'd find all kinds of symmetries and geometries in nature's crystal structures."

Professor Weintraub entering the fray was almost like piling on.

"Angela? May I say something about methodology?"

"Of course."

Weintraub took a moment to polish his glasses and perhaps his argument.

"Dr. Eklund, you mentioned Egypt and the Mayans. And correct me if I'm wrong—you knew what kind of shapes and alignments you were looking for, almost like a template. And knowing what you hope to find builds in bias, which is bad science, frankly . . ."

▼

Winston stopped the tape. Eklund had been effectively marginalized, but still, the man was a loose cannon. Why NASA tolerated somebody like this on its payroll was baffling.

"Christ." He finished his martini and again picked up the phone.

Fortunately, this was but a small irritation at the end of a very good day. The analysis of the data set from the full-scale test of Project Orion by Defense Intelligence, NASA, and their partners in the Ukraine had been positive across-the-board. They had finally done it, made the first giant step toward realizing the promise of Ronald Reagan's Star Wars vision, the Strategic Defense Initiative. It was a major achievement he would enjoy reporting directly to the President, though not with that particular spin on it.

He punched some numbers on the secured landline and waited.

There was still a lot to do besides leading the reluctant Occupant of the White House to water. On the Hill, there were armed-services chairs to convince, and key people at State. And there was still the Sokoff problem, the President's mush-mouthed fixer and whatever he thought he was doing, sniffing around. But it was late, and Winston didn't want to get the wheels started on that.

He could take care of one item, however, without losing any sleep.

Wiping his mouth with a sharply creased linen napkin, Winston knew he was probably getting NASA Administrator Vernon Pierce out of bed. But he didn't really give a shit.

"Vern, you awake?"

18

With her Beanie Bullwinkle presiding, Angela sat next to Miriam and watched Dr. Stephen Weintraub set down his glass of Chardonnay from the green-room buffet and give his attention to the TOLAS photo of Mars on Angela's computer.

"Well," he said, noncommittally. "And there was no note, nothing?"

In buoyant spirits at the wrap party, the professor had been happy to do them a favor. Dr. Winnick had been charming and generous to him about his work at NASA and Cornell, and Angela made him feel quite at home. Weintraub hoped some of his colleagues at the university would tune in, though he'd be sure to get his share of jealous ribbing if they did.

"What you see is what we got," Angela said, observing the professor as he scrolled down the high-res image with Holmesian thoroughness.

"And you're not going to tell me anything more about it?"

"Nope."

Angela and Miriam had agreed in advance that they should say as little as possible. And certainly nothing about *Mars Observer*.

"The guys at Goddard thought it looked pretty good," Miriam offered.

"Oh, it's better than good." Weintraub nodded. "It basically looks like imaging data from the *Mars Global Surveyor* mapping program. Formatting is correct for *Mars Orbital Camera*, resolution, pixel count . . ."

"What about the pyramids?"

"Oh, I can't confirm CGI without being in the lab. I imagine somebody's having some fun. Whoever it is, he doesn't seem to have gone beyond the limits of the instrumentation, which is smart. The MOC specs on *Surveyor* are identical to what we had on *Mars Observer*. I could probably order this frame from Malin Scientific for you, then use the original to compare . . ."

Weintraub scrolled to the right-hand bottom edge bearing the mission code and promptly froze.

Angela and Miriam waited out his initial reaction with small pangs of guilt that showed a nice spirit. Weintraub shot them a look.

"You saw this at Goddard?" His voice sounded strained and he cleared his throat. "Stupid question. I'm guessing this is what you really wanted me to see."

"The mission code." Angela could see he was upset, but forged ahead. "Eklund and a planetary geologist, John Fisher, put it up on the mainframe and enlarged it until it fell apart. Seemed like they were pretty thorough."

"And their position is what, exactly?" Weintraub sounded a bit sour about it. Angela gave him the facts.

"They could find no obvious tampering. No hard edges suggesting inserts or pasting, no evidence of erasure or blurring behind the numbers, which I understand you'd expect if they were superimposed. They could not prove it was a fake."

Weintraub fell silent. Miriam put the unspoken question to him.

"Professor, is it possible that *Mars Observer* was not lost?"

"No, I was there. It was lost. We lost it . . ."

The scientist's expression darkened as he turned back to the TOLAS image, seemingly too involved with his own emotions to invite further questions.

It wasn't possible that he could have been this grossly deceived. How could NASA have lied, not just to him and everyone involved with the Observer *mission, but to the world? But if this capture was real, the evidence spoke for itself. The* Mars Observer *imaging had represented the fulfillment of his life's work. How dare they just take it away? What gave them the right?*

Weintraub was not naive. He knew NASA, the institution, had always played for its survival in a larger game: a lopsided tug-of-war for preeminence in space with the Department of Defense. This had been true from day one of NASA's inception as a civilian agency. So there were institutional reasons to suspect the Pentagon, in concert with the NASA, of asserting primacy in the name of national security. Weintraub began to suspect that a "sacrifice" had been demanded and NASA had been obliged to give up *Mars Observer*.

Control. It's all about control.

He wanted to take this *Mars Observer* image and go wave it like a bloody shirt in front of Vern Pierce, the NASA Administrator, just to see the look on his face. But he knew he would never do any such thing.

He had too much to lose, even at this point in his career. Didn't he?

Angela tried to pull Weintraub back from his thoughts.

"Professor, during the Gulf War the Pentagon secretly commandeered four NASA satellites and redeployed them over Iraq, isn't that true?"

Miriam glanced at her partner, wondering where she'd dug up this cogent bit of info, or if she was just winging it. Weintraub nodded.

"For military surveillance, yes."

"And the Pentagon instructed NASA to lie about it to the media, so they told CNN and the *New York Times* that the satellites had been "lost," which was how it was reported to the public."

"For reasons of national security. Point being?"

But the Professor seemed unwilling or unable to continue.

"I'm sorry," he said, getting to his feet. "I think I should go."

"Please." Angela stood with him. "I know this is your work and it has to be upsetting, but hypothetically: Could the government remotely take over a NASA satellite and continue to run it 'in the dark' for its own purposes?"

Miriam got up on her feet, too. Weintraub winced as if his stomach had cramped.

"Could it? You mean is it technically feasible? Sure. Sure they could. Easy as changing a phone number. But would they? I can't tell you. Go ask DOD. Ask the NSA. That's one reason I went back to teaching. It's all about the militarization of space now. There is so little pure space science being done. It's not about space science. It's about control."

The professor looked for a moment like he was about to say more, then turned for the door as if he'd already said too much.

"Wait. Stephen, please," Miriam said, touching his sleeve. "It was an honor to have you on the show and we can only imagine what your feelings might be, but if someone of your stature would be willing to offer an expert opinion . . ."

"We're not asking you to get involved in the politics," Angela added, knowing instantly it wasn't true.

Weintraub laughed out loud. It was a bitter worldly little bark, full of scorn: authenticating this image could be the most political thing he'd ever do.

"Please," he said. "Take it to the office of the NASA Administrator, walk it in to Vernon Pierce, lay it on his desk, and then walk away. In your business I'm sure it's very valuable to have powerful friends who owe you a favor."

▼

It wasn't until the angry slap of Weintraub's wing-tipped shoes down the corridor had completely faded that either one of them could speak.

"Well," Miriam said, breaking the silence. "I think that went rather well, don't you?"

But Angela seemed momentarily immune to smart remarks.

"I think we just got our authentication, Miriam."

"Is that what that was?"

All Miriam could see was that they had alienated a very important member of the nation's science community and had nothing to show for it.

"You saw it." Angela gestured at the door Weintraub had disappeared through. "How much more confirmation do you need? The man is freaked."

"I'm a little freaked myself," Miriam said. "Because our key satellite imaging expert will probably not even be returning our phone calls, much less going on record with his expert opinion. Which puts us at something less than square one, kid."

"Not necessarily." Moving back over to the computer, Angela went on-line and began searching through the hundreds of TOLAS bulletin-board comments.

"We needed to know if this was a hoax, right?"

"Right. And?"

Miriam looked at the clock, feeling suddenly dead tired as Angela scanned for signs of Deep Cosmo in the postings. Nothing. She turned to her partner.

"Look, Miriam, this is huge. I mean Watergate huge." Angela's face was a study in quiet, clear determination. "We didn't get exactly what we hoped for from Stephen. But we got something incredibly important. We got a big, dark *yes*. Confirmation, for you and me personally, that we are not wasting our time, we are onto the science story of a lifetime."

Miriam nodded. Part of her was still being dragged kicking and screaming to that same conclusion. But the preponderance of evidence was becoming hard to deny, even if she saw herself as playing Scully to Angela's Mulder.

"Was that true about the satellites and the Gulf War?"

"Absolutely."

"Jesus."

Miriam knew what her partner wanted from her. This was a *moment de vérité* in another way, too. Angela was outgrowing *Science Horizon*. The two of them would either go forward together on this career-making story, one hundred percent, and become prime-time players, or probably not last much longer as partners. Miriam sensed this, whether Angela did or not.

Accomplished and diligent, Miriam occasionally felt a bit jealous of Angela's passion about all this, even as it blew past all apparent stop signs. But as she affirmed her own commitment to go the distance on this story, part of her was hoping some of Angela's enviable, sometimes naive fearlessness might rub off.

"Watergate huge," Miriam repeated the phrase. "Which one would that make me, Woodward or Bernstein?"

Angela furrowed her forehead, remembering *All the President's Men*.

"Did Redford play Carl Bernstein?"

"No. Dustin Hoffman."

"Then I'm obviously Bob Woodward."

"You just won't kiss my ass for a second, will you?" Miriam said, doing a nice slow burn. Angela laughed, gave her a hug, and grabbed the Beanie Bullwinkle.

"Want to see me pull a rabbit out of a hat?"

She then looked her producing partner in the eye, as an ally and a battle-tested friend, and paraphrased Bobby McFerrin and JFK, back-to-back.

"Don't worry, be happy. We will do these things not because they are easy, but because they are hard."

"But first we have a sit-down with the suits." Miriam nodded. Angela was very glad to see Miriam was in with both feet and already thinking several moves ahead. Not like someone afraid to move without a panoply of lawyers nodding yes. More like a woman scheduling a nail appointment before going into corporate battle.

PART

III

We often forget how much unites all the members of humanity. Perhaps we need some outside universal threat to make us recognize this common bond. I occasionally think how quickly our differences would vanish if we were facing an alien threat from outside this world.

—President Ronald Reagan
United Nations General Assembly
September 1987

19

1973/Sinus Medii/the Moon

Setting up the last of the seismic sensors, they were unprepared for that first moment when the Earth rose up into view above the cratered lunar surface, achingly blue and gibbous in the pitch-black sky. Commander Jake Deaver dropped the hammer he'd been using and stared.

"Good God Almighty . . ."

The installed sensors registered the tool's impact like a mini-moonquake.

"Commander? Uh, we failed to copy. Over."

But Jake had stopped hearing the mission director at Johnson Space herding them through the choreography of their science schedule, stopped doing anything at all beyond just standing there, bearing witness to Earthrise.

He could feel his heart beating in his throat and hear the sound of his lungs inhaling and expelling the monitored mix of breathable bottled air. His eyes welled up, but he couldn't wipe them clear.

"Commander?"

Blinking rapidly, Deaver decided he needed to see the world just as it was and lifted the gold visor on his helmet.

"Houston, we have Earthrise . . ."

"Copy that. Commander? Check your visor. Over."

"Augie?" Jake pointed a pressurized glove.

"I got it." Augie focused a hand-wound eight-millimeter Kodak camera on the rolling lunar horizon just as it completed the full revelation of their home world.

"Commander? We show your visor in the up position. Over?"

Jake purposely ignored the transmission and allowed himself a good look around: unfiltered, the colors on the lunar surface were intense. What had only been dark shadows inside several surrounding craters were now plainly seen as pools of deep violet, and as he looked around he noticed a faint dusting, like indigo snow, on the worn-down lunar hills.

"Uh, Houston? Repeat the question. Over."

"Commander? Check your visor. Do you copy? Over."

Looking down, Deaver noticed how his own shadow was not black, as it would have been on Earth, but a curious rainbow of color, eerie and magical. The shifting spectrum of shades reflecting and refracting all around him made the moonscape intoxicating and surreal.

"Jake?"

"Visor check, copy that."

Whatever happens, it was worth it, Deaver thought, pulling the gold faceplate back into position, thrill-drunk as the Dog Star, Sirius, winked up over the horizon, trailing Mother Earth on a short leash.

"This is amazing . . . awesome . . ."

Something caught Jake's eye and he plunged his gloved hand down into a mound of what looked like lavender beach glass heaped at his feet and extracted a blade-shaped indigo shard. He called over to his partner.

"Augie . . . I think you want to get this."

Standing under the hard black sky, Deaver lifted the shard up in both hands like an ancient Egyptian priest making an offering to Ra, the sun god of the Followers of Horus. He seemed transfixed with awe.

"Podnah . . ." Augie panned the windup Kodak. Gold threads in the Apollo mission patch on Deaver's shoulder flashed in the sun, the embroidery depicting the three belt stars of Orion. He held the glass shard very still.

"Can you see?"

"God, yes. Look at that . . ."

Augie zoomed in and Jake presented various angles on the indigo silica to the lens, but not to the billions back home. Like so much about

America's last mission to the Moon, this film footage was destined to remain an Official State Secret until "the appropriate time," however that would be determined.

The lunar shard would be brought back and preserved, then taken out and digitally photographed when that technology was developed in the '90's and then secreted away again, in the most highly classified domain of the U.S. National Archives.

But Deaver and Blake would remember that moment of Earthrise at Medii the rest of their lives. Well into the twenty-first century, Jake in particular would return to it in dreams, and even fully awake, he'd find himself going back, imagining himself there and thinking about it, whether he wanted to or not.

20

February 1/Boulder, Colorado

Thinking.

Inside Naropa Institute's colorful Dharmadhatu Temple, former Apollo Commander Jake Deaver was sitting cross-legged on a Zabuton pillow, surrounded by fellow Buddhist students and trying desperately not to nod off.

Thinking.

He shifted his knees and brought his wandering mind back to his out-breath.

Jake Deaver was long retired from NASA and the military and well into a third career as a teacher at the University of Colorado at Boulder. His short-cropped hair was textured with gray. The face it framed was lined and well worn, like the visage of some forgotten Roman general cast in silver coin and rescued from the Aegean by treasure hunters.

In repose, he might have been considered flat-out handsome, even at this distance from a glory-drenched youth. But Deaver's lopsided smile, when it surfaced, played against that, revealing a fundamental lack of vanity. At least in regard to his looks.

Espresso, he thought, almost smelling it, like the faint odor of a skunk wandering down from the hills outside Boulder. *My kingdom for a double espresso.*

Thinking.

He labeled this mental digression and returned his attention to his breath.

At one end of the high-ceilinged meditation hall, the Kharmapa, a visiting lama and lineage holder of the Khargyu School of Tibetan Buddhism, sat in meditation among the brightly robed monks of his order, a Vajrayana sect long exiled into northern India by the Chinese Army.

Jake became momentarily aware of the colored silk banners, Tibetan prayer flags, and traditional *thangka* paintings hung from red-and-gold-enameled beams, and of the presence of His Holiness, the reincarnated Khargyu master's proper appellation.

Thinking.

Deaver refocused on his breath and struggled to ignore the tingling sensations as his limbs began falling excruciatingly asleep.

It was his knees. An awkward jet-training parachute jump in '66 at Wright-Patterson AFB was the primary suspect, an event so far in the past it might as well have been from another life.

Physical discomfort aside, Tibetan Shamata sitting practice was especially difficult because of the tendency of people to get bored out of their skulls, which meant their minds would constantly be wandering off into memories, feelings, daydreams, and every imaginable fantasy.

The trick, as taught by Rinpoche, Jake's meditation instructor, was to mentally label whatever came up during sitting practice as *thinking*. Then, without judgment, to gently redirect your attention back to that ineffable human activity that was always occurring in the present: your own autonomic breath.

This was intended to help one rediscover the subtle, ordinary, but powerful state of *being present* or in the *now*. To see how thoughts arise out of nothing, manifest in living color, then return to nothingness. It also created the opportunity for the Shamata practitioner to recognize the repeating patterns of ego expressed in the human mind's machinations, and see a lot of embarrassing shit about one's self without jumping up and running off screaming—hopefully. And for Jake Deaver, at this point in his life, that was truly the ongoing challenge: consciousness . . . the final frontier.

Thinking.

He felt firm feminine hands on his back and neck that he recognized as belonging to Maeera, a dancer from New York and a Dharmadhatu meditation instructor. Her strong deft fingers pushed and pulled on him, effecting small but precise adjustments in Jake's posture before moving on to help others.

Maeera would later be teased that her alignment of Jake's lean athletic body and all-too-military spine had just been an excuse to lay hands on the astronaut. The Buddhist community, or Sangha, was spiritual and disciplined but not at all prudish; the lamas themselves seeming to be unimpressed with the notion of celibacy. And Deaver was no stranger to gossip.

Thinking.

A Tibetan brass-bowl gong sounded twice, the ring-off reverberating as designated monks and students got up to lead walking meditation. Jake stood up on pins and needles, utterly unable to feel his feet, and made himself move. Limping along in silly agony, he shuffled into a long line filing around the room and passed the raised platform of His Holiness, the Kharmapa.

At the end of the hall, tapping the shoulder of a hosting American student with his ornate ceremonial fan, the Khargyu lineage holder pointed in Jake's direction down the approaching line. The *tulku*'s mischievous eyes wrinkled, his voice raspy from hours of song-chant, which, for the visiting monks, had begun long before dawn.

"Moon Man," the Kharmapa said in Tibetan, and waited as the flustered suit-and-tie Buddhist searched his modest Tibetan vocabulary.

"Ah! Moon Man! Yes." The student laughed, working it out, and then froze for a moment, unsure if laughing was appropriate.

But the high lama simply sat in his traditional hat and robe, twinkling happily, and none of the attendant monks offered a reproving look.

By the time Jake had shuffled around in front of the Kharmapa, some feeling had returned to his extremities; at least he would probably not fall down.

"Your Holiness." Deaver bowed slightly, his hands together.

"Moon Man." The Kharmapa bowed back, speaking hoarsely in English.

His smile beamed beatifically, as if he was recognizing a saint or a long-lost relative from another life. His Holiness then nodded his closely shaved head, and with sly piercing black eyes he blessed Jake and then gestured for him to come nearer. It was both an invitation and a royal command.

Deaver approached, understandably wary of those extremely intelligent-looking eyes. But the Buddhist master simply radiated unaffected compassion. And then leaning forward and touching foreheads with Jake, he whispered into his ear.

"Moon Man. Time to take another walk."

It was as if Time had somehow stopped. The words had both literal and metaphoric meaning, but Deaver was experiencing something more: a vivid super-string of unfolding chaotic images mixed with waves of emotion that resonated through him, uncensored and charged with an indescribable oracular power. It was quick, quasi-psychedelic, and it left Jake speechless.

Time to take another walk.

Managing to mumble an awkward thank-you to His Holiness, he rejoined the rest of the practitioners for walking meditation in a state of turmoil.

Time to take another walk.

What the hell had just happened? It was as if the Vajrayana master had given him a brief inchoate glimpse of multidimensional Reality, tearing open the seemingly seamless fabric of space/time and laying the illusion of the senses bare for only a fraction of a moment.

But that had been quite enough. Whatever hard-won peace Jake had acquired through years of sitting practice and other devotions now seemed absurdly delusional: just another ripe field of play for spiritual materialism. The ego's pride in the acquisition of skills or accumulation of spiritual experiences was a classic pothole on the path of dharma.

Seeing with stark clarity, in that instant, how this phenomenon of ego had manifested in himself was both liberating and deeply embarrassing.

Chagrined awake, he thought.

He felt ungrounded now and almost comically sorry for himself. He wanted to go, just get the hell out of there. Or rush back and pepper the Kharmapa with questions.

What the hell just happened there? Was he supposed to do something or "get" something? Was there a Tibetan name for it, what he just experienced there? And what exactly was that supposed to mean: "Time to take another walk"?

But then the bowl gong sounded the end to walking meditation and the Sangha members drifted back again to their *zafu* pads. Unpersuaded by any impulse to do anything else, Deaver took his spot among the others inside the crowded Buddhist temple, adjusting his legs under the Zabuton pillow.

Then, with a practiced effort, he resumed the three-thousand-year-old Tibetan discipline of following his own breath.

Thinking . . . thinking . . . thinking . . .

21

Parked outside the Dharmadhatu in downtown Boulder, the two plain-clothes FBI men in their burgundy Chevy program sedan were bored to death and tired of being made for narcs.

Waiting for Commander Jake Deaver, USN, Ret., to finish whatever the hell he was doing in there, they were continually being pinned by passing CU students who would then scuffle off in burgeoning paranoia about their current source for Ecstasy and reasonably priced weed.

"On-sight prevention," Agent Stottlemeyer said.

"Yeah, right." His partner, Agent Markgrin, took his word for it from behind the financial section of the *Denver Post*.

Field agents Stottlemeyer and Markgrin were not staked out in the little college town of Boulder, Colorado, to interdict a scourge of psychotropic drugs. A certain incident last summer involving trespassing, mushrooms, and a private cow pasture notwithstanding, they were keeping an eye on former astronaut Jake Deaver under what the two men liked to call the government's Witless Protection Program.

On a recent trip to Egypt, the astronaut-turned-history-teacher had apparently been present during a tragic and calculated paroxysm of radical Muslim xenophobia: a terrorist attack that left dozens of mostly Russian, Georgian, and Ukrainian visitors injured and four Egyptian policemen killed outright. Already crippled by the regional violence and instability among its Middle East neighbors, the National Tourism Bureau in Cairo would be a long time recovering. Commander Deaver, however, had escaped harm. And as far as Agents Stottlemeyer and

Markgrin and even their superiors in the Denver field office were concerned, that should have been end-of-story.

The powers-that-be inside the Hoover Building in Washington, D.C., however, obviously disagreed.

▼

"My turn to check the alley for ragheads and car bombs." The stocky agent Stottlemeyer smirked over at his partner.

"You be careful out there," Markgrin said, flipping to the tech-stock index below the fold.

Stottlemeyer had not been spurred to action by any real hope of squelching international terror in the mean streets of Boulder, Colorado. Mostly the G-man was moved by the dead nerve endings in his ample derriere and the sight of a pair of laughing co-eds jaywalking across the street to the local Starbucks, a situation plainly calling for a fresh cup of coffee. He checked his teeth in the rearview mirror, looking for nasty food bits, and then squeezed his thick torso out from behind the steering wheel.

Behind the dull tail job, there was method to the madness, or at least a rationale. Hustled out of Egypt by the CIA head of station aboard an Exxon company jet, Deaver had left the embassy folks more jittery about Deaver's presence at the attack than about the violence itself.

Twenty-two hospitalized Russian Federation tourists on five-day packages, air included, at $500 per person/double, along with four dead Egyptian policemen was terrible, but finally not the issue. The issue was Jake: Was it just a coincidence or had an American space hero been targeted in the incident? The potential for political exploitation was certainly there; in Egypt's ongoing secular/religious power game, an attack on Deaver might have been designed to set certain actions in motion.

Had former Apollo Commander Jake Deaver been deliberately targeted for assassination, the United States would have been "invited" by the embattled Cairo government to "offer assistance" in hunting down the Pan-Islamic terrorists presumed responsible. And if the FBI and the CIA came rushing in, wasn't this just the kind of move that the most radical anti-American mullahs and clerics could exploit to the hilt? The Caireen news headlines practically wrote themselves.

INFIDELS PURSUE EGYPTIAN CITIZENS ON THEIR OWN SOIL!

Public outrage, massive street demonstrations, more inflammatory antigovernment rhetoric in the mosques. And the last thing Washington wanted to see in Cairo was a coup that brought fundamentalist Egyptian *jihadis* to power.

Fortunately, though, Deaver had not been harmed in the attack at Giza, so the adept U.S. ambassador at the scene made quick calls to Western media moguls, who used their influence with CNN, the Russian news people, and regionals like al-Jazeera, until a full lid was brought down: Deaver's presence during the tragedy went unreported.

Still, even with Jake safely home and teaching again at UC–Boulder, someone high up in the intelligence food chain in D.C. had apparently decided that the situation bore watching.

"Want anything?" Stottlemeyer said, indicating the Starbucks and pulling on a mustard-stained Rockies warm-up jacket.

"A tall Americano. And a biscotti." Markgrin barely looked up, continuing to track his tech-heavy nest egg on the NASDAQ roller coaster.

"Jesus." Stottlemeyer rolled his eyes and leaned down to look back at his partner through the driver's-side window. "Coffee and a doughnut would just be too much of a cliché, wouldn't it? Whoa! Hate to be mistaken for cops."

Markgrin put down the *Post*. The town-and-gown bit was a running gag. Both men had degrees. Only Stottlemeyer had had to earn *his* education scrambling for loans and scholarships, and working his butt off nights and weekends. It was a hardship that made him feel both self-made, as they used to say, and proud, but also a bit defensive, with a slightly righteous sense of personal "street cred" next to his Ivy League partner, whatever that was worth.

"Starbucks doesn't carry doughnuts," Markgrin said. "Anyway, biscotti is hard, so it dunks better. Trust me. I have a great catholicity of taste."

Stottlemeyer smiled and zipped up his baseball jacket.

"Aw, fuck you *and* the Pope. Plain or chocolate?"

22

Sandia Research Labs/New Mexico

Escorted into the Sandia Labs by a delegation of scientists, Sandy Sokoff made it an aggressive, high-profile entrance. The President's Marine One helicopter that had delivered him was instructed to keep its engines warm, at the ready to whisk him off to Los Alamos, Raytheon, and the other top-secret facilities on his itinerary. The hulking chopper hunkered down on the landing pad, radiating a sense of urgency and command authority.

Sokoff thought a little big-swinging-dick ostentation was in order to inspire fear and, hopefully, cooperation at one of the nation's most insular and tightly guarded weapons plants.

Half science compound, half classified military base, Sandia Labs was home to the development of the next three generations of high-tech American weaponry, about which the new President and his personal counsel knew almost nothing. And once inside, Sandy expected to encounter institutional reluctance as far as the divulging of any details. In that, he was not disappointed.

"Project Orion," Dr. Milton Krantz, the senior project manager, addressed Sokoff from across a long conference-room table. "Well, we did design work for something like what you are describing. It was a prototype ELF, Extreme Low-Frequency scalar-type transmitter."

"Who commissioned it?" Sandy said, making notes on a yellow pad. He knew who had assigned the Orion contract to Sandia Labs. He just wanted to see how forthcoming Krantz intended to be.

"The Navy." Krantz shot the cuffs slightly on his white lab coat. "We were given certain specifications after initial consultations. The lab was then tasked with developing a solution for long-range submarine communication; bouncing extreme-low-frequency signals off the upper atmosphere. Very interesting problem, hadn't been done before really, but in the end, it did prove technically feasible."

"Long-range data transmission without satellites."

"Yes. Think of it as high-powered sonar. In case, for whatever reason, in time of war, our satellites were down. But like I say, it wasn't called Project Orion."

"No, you probably knew it as part of the HAARP project." Sandy rubbed his ear, looking up at the half-dozen other scientists seated at the table, ready and waiting to field any technical questions he might have. "Up in Alaska."

"That's correct."

Krantz looked wary, wondering what the agenda was here. Maybe more grief about beaked whales beaching themselves with bleeding inner ears after Navy testing of the new sonar they'd developed. In any case, the President's counsel was behaving more like a prosecutor than a fact finder.

"Now, in your opinion, Doctor, could this extreme-low-frequency or ELF technology also be used as part of a space-defense platform?"

The senior project manager smiled, visibly shifting gears.

"Mr. Sokoff, if a Sony PlayStation can be used for missile guidance . . ." Krantz offered an insider's Gallic shrug and looked at his hand-picked colleagues around the table. They chuckled on cue.

Rather than disarming Sokoff, the glib reference to the ban on exporting game modules to rogue nations only pissed Sandy off.

"Dr. Krantz." Sokoff's peremptory tone was as sobering as a congressional subpoena. "The President of the United States has tasked me with bringing him up to speed on all Unacknowledged Special Access Projects, past and present. This is not an idle curiosity, it is a matter of national security. What do you know about USAPs here at Sandia Labs? And would you characterize this ELF project or any aspect of ELF technology as a USAP?"

Sandy watched the smiles disappear around the long table and felt the room temperature drop about ten degrees. President Carter had given him a few key leads, and this one had struck a nerve. Dr. Krantz, however, had a ready answer.

"We handle no such programs at Sandia Labs, to my knowledge."

Sandy had ferreted more than a few bureaucrats out of their bunkers during his years as a congressional investigator. Careful language was no refuge.

"Is there something inadequate about my level of clearance, Doctor?"

"You're authorized above top secret, Mr. Sokoff," Krantz said. "But I can assure you, no Project Orion or any other special-access contracts are being worked on at this facility."

"To your knowledge. Is there someone who might have more complete knowledge?"

It was a deliberate needle designed to prod Krantz higher on his horse.

"As senior project manager, I supervise all the science being done under this roof. There's nothing I wouldn't know about, if it was going on here."

"Then you would know if the ELF technology you developed for Navy subs had a dual military purpose."

Krantz's self-assurance wavered.

"What exactly do you mean?"

"It's a simple question, Doctor. Could the high-powered extreme-low-frequency transmitters developed here on your watch have both overt and covert applications?"

"Mr. Sokoff, with all due respect, if you are asking me to speculate on some convoluted hypothetical—"

"A yes-or-no answer will suffice," Sandy said.

Sokoff was blunt, intentionally disrespectful. Krantz found being spoken to like this in front of his subordinates galling. He took the offensive.

"The answer to your question is yes. Yes, of course. Anything and everything we do may have dual purposes. Please explain that to the President. You'll find it's true at every lab in the country; that's just how it is. We're given certain specifications, a time frame, and a budget. We do the research, we do the science, we gain the knowledge needed to solve a given problem. How that knowledge is applied after it leaves this facility is not our concern. What NAV/INT or the NSA does with the fruits of our research is beyond our control. Not to mention way beyond my pay grade to speculate."

Sandy waited a beat or two, letting his dissatisfaction and disappointment become more pointed, more evident. He then stood up and gathered his things. When he spoke, it was with the assurance of someone who knew or would soon know where all the skeletons were hidden.

"Dr. Krantz, you and your people have seventy-two hours to do better than this, and I suggest a top-to-bottom. On behalf of the President, I can also assure you that if you fail to cooperate fully with the White House on this, if we determine that for whatever reason you are being less than forthcoming, every sustaining government contract at Sandia Labs, everything bid on by you during this administration, will come under immediate negative review."

The shocked silence around the conference table spoke louder than words. Sandy extracted a business card from his wallet.

"And please, let's not have any explosions or burst water pipes or other regrettable accidents resulting in the loss of key files and documents. The President hates having his intelligence insulted. And so do I."

It was a little over-the-top, but what the hell. Sokoff tossed the business card down in front of Krantz, as if paying off rough trade with chump change.

"This is my direct line at the White House."

Sokoff's phone actually rang in the Old Executive Office Building via the White House switchboard next door. But he had made his point.

Striding out to the Marine One helicopter with the presidential seal on the side, he wondered whether Dr. Krantz would realize his little slip.

What NAV/INT and the NSA does . . .

Naval Intelligence being in the loop on a sub communications research contract was to be expected. The National Security Agency, however . . .

"Our friend Bob." Sokoff mumbled it under his breath.

Ducking down beneath the whirling whine of the chopper, he snapped open his cell phone and hit the autodial.

"Mrs. Travers," Sandy shouted it out over the prop wash. "Tell the President I'm up to my knees in prairie pizza out here. I'll call him back on a landline."

23

Los Alamos, New Mexico

As the President's counsel took his one-man-show farther up the road, he was not strictly speaking alone. From a greater distance up the high desert hill than he would've liked, the intelligence officer assigned to follow Sandy Sokoff leaned across the hood of a dusty silver Crown Vic and studied the helicopter pad at Los Alamos through Zeiss binoculars.

He could not get much closer without drawing attention. Switching to a Nikon digital camera with a kick-ass custom zoom, he documented each person who came out to greet the President's counsel and escort him inside the facility. He recognized the Chinook's pilot and copilot as two of the six on 24/7 rotation for the President, and took shots of them, too. He also noticed how the Secret Service seemed conspicuously absent.

The officer then settled down to wait and see what he could learn from Sokoff's departure.

24

February 2/Dunsinane, Antarctica

Emerging from the Antarctic ice, it was erect on all fours, with an astonishing look of sentience in its wet black eyes. Frozen dead standing up, with a rack of antlers cocked back at an angle, the caribou seemed afraid, as if listening to the sound of the end of the world. The National Science Foundation team now carefully releasing it from eons inside the glacier was ecstatic.

Mastodons had been found like this near the Arctic Circle, fully upright with a stomach full of freshly cropped grasses and flowers, as if mysteriously flash-frozen with the cud still in their mouths. But nothing like that had ever been found near the South Pole.

At least, not until now.

Thanks to Captain Wesley Bertrand and his crew, 99.9 percent of the radioactive ice at Dunsinane and the hot nuclear drill itself had been safely retrieved, contained, and removed. Trace contamination remained, which caused some wringing of hands, but not enough to warrant shutting down the dig.

So, with strict protocols and new biohazard protections for the science team, the Antarctic prehistoric forest was opened for study.

Running heavily insulated power lines down to an exposed section of ancient trees, the scientists in their bulky "clean suits" used handheld hair dryers to melt the last inch of ice from the upright caribou corpse.

Matted wet fur dusted with a curious layer of fine black carbon began to smell as it thawed. It would be easy to get an accurate dating, but the NSF team already had a pool going with their bets. Most hovered around 10,500 B.C.E., give or take a century or two.

Antarctic ice-core samples taken in 1998 had thrown paleoclimatologists one looping big-league curveball. The samples showed that around 12,500 years ago, the Ice Age abruptly ended with extremely rapid global warming.

This dramatic climate change version of Earth history shattered the mainstream gradualist models taught in Western universities. Subsequent Greenland and North Pole core samples confirmed an overall fifty-nine-degree increase in average daily temperature during one fifty-year period; a radical change in a geological blink of the eye.

For the human population, circa 10,500 B.C.E., that would've meant a catastrophic melting of glaciers around the world, lending a whole lot of historical credibility to the Noachian myth of the Great Flood.

But what had caused the heat-up, what was the trigger? Had an immense Earth-crossing comet or bolide slammed to ground, kicking off enough volcanic eruptions to dwarf the carbon dioxide pollution pumped out by mere superindustrial man? Carbon levels in the core samples at least raised the suspicion.

In any case, the Academy of Sciences acknowledged that around the year 12,500 *something big happened* and thousands of species of plants and animals were wiped out. For Homo sapiens, that most adaptable of mammals, it had been yet another near-extinction event to survive, like the Ice Age itself.

And for the twenty-first-century scientists at Dunsinane, bent over their emerging caribou buck like Moses' lost Israelites anointing a fatted calf, the prehistoric biosphere beneath their feet was an unfolding mystery with a hundred questions for every solid answer.

25

Goddard Space Flight Lab

"Richard? Close the door, would you?"

The normally breezy and cordial NASA project manager was all business.

Eklund closed the door, surprised to see a stenographer perched with her machine next to the manager's desk. Beside her was a wiry man in a dark suit who looked as though he spent all his spare time on a stationary bike when he wasn't working for the federal government.

Eklund knew this couldn't be good.

"Agent Turner, this is Dr. Eklund." The NASA manager made the introductions. "Agent Turner and Ms. Stegman are with the FBI. The Bureau is assisting Administrator Pierce, who requested this meeting. They just want to ask you some questions."

Agent Turner and Ms. Stegman shook hands with Eklund as if he might have a communicable disease. Turner took charge of the questioning.

"Please have a seat, Doctor. We're required to record all interviews. Uh, 'February second, Goddard Labs, Agent Turner interviewing Dr. Richard Eklund.'"

Eklund noticed the tape recorder and its little omnidirectional microphone and sat down. He then responded to a wide-ranging set of prepared questions for the next fifty minutes and change.

Curiosity concerning the tenor of his remarks on the *Science Horizon* program was expressed, especially his criticisms direct and implied of

NASA and Malin Scientific, the imaging contractor for *Mars Surveyor*. Past conflicts with Goddard Space Flight management were revisited and discussed. An accounting of his hours was requested, especially non-NASA activities involving the so-called Mars Underground and the use of Goddard equipment and facilities, along with a complete description in writing of his contacts and conversations with Ms. Angela Browning and anyone else in the media with whom he had any kind of contact or correspondence.

Had the bow-tied research scientist been suspected of planning to bomb the building, the interrogation could not have been more thorough.

They also quizzed him very closely about his colleague John Fisher; what the planetary geologist had told him about his classified work at the Pentagon, whether Eklund thought Fisher was unhappy, disgruntled, having money problems, family problems, drug problems, health problems, sex problems, etc.

When it was over, Agent Turner showed him a copy of the nondisclosure agreement that Eklund had signed when he was hired by NASA and reminded him of the penalties for violating it. He was then thanked and dismissed.

Eklund stood up to go, his mind racing. He had remained polite and cooperative, and except for leaving out any mention of TOLAS and the *Mars Observer* data, he'd been absolutely truthful. But he could tell they suspected he was holding out on them. Or maybe that was just an interrogation technique.

In any case, he left for an early lunch in his aging red EV-1 feeling frightened, shaky, and drained.

What the hell was that all about?

Only paranoid-sounding answers came to mind until he remembered he needed to call John and give him a heads-up. But maybe not on a cell phone.

John is going to shit.

Using a pay phone at a gas station where his electric car was quite a novelty, he got Fisher's voice mail and a thin robotic-sounding recorded announcement.

"Dr. . . . John . . . Fisher . . . has been transferred to . . . NASA/AMES at Moffet Field, California . . . There is no new number at this time."

Eklund hung up, struggling with a nauseating sense of vertigo, as if a gaping crevasse had just yawned open beneath his feet. And for the first time since he'd had root-canal work done in the '90's, he decided he needed to take a personal day.

26

Corporation for Public Broadcasting/Washington, D.C.

In the twelfth-floor wood-paneled office at the Corporation for Public Broadcasting building on Pierre Street near the bridge, Arthur Maclewain tossed the TOLAS CD back across his mahogany desk like a radioactive Frisbee.

"We can take your word about what's on there. Any response yet from this Deep Cosmos?" Leaning back in his leather desk chair, the senior attorney at CPB Legal made a steeple of his manicured fingers.

Seated opposite him and next to Angela, Miriam wasn't sure if the lawyer's pose was an affectation or a cliché, then decided it could be both.

"Not yet," she said, ready to rumble in her DKNY suit.

"Just as well." Maclewain rocked slightly back and forth. "Even a superficial reading of the law—re: the publishing or broadcasting of classified government documents—puts us in a world of hurt."

From a dollar-green tufted leather wing back off to the side, Marvin Epstein, an associate sitting in for the Washington, D.C., affiliate, nodded in agreement. But Miriam and Angela stayed focused on Maclewain. Both looked angry.

"Who said it was classified?" Angela said, reacting first. "If you looked at it, you'd see there's nothing on it that says it's classified."

"Oh, I think a federal judge would find that a bit disingenuous, don't you?" Maclewain said with a sly smirk. Miriam knew a smirk when she saw one.

"Disingenuous? Come on, Arthur, cut the crap. Either it is or it isn't. Either it's classified information or it's not. Why should we presume a photograph of Mars is classified, for God's sake?"

"Shall we call the Department of Defense and ask them?"

"Hell no."

"Well, if you're afraid to ask the Pentagon if it's classified because you think it might be classified, then you damn well better behave as if it is classified. Next?" Maclewain raised an eyebrow that reminded them that time was money and they were on their employer's dime.

"Hold on a second." Angela took a breath, trying to rein in her anger and frustration. "Wait, wait, wait. You're talking preemptive self-censorship by a media journalist, which is de facto abridgment of free press and you know it."

"I don't see a constitutional argument."

"Well, what's the law here, damn it?" Miriam almost shouted it. "When does the government's right to keep a secret supersede free speech, free press, and the people's right to know?"

Maclewain swiveled slightly to include his young associate.

"Marvin?"

"Whenever the Supreme Court says it does," Epstein said. "And anyone who helps broadcast state secrets or analyze classified documents for attribution like this Dr. Weintraub? He's looking at the same ten years plus that you are."

There it was: imprisonment and fines. It was their job to say it, but Angela thought it was also being used to try to scare them off course. She stared at Epstein.

"That doesn't answer the question. State secrets are state secrets because somebody has decided that our national security will be harmed if they are not kept secret. So, the question is, how the hell can a NASA photograph of Mars be a state secret? What can the government possibly be trying to hide that would be a matter of national security? They can't make a sources-and-methods argument, it's a NASA satellite photo. I think we're home free. They have to know that if they did come after us, they'd be begging the question! The whole world would want to know what was on Mars that the U.S. government did not want the public to see. Anyway, Weintraub declined."

"Probably signed an open-ended nondisclosure. I don't suppose you asked him that," Maclewain said. Angela just stared across at him.

He just resets to smug, Angela thought, and imagined vaulting across the barrister's desk and ringing his condescending neck. Miriam jumped in.

"No, we didn't ask him about the terms of any agreements, but answer me this: Why would Justice even go after Weintraub in the first place? We were only asking him to give his opinion as a satellite imaging expert."

"For the record. In public. On-camera. On *Science Horizon*." Maclewain shook his head and turned to Epstein, who was nodding in agreement.

"Yeah, that's like saying he was just casing the bank for you," Epstein said. "You're the ones actually stealing the money."

Before Angela could explode, leaving attorney entrails all over the wood-paneled walls, Miriam held up her hands like a traffic cop.

"All right, fine. You've told us all the good sound reasons why *Science Horizon can't* break the greatest science story ever, smash the all-time ratings record for market share on public-service television, and win every broadcast award going while we're at it. Now tell us how we *can*."

The two men frowned, thinking it over. Epstein shrugged.

"Big guns," he said.

Maclewain leaned way back into his leather desk chair and made another Christ's Church of his well-tended fingers.

"Big *honking* guns."

27

Miriam and Angela took their lunch on the run as they hurried back to their own turf and the PBS tower.

"Well, stature-wise, there's Stephen Hawking. He'd see us. And Dr. Kaku at NYU. You like his take on multidimensional universe stuff." Miriam licked cream cheese off the edge of an everything bagel as they walked.

"Hawking, I can see. Kaku is good, but I don't know..." Angela tossed her empty yogurt cup into a green recycle bin and wished she'd had a bagel, too.

"What about what's-his-name? Einstein Chair at Princeton."

"Look, forget academic stature a second. Let's talk about clout: senators, congressmen, people who can give us some actual political cover. Somebody like a John Glenn—"

"There is no one *like* John Glenn." Miriam laughed.

"Well, there's gotta be somebody on the House Committee..."

"Chairman Phillip Lowe."

"You know him?"

Miriam gave up a half smile.

"I think the congressman'll return my call."

"Hold that thought."

Pushing in the doors of the tower-building lobby, Angela changed trajectory, veering over to the reception desk. An intern looked up from sorting the mail.

"Ms. Browning? You got a package while I was at lunch."

She held up an opened, eight-by-ten manila envelope with "ATT:

Angela Browning c/o *Science Horizon*" neatly typed on a plain white label.

"There's a cancel, but no return. You still want it?"

"Sure. What the heck."

The receptionist handed it over and returned to her stacks of mail. Angela held up the anonymous envelope for her partner to see.

"No name. No return address. Deep Cosmo strikes again."

"Ya think?"

Miriam watched closely as Angela tore it open. Inside was one item: a black-and-white photograph of two unidentified astronauts standing on the Moon. In the top margin eight words were scrawled in quotes. Angela read the caption.

"And good luck, Mr. Grotsky, wherever you are."

They quit the reception desk, puzzling over the otherwise unremarkable Moon picture all the way to the elevators.

"This is it, Miriam. I can feel it. We're in communication now. We're having a dialogue. It's like a puzzle and he wants us to put it together. So, who's Grotsky? Right?" Angela punched the up button several times, her mind already at work on how to start tracking the man down.

Miriam nodded, more wary than her partner, but still intrigued.

"Exactly. Who the hell is Grotsky?"

28

February 3/the Blair House Mansion/Washington, D.C.

Blair House, the historic vice-presidential residence, was still impressive with its eighteenth-century Franklin crystal chandelier, appropriately electrified and blazing away in the atrium. A gift from the People of France, who had so adored the great American ambassador and scientist, the Franklin chandelier was holding elegant sway over the jointly hosted NASA and U.S. State Department revelry below.

Back from McMurdo Station via New Zealand, Colonel Augie Blake looked resplendent in his Marine dress whites. Though the Blair House bash swirling around him was officially in celebration of the latest module linkups on Space Station Alpha, Augie was inwardly hoisting his glass of Perrier to the successful evacuation of his kids from the South Pole. The program's Extreme Environment trainees remained in quarantine at Auckland, suffering more from boredom and disappointment over their truncated mission than anything else.

"Thank you, God," Augie said out loud.

Reflecting on how working a big old Washington party was a far less onerous duty when you didn't have to fake feeling good, Augie looked happily around at the assembled elite roaming the glossy two-hundred-year-old parquetry. Canapés in hand, they were a noisy rainbow of polished players, military and civilian alike, representing the eleven nations who were contributing treasure and expertise for a share in the glory and high-orbit science harvest of the International Space Station.

But one face in particular separated itself from the glitterati and made Augie smile.

Turned out in a Givenchy dress she was unlikely to be allowed to write off, Ms. Angela Browning, of *Science Horizon* fame, looked quite stunning as she chatted up the C-SPAN crew covering the event.

Blake strained to eavesdrop, but whatever Angela was laughing about was drowned out by several rowdy broad-shouldered cosmonauts wolfing down Black Sea caviar appetizers at the bar with a pair of half-lit taiko-nauts from the People's Republic of China.

"How you say? Fish egg!"

"Beluga!"

"Ah . . . smelt!"

"No, no, no . . . Beluga! Beluga!"

Augie moved to a better vantage point, away from the loud space pups, observing from afar the beautiful and apparently unescorted Ms. Browning.

In an adjoining room, a rising young soprano from the current Kennedy Center production of Donizetti's *Lucia* could be heard singing the mad-scene aria. It was colorful and spirited, but not in any danger of putting Sutherland's truly harrowing rendition into eclipse.

Turning away from the C-SPAN crew and negotiating her way through the crowd, Angela captured a glass of Blanc de Noirs from a passing tray and hovered for a moment near a cluster of tables packed with august members of the American astronaut pantheon: the Mercury, Gemini, and Apollo alumni, in particular.

Then Colonel Augustus Julian "Augie" Blake was at her elbow.

"Ms. Browning." Augie beamed in open admiration, offering his white-gloved hand with a courtly bow that would not have been out of place at a Savannah tea party before the War Between the States.

"Colonel Blake." Angela blessed the enduring power of the *little black dress*, resisting the temptation to curtsy as Augie continued making a fuss.

"Ms. Browning, may I say that whoever cut that gorgeous shot of crepe de chine should be paying you *beaucoup* to wear it. You're makin' him look like a goddamned genius."

Angela blushed down to the black pearl choker she had borrowed from Miriam for the occasion. Now she *did* feel like Scarlett O'Hara.

"Thank you, Colonel. And it's Monsieur Givenchy who deserves the couturier props. But you're looking quite spiff tonight yourself." She waved at the medals on his whites and sipped her bubbly. "No saber, though, I see."

"No, no. Ribbon ceremonies and funerals aside, I'm afraid a close shave pretty well exhausts my repertoire with a blade."

"Oh, I've heard about some of your close shaves." Angela gave him a look, seeming to enjoy teasing him. "Not counting your infamous Moon landing."

Augie attempted to demur.

"I'm afraid my reputation exceeds me."

"I'm thinking about a certain May Day embassy party of legend and lore. You and Commander Deaver matching Stolis with the comrades?" She laughed, sliding a glance toward the cosmonaut cutups over at the bar. "In that, I'm afraid, it's the Russians who have the Right Stuff."

Augie took the jabs in good humor, just happy to be on the survivor's side of a bad-boy past. Rumor had implicated both Blake and Jake Deaver in a May 1 commemoration-cum-drunken-brawl hosted at the then Soviet embassy in 1972. The debacle had reportedly featured call girls seen exiting via the windows in various states of dishabille, damaged priceless Russian art and antique furnishings, several cosmonauts with inexplicably self-inflicted wounds, and a morning-after flurry of official apologies and hefty reparations.

"May Day, May Day." Augie laughed, holding up his Perrier water in surrender. "I can't speak for old Flaky Jakey, but for myself I just take it one day at a time now, darlin'."

Glancing across the crowded foyer, Augie caught the eye of the tuxedoed Representative Phillip Lowe, the powerful chairman of the House Committee on Space attending with his wife. He gave them a wink and a wave and they raised their champagne glasses in return, including Angela in the room-spanning toast.

She returned the salute and reminded herself to go say hi. Miriam had already set up a meeting in Lowe's office, and trolling for other potential *big guns* was Angela's primary mission tonight. She turned back to Colonel Blake.

"And what about Commander Deaver?" she said, curious about the Apollo alum now that Augie had brought him up. "Is he here tonight?"

Angela was conscious of working the little black dress a bit, but with negligible shame.

"Jake?" Augie made a face. "Aw, this kind of soiree is not exactly Jake Deaver's cup of herbal tea. Maybe if they were serving hashish brownies, and even then . . ."

Angela heard a certain edge creep into Augie's voice.

"So, Augie Doggie and Doggie Daddy still stay in touch?"

"That's not really on either of our agendas," Augie said, sounding sorry he'd brought it up. Angela was about to pursue it anyway, when she remembered the news story about the astronauts evacuated from the South Pole.

"Colonel, I understand you had some excitement down at McMurdo . . ."

"Not really . . ."

But Augie's attention was distracted. Angela turned to see a knot of half-lit cosmonauts and taiko-nauts gesturing insistently, calling Blake over and including Angela in the invitation. Augie gave them all a wave as NASA Administrator Vernon Pierce appeared over at the bar, passing out vodka shooters to the whole space fraternity.

"Ah, well," Augie said, reluctant but resigned.

"Duty calls?"

"Care to join me?"

Despite or maybe because of Augie's valiant effort at evincing a Pagliacci hopefulness, Angela knew it was more good manners than a real invitation. And much as she might have been amused by the Asian space brothers and the hearty partyers of the former Evil Empire, she graciously declined.

"But thank you," Angela said, offering her hand. "By the way, was there ever a cosmonaut by the name of Grotsky?"

"Grotsky?"

"Maybe back in the late '60's, early '70's."

"No, I don't believe I ever knew a cosmonaut by that name." Augie made a show of searching his memory. "You might query the comrades . . ."

"No, no. I'm sure it was before their time."

"Well, then, *dosvedonya.*" He kissed her hand with practiced gallantry and then leaned close, drawling into her ear. "You take care, now . . . y'hear?"

Augie flashed a kind of enigmatic smile and disappeared with his glass of Perrier into the big-shouldered crush of Russian and Asian uniforms.

Angela felt a mild frisson down to her noire Ferragamo heels.

You take care, now . . . y'hear?

What did he mean by that? She felt another shiver, a chill presentiment that could have been just paranoia. Then Angela shrugged, deciding in the spirit of Occam's Razor that the simplest explanation was the best: Colonel Blake had been merely flirting with her, in his southern-gentleman style.

Accepting a Maryland crab cake from a swallowtail-coated server, Angela regrouped: there were people to meet, tables to work. But as she scanned the room, Augie's comments about Jake Deaver suddenly came back to her.

Hashish brownies? She laughed to herself, nibbling on the crab cake.

Colonel Augie Blake had been a hell-raiser back in the day, but he was much more of a NASA poster boy at this point. She had been toying with the idea of showing him the *Mars Observer* stuff, but her instincts now told her maybe not.

Commander Jake Deaver, however . . .

She tried to remember what she knew about him: dropping out of the space program, becoming a college professor out in Colorado. What did he teach?

Feeling eyes on her all-but-naked back, Angela glanced toward the tables reserved for Mercury, Gemini, and Apollo alumni and recognized one of several famous faces unabashedly appraising her from the inner circle of the most exclusive men's club on Earth.

Commander Edgar Mitchell. Sixth man to walk on the Moon.

The distinguished astronaut smiled at her. Angela smiled back. And executing a graceful turn in the wildly successful little black dress, she carried her empty champagne glass over to where the silver-haired Commander Mitchell and his friends were already getting to their feet.

As men of that great generation were still wont to do in the presence of beauty.

29

February 4/Arlington Country Club

The Arlington Club golf course was not normally open in February, but unseasonably mild weather was bringing the hackers out. At 7:00 A.M. on a weekday, however, Bob Winston, J. B. "Clay" Claiborne, a heavyset TRW lobbyist, and NASA head, Vernon Pierce still had the first tee all to themselves.

"Just wanted to give you a heads-up," Winston said, addressing Vern Pierce and practicing his swing.

"About what?" Pierce kept it casual as he picked out a driver.

The aerospace lobbyist, Claiborne, turned out in designer golf wear that did nothing for his paunch, stood discreetly apart, swinging a Callaway club and pretending not to eavesdrop.

"PBS science journalist Ms. Angela Browning," Winston said.

"*Science Horizon*. What about her?"

To the east, the spire of the Washington Monument could be seen poking up above a row of skeletal cherry trees, almost in perfect alignment with the flag on the far green. Winston took a practice swing, just clipping the wet grass.

"She called Commander Jake Deaver at the crack of dawn this morning, and then booked a red-eye to Colorado."

Vern Pierce pulled on his gloves. He hated shoptalk when he was trying to enjoy himself. But Winston seemed determined to turn a little early-morning golf into exactly what Samuel Clemens had once called it: "a good walk spoiled."

"So?" Pierce shrugged. "Maybe she's doing a show on astronauts."

"Maybe," Winston said without conviction, cleaning his spikes with a Popsicle stick. Staring hard down at his Slazenger, the national security adviser then teed off, only to see the ball slice and carom off the fairway.

"Shit."

Winston scowled at his club, as if the fault lay in the design. Pierce looked at Claiborne, TRW's man in the capital: he'd seen it, too, but the lobbyist kept a straight face. Clay was there because he needed Winston's support for his company's military satellite contracts. There was no percentage in twitting the man about sportsmanship.

"Look, Bob," Pierce said, stabbing a tee into the turf, "I wouldn't worry about Jake Deaver for two seconds. Nobody's strayed from the reservation in thirty-some years and I don't know why they'd start now."

Pierce set his feet and swung his Big Bertha. The ball was high, wide, and slicing handsomely when it disappeared like Winston's Slazenger into the bordering trees. He shook his head.

"Crap."

"In any case, Vern," Winston said, lowering his voice, "we'd like you to have a little sit-down with Admiral Ingraham."

Pierce looked bewildered.

"Ingraham?"

Claiborne, the veteran lobbyist, teed up, making a show of giving the two men their privacy by taking his practice swings with fierce concentration.

"What's going on, Bob?"

"We've asked Jim to oversee the restructuring at JPL."

"Jesus." Pierce sounded as stunned as he was.

Admiral James T. Ingraham was a big-time spook. Former chief of Naval Intelligence. Former head of NSA. And his fait accompli posting to the top spot at the Jet Propulsion Lab, traditionally part of NASA's turf, had occurred without consulting the NASA Administrator. Pierce felt impaled.

"When did this happen?"

Vernon Pierce didn't have to ask why. After corrosive public hearings on Capitol Hill during which NASA was raked over the coals for its numerous and expensive Mars mission failures, a list of congressional recommendations was put in place that included provisions for enhanced oversight. But bringing Admiral Ingraham into the mix by intel fiat was almost a slap in the face. Winston made an effort to smooth ruffled feathers.

"Vern, it's just a preemptive shot across Phillip Lowe's bow. We don't want Congress to think it's their job to fix NASA, do we?"

Clay Claiborne launched a clean, straight tee shot that would give him a look at par. Winston and Pierce broke off their sotto voce conversation and nodded in admiration.

"Beautiful."

"Nice shot, Clay."

"Thanks. Vern? Can we talk about this Sokoff character?" Claiborne asked.

"Sure."

The two men grabbed their golf carts and hiked off across the fairway with their heads together. Pierce felt sick to his stomach.

Admiral James T. Ingraham. Son of a bitch.

Under pressure from Winston, he'd broken up the partnership of Eklund and Fisher over at Goddard, though he had doubted the necessity for doing so. And he'd make a few more eyewash moves that would chill out the so-called Mars Underground crowd, just to show he was "buttoning down his shop." But bringing Ingraham on board, for Christ's sake? Why couldn't they just let him do his job?

Son of a bitch. Pierce took a deep breath. Just because he knew why it was happening didn't mean he had to like it.

Aw, hell, save your powder for a more important fight, he told himself. There was real science to do that needed real budgets, and if he didn't bitch and moan over something he could not change anyway, he'd have more chips to cash when approval time came. Besides, any one of a dozen potential events beyond the horizon could take the heat off and make all this paranoic pressure go away.

One good crisis in the Middle East or North Korea and Bob Winston and his hardball go-go boys will all get too damn busy to be backseat-driving the fucking space program.

Pierce cursed under his breath and trundled his cart out toward the trees, perversely wishing for a rogue dirty bomb to go off in some place like Kashmir or Tel Aviv or the Korean Peninsula. Once off the green in search of whitey, hacking at the weeds with his three-iron, the NASA chief suspected he was not going to get that lucky.

30

Office of the Jesuit Counsel/Washington, D.C.

"Father, I understand you've been called upon from time to time to use your good offices with the Vatican on behalf of the government here in Washington."

"I've had that privilege, Mr. Sokoff."

The worldly, white-haired chief counsel for the Jesuit order was having the very odd presentiment that somehow God had brought Mr. Sokoff to his office. Kilgerry was not a lapsed Catholic by any means, though if faith can be tested, his certainly had been throughout much of his forty years in the capital.

But at age sixty-five, Harvard Law and Divinity School alumnus Michael Joseph Kilgerry tended to invest his faith more actively in the people through whom God worked than in prayers for intervening miracles by the Almighty himself. With this as his guiding view, Father Kilgerry was predisposed to look upon the President's emissaries, be they atheist, agnostic, or practicing Jew, as equally viable vessels.

"How can I help our new President?"

"Father, do you recall a congressional officer acting for a House subcommittee and President Carter, sometime during the first year of his presidency, who came to you with an unusual intercession request?"

"I do, indeed. Her name was Keating, I think."

"Carol Keating."

"Yes. Very earnest, well organized. The White House was interested in obtaining copies of certain Vatican documents and she asked me if I would be willing to act as liaison to the Holy See. I said yes, of course."

"And were you able to help her, at that time?"

With his back to the view of the Jefferson Memorial that his leaded-glass windows afforded him, Monsignor Kilgerry seemed to regard Sokoff with growing affection.

"I communicated with Rome, requesting certain 'sensitive' material from the Vatican Archives, which, as you may imagine, are quite vast and go back many hundreds of years. But—we were denied."

"Had that ever happened before?"

"Never." Kilgerry leaned across the antique desk. "We had never been denied access before and certainly not when requested by a sitting President of the United States."

Kilgerry, or Father Michael at the time, had waged quite a campaign within the order, trying to get that decision reversed, but the Holy See had not been susceptible to appeal.

Sandy Sokoff didn't know about Kilgerry's youthful battle on behalf of President Carter, but he had begun to feel he was in the presence of an ally.

"Why do you think that happened?"

"One must assume it was the subject matter of the documents."

The two men looked at each other, neither one needing to pronounce the nature or category of the subject matter out loud. Sandy spoke first.

"And was that the end of it, as far as you know?"

"No, like I say, Ms. Keating apparently took her charge very seriously and I did meet with her on one other occasion, at her invitation and not in any official capacity. I suppose she trusted me."

"She showed you some documents from the National Archives," Sokoff said. "Things relevant to her request for material from the Vatican. Would you be willing to share with me, and possibly with the President, under the protection of executive privilege, what you saw?"

Kilgerry took a moment to gather his thoughts. He was not frightened or being coy; there was an ethical issue.

"Mr. Sokoff, Ms. Keating was under no obligation to do what she did, but she knew I would be interested and chose to trust in my discretion.

I would hate to cause her even the smallest amount of grief by violating such a confidence."

"I'm afraid Ms. Keating passed on in 1999."

"Ah. Then she is beyond our harm." Kilgerry closed his eyes as if saying a small prayer, then opened them and rose to his feet. "Well . . ."

Coming around the beautifully inlaid Italianate desk, the learned Jesuit motioned Sandy toward his private library and the overstuffed chairs of that sanctum sanctorum.

"I have often wondered whether this day would come. May I offer you a glass of sherry?"

▼

Across the street, in a navy-blue Chrysler minivan with blackout windows, DirecTV graphics, and a high-powered saucer-shaped receiver on the roof, the signal degraded rapidly as Monsignor Kilgerry and his guest moved away from the window glass that had been amplifying their conversation.

"They're moving."

"Jesus, Mary, and Joseph."

"Oh, shut the fuck up."

The two operatives warming their hands on thermos coffee listened closely on Koss headphones, boosted the gain until the white noise hurt, and finally logged in the time when they lost audio.

They didn't know if anything they had on tape had any intelligence value. But they were pretty sure that what they were *not* getting was probably pretty hot.

31

February 5/Ft. Meade, Maryland

At the cortex of the National Security Agency headquarters in Ft. Meade, Maryland, a tidal wave of intelligence data from every country in the world came crashing into the wall-sized banks of series-strung super computers every second of every day.

Gossip, rumors, misinformation, disinformation, satellite imaging, terrorist eavesdropping, all of it was part of an encrypted intel-acquisition system managed and maintained by a small army of analysts and tech wizards around the clock.

Gathering data was not the problem. The problem was determining if any of these words and sounds and pictures *meant anything* in terms of potential threats to America. And the ongoing urgency of this problem required the collective brainwork of human analysts and linguists the same as it always had.

The epicenter of the NSA that served that collective brain was a room that had always been called the Black Chamber, ever since the Nazi-busting cryptology heroes of the Army's Secret Service first moved here to Ft. Meade in the '50's and set up shop to fight international communism.

Flown in from touring his new JPL offices at Cal-Tech in Pasadena, Admiral James T. Ingraham, former NSA spy chief, had chosen the Black Chamber for this meeting. Not just because it was probably the most electronically secure place on the planet, but because it felt like home.

During his tenure here, he had been a hands-on leader who knew the capability of his men and women and the reach and limitations of their machines and had set a high standard for productivity.

Flanked by his aide and a much-decorated Defense Intelligence officer, the Admiral now looked around the windowless conference room, next door to his old stomping grounds at Operations.

Bob Winston had assembled execs from Rockwell, Lockheed, Raytheon, Boeing, Sandia Labs, and Los Alamos for this meeting but it was the Admiral's show.

"We all know the future is arriving at the speed of light." Ingraham inclined his head, acknowledging Clay Claiborne and the photon laser weapon designed by TRW. "Nevertheless, I understand concern has been expressed about the delay in the decision about Orion and also about former Senate investigator Sandy Sokoff, who is presumably acting for the White House. Well, I'm afraid Mr. Sokoff's learning curve is rather steep. Sort of like a blind puppy groping around inside a black box. In any case, let me assure you we are one hundred percent on track. Let's not get overanxious in the stretch drive. Believe me, if any kind of bogey seriously shows up on the radar, we will be *on* it. In a decisive and robust a fashion. But, again, that is not the case."

As always, the Admiral projected a commanding presence, but Clay Claiborne shifted in his chair, not entirely mollified. Winston noticed his discomfort.

Despite the link time invested, he still had his hands full trying to finesse TRW, which had over a billion dollars at risk with Project Orion, the most of anyone at the table. There'd be a hell of a charge against their bottom line if Uncle Sam changed its mind.

"And in terms of the decision vis-à-vis deployment of Orion, we still have almost ten days remaining." Ingraham addressed the group, making it sound like an eternity. "According to the Old Testament, the universe was created in less time than that. And let me remind you, the President's support of discretionary funding and ongoing development is not in play. Thanks to the persuasive powers of R. Cabot Winston here, a better man than I am when it comes to diplomacy, the White

House has already signed off, and nothing Sokoff is doing or not doing is likely to reverse that."

"Besides, he only reports to the President of the United States," Winston added, with his razor-blade smile. "Not to the *Washington Post.*"

This provoked the intended chuckle and a more general sense of relief, except from Claiborne.

"Admiral, I hear what you're saying. I just can't help wondering: When are we going to be able to do the business of protecting the United States of America entirely in the light of day? When are we going to be able to stop having to hunker down behind closed doors like this, with our collective necks on the line, waiting to get blindsided?"

It was an impolitic if not rude question, but all the assembled aerospace reps turned to the Admiral, glad it had been asked. Ingraham had an answer.

"When the civilized world is a safe and sane place to raise our children and all of mankind can live free from threats of mass destruction."

His face had become implacable. Hand-holding these whiny defense-industry fat cats was the worst part of having to deal with the private sector.

"In other words, for the foreseeable future, we must stay the course, whatever that requires." Ingraham glanced meaningfully at the DIA man seated next to him who immediately stood to attention. The Admiral surveyed the table, making eye contact with each man, including the subdued if not satisfied Clay Claiborne.

"In defense of the Republic, gentlemen, the President's hands must not be tied. Not even with his own rope."

The Defense Intelligence officer nodded at Ingraham, tucked his hat under his arm, and quietly quit the room.

There were no further questions: this was how things got done. The Admiral knew from the quality of the silence around him that every man in the room understood something had been set in motion: an executive action directed at resolving their anxieties and concerns.

Of course, no one would have admitted to such an understanding. And none of the aerospace lobbyists who had come to press their interests had any desire to imagine, must less be actually told, exactly what action was being taken on behalf of those interests.

They just hoped it worked.

32

The University of Colorado at Boulder

As she entered the UC–Boulder parking lot nearest to Jake's lecture hall, Angela was not particularly aware of the fresh-faced young man in the ten-year-old Subaru beater who had followed her Avis Cavalier from the Denver airport.

Having sat on the tarmac in D.C. for an hour and a half—God only knew why—she was late for Deaver's class and oblivious to Subaru Boy falling casually in behind her as she hurried across the campus set down in the foothills of the Rocky Mountains.

Finding the right building, Angela slipped into the back of a packed amphitheater-style hall and let her eyes adjust to the low lighting. Down front, at a lectern defined by a tiny desk light, Jake was well into his talk, showing museum-quality transparencies of Mayan and Egyptian hieroglyphs on a theater-sized screen behind him.

"Damn."

Angela shucked off her parka and looked around, but every spot in the five-hundred-seat auditorium seemed taken.

"So, we have a mystery, don't we?" Jake was saying, stacking his note-cards and indicating the projected hieroglyphs. "Two highly evolved cultures with remarkable similarities on two different continents, separated by thousands of years and an ocean that ostensibly would not be crossed until the Vikings."

Behind Angela, Subaru Boy made an entrance wearing an artfully sheepish expression. He then moved off, looking for a seat, like just another undergraduate late for class. Angela stayed standing, intrigued more by Jake Deaver himself than by the images of Olmec stelae and pharaonic carvings that illustrated his lecture.

▼

"Let's look again at what the Mayans and Egyptians had in common: pyramid-shaped monuments oriented to the cardinal points, the solstices, et cetera. A similar and extremely sophisticated mastery of geometry, astronomy, engineering skills, art, and architecture. Shared elements of architectural style, decorative symbology, and pictographic language, not to mention similar origin myths about where all this knowledge had come from. Can we have the lights, please?"

As the students applauded, Jake looked out and recognized *Science Horizon*'s Ms. Angela Browning at the back of the room. She gave him a sorry-I'm-late smile and a quick wave. He smiled back, deciding she was even more attractive in person than she was on television, which made him a little nervous.

"Now, the question is," Jake continued, "do all these cumulative little coincidences suggest contact? Some kind of a link between seventh-century Mayan civilization in the Americas and Egyptian culture in North Africa thousands of years earlier? I'm inclined to argue that they do, and what the nature of that contact or connection might be, we'll be going into after you've read West, Hancock, and Bauval . . ."

▼

Outside the auditorium the two Fibbies, Stottlemeyer and Markgrin, had already made a perfunctory sweep inside the hall, missing Subaru Boy (though he easily made *them*) but noticing Angela. At least Markgrin did.

"Yeah, *Science Horizon*. Wonder why she's here. You watch PBS?"

"Fuck no." Stottlemeyer pulled his collar up and sucked down smoke from the last of an unapologetic Marlboro pinched like a hot-running reefer between his thumb and index finger. Markgrin wouldn't let him smoke in the car.

"Man, there's this jazz series with Wynton Marsalis," Markgrin said, leaning upwind of his partner's smoke and checking the time on his

Kenneth Cole watch. " 'Sax Giants of Jazz' or something. All this early film on bop and bebop, Rahsaan Roland Kirk, Wayne Shorter . . ."

"Aw, that stuff sounds like somebody squeezing a cat."

Stottlemeyer spat a plume of smoke out of the side of his mouth and then got ready to roll as kids began pushing their way out of the lecture hall.

"Gimme Bird playing straight ahead. Hell, gimme Clarence and 'The E Street Shuffle' . . ."

33

Dunsinane, Antarctica

"I think I see something." An Army engineer wearing bio-iso gear pointed at a blurry shadow in the wall of shadows that was the glacier-entombed forest.

The prehistoric caribou they had already liberated was wrapped in a space blanket and carefully tied to a sled. The Science Foundation team had then moved on to a deep translucent blue seam in the ice that proved to be a window on the rest of the ungulant herd standing poised in suspended animation, as if waiting for time to start again.

But that's not what the engineer was looking at.

"Can we have the laser over here?"

White light thrown into the glacier just increased the whiteness that was reflected back, sort of like driving with high beams in a heavy fog. But a ruby laser light had proven very effective.

A paleoglaciologist heading the science team obliged.

"Show me where."

He painted the area with the red laser. They could just make it out, protruding from behind a boulder: a dark, sharply pointed object about six inches in length connected to a longer shaft.

"Holy shit. Everybody, come over here."

Tuning the laser to the warm end of the spectrum, they saw a chipped stone blade connected to the shaft of a spear. The shaft itself was etched with colored markings and disappeared behind a rock. All the way back to whoever had been out hunting caribou in this inexplicably temperate region of the Earth circa 10,000 B.C.E., now located only a short walk from the South Pole: Dunsinane Man.

34

"So, tell me," Angela said, cradling a second glass of Pinot Grigio in the kitchen of Jake Deaver's A-frame cabin outside Boulder. "Is it true?"

"Probably." Jake made a mock-wary face. "Can you be more specific?"

Deaver had cleared what was left of the reheated meatless lasagna and goat-cheese salad, bused their dishes, and set coffee brewing on the kitchen counter. Beeswax candles made a flattering light, bouncing off the skylights and the warm wood walls.

Angela grinned at him, enjoying both Jake and his impromptu dinner.

"Did you really get arrested in a cow pasture doing mushrooms with a bunch of college kids?"

Her reporter's chops were showing, but it was amusing what a little digging could uncover.

"We were cited by a sheriff for trespassing," Jake confessed, drying his hands on a kitchen towel and rejoining her at the table. "But I talked the owner into dropping it. As far as the mushrooms, they couldn't technically charge us."

"'Cause you'd eaten the evidence."

"*Gate, gate, parasam gate* . . . gone, gone, all gone."

He mimed the gestures of a Tibetan *tulku* blessing. It was simple, well observed, and Angela laughed out loud: she was finding former Apollo Commander Jake Deaver rather charming and interesting company. He didn't seem to be working at it too hard, though she could feel he was attracted to her.

Before she left Washington, Miriam had teased her, offering the opinion that there had to be something irresistibly sexy about any man who'd walked on the Moon. Angela had felt obliged to point out the age difference, among other things. However, sitting in his kitchen, she was conscious of something about Deaver that she'd been trying to put her finger on all evening, something besides Right Stuff glam, academic smarts, and a self-deprecating style. He had a brooding quality at moments, as if he'd been deeply wounded in a way that had yet to heal, but that was not it.

Masculine grace, she decided, sipping his Italian table wine. *That's what it is. Masculine grace.*

She felt unexpectedly at ease with him and wondered why that was such a rare thing, at least judging from the men she'd been involved with. Maybe it just had to do with experience and confidence or just having nothing more to prove. The ambitious young professionals she dated, whether in journalism, science, or politics, often came to resent how she put her work and her career first in the same way they did; some were even uncomfortable with Angela's more visible success. Jake, though, seemed beyond the pain of all that Sturm und Drang, which was refreshing.

For his part, Deaver saw Angela as flat-out beautiful and a born flirt, who just might have the smartest green eyes he'd ever seen. He chastened himself not to mistake her teasing for mutual interest, but he liked how she laughed from way down in her stomach and seemed to have a sense of humor about herself, too.

"Don't tell me you never got high," he said, turning the tables.

"In college! That's my story and I'm stickin' to it."

"What? Weed? Ecstasy? Beer?"

"Oh, yeah. Par-tee! And diet pills during finals, like everybody else. I was curious about 'shrooms, actually, but I guess I was never in the right situation or with the right person to want to do it."

"But you didn't come all the way out to Boulder to score mushrooms."

Deaver had naturally been curious ever since Angela had declined to say exactly *what* it was she wanted to see him about over the phone.

"Nope," she said. "That's not why I came to Boulder."

Angela searched Jake's eyes in the live light, as if needing a last sign.

"All right, here's the deal," she said, taking the leap. "I want to show you some photographs that may or may not be classified documents."

Deaver felt his own guard going up, but his voice stayed neutral and open.

"Photographs of what?"

"In a sec. If you agree to look at them, I'll tell you how we got them and what we've done so far in terms of authentication. What I'd like from you is your take on what it is you see, and any ideas you might have about where these pictures might have come from, et cetera. But whether you look at them or not, I need to be able to count on your discretion."

Deaver was glad he hadn't had much more wine with dinner.

"What kind of classified?"

"CIA, NSA, DOD, I don't know. Top secret."

"Are they stamped 'top secret'?"

"No, but the lawyers at PBS say we should behave as if they were."

"What else can you tell me without going into the classified part?"

"One picture is of Mars and one is of the Moon."

Jake felt a quickening, like the adrenaline spike from a small freshet of fear. He could stop it here, right here and now. He could protect himself completely by just saying no. Of course, he knew he would feel like shit, but it wasn't the first time that had ever happened, and why should he trust this woman? Just because he was attracted to her? That would be pretty stupid.

Moon Man . . .

Remembering the voice of the Kharmapa whispering hoarsely in his ear, he relaxed a little and almost laughed out loud.

Moon Man, time to take another walk.

Deaver studied Angela's face for a moment, like a condemned man unsure whether he beheld a messenger of deliverance or an escort to the Tower. Or both in one. He was not a hundred percent sure where this was going or what it would lead to, but the sense of danger was real enough. Even so, the impulse to turn away this earnest beauty felt suddenly like a betrayal. Not a betrayal of Angela but of his most essential self. Or at least what he thought he liked most about himself. And whether he was trusting Angela too quickly or not, he trusted that feeling.

"Okay, let's see them," Jake heard himself say.

"Great." Angela offered her hand on the bargain. "You run Macintosh?"

35

NASA Station/West Australia

"Can you hear me now? Colonel Blake?"

The Aussie grad student and aspiring astronaut candidate yelled into the cell phone, steering his faded, aging Ford truck down the sun-slammed, wavery licorice blacktop road. Augie's voice was breaking up.

"I'll have to call you from the station . . ."

Two hours west and south of the University at Perth, Jonathan Quatraine rang off, hurtling on through the outback heat and trailing a plume of dust. It was easily 110 degrees, with the windows down.

He checked the odo and squinted out the windshield, keeping watch for a little blue-and-white sign that would probably say NASA on it.

"Shite. This is the back of beyond, eh?"

The overloaded red pickup hit a pothole and shuddered, sending a nasty jolt into the cab. Jonathan slowed down, glancing at Hudson, a four-year-old Labrador retriever, riding shotgun beside him.

"Sorry. Huddy? Care for a cool one?"

His sense of balance unfazed by the road's bumpy assault on his four-legged center of gravity, the chocolate Lab perked up at the offer. In lieu of long-deceased air-conditioning, Jonathan kept them both hydrated with Broken Hill lager and handfuls of ice.

"Amber fluids it is." From a plastic cooler on the floor, he fished out a beer, secured it between his thighs, and fed some ice to Hudson. Then he saw it.

"Hold on!" Jonathan stuck his arm out across the dog's chest and stood on the truck's aged disk/drum-brake combo, coming to a stop twenty meters past the NASA ground-station turnoff.

Eyeing the ninety days of provisions still bungied down in the truck bed, he checked the time and his unflappable companion.

"No worries, Hud. Just chuck a yewy, right? Right!"

January was the hot season down under and he was excited about winning the NASA summer job: former Apollo astronaut Augie Blake had even come to Perth and personally recruited the grad student from over two hundred applicants.

"Here we go, mate." Jonathan graunched his balky shifter into reverse, backed up past the blue NASA down-link sign, and turned off into the bush.

Less than a mile beyond, a huge gray dish peeked up over a stand of eucalyptus hiding the cinder block building that would be Jonathan's home for the next three months.

36

Using the dual-processor Mac in his office, Jake had put the TOLAS/ *Mars Observer* photo up on a high-res flat-screen monitor. From her perch in a refinished captain's chair, Angela had observed his reactions to the Mars anomalies and fielded Deaver's technical questions, some of which she could not answer.

Then she had one of her own.

"Jake?"

"Yeah."

"You didn't send this to me, did you?"

"Nope." He turned to face her.

Angela knew he was telling the truth. But now he was looking at her, again with those wild-blue-yonder eyes, as if trying to divine her intentions, or testing her integrity, her character. It was a bit unnerving.

"What?" she said, shifting in her seat.

Jake leaned toward her, his voice as intimate as their proximity.

"Knowing changes everything, doesn't it?"

There was an impish quality that rode along with the intimacy. Angela smiled and nodded, as if they were now part of a secret society of their own making. An unspoken trust was there, too, but there was more.

"Yes. Knowing changes everything."

Jake leaned back and cocked his chin in the direction of her prodigious shoulder bag.

"Let's see the other one."

Angela produced the second image, showing two astronauts on the

Moon. She noticed his posture, how he became tense and still, losing the more playful quality he had flashed before as he began looking closely at the lunar photo.

"And you think this is from the same guy."

"That's my guess."

Deaver read the handwritten caption out loud.

"And good luck, Mr. Grotsky, wherever you are . . ."

Angela told what she knew.

"I searched the employee databases at NASA and at JPL in California and couldn't find any Grotskys. Then we tried looking up all the cosmonauts from the '60's on, but as far as we could tell—"

"Stop . . . hold on a second." Deaver struggled to keep a straight face.

"What? You think that's stupid?"

"No, no, it's just Grotsky . . ."

Jake was laughing out loud, like some kind of inside joke had been played more or less at Angela's expense, and something about it really pissed her off.

"Then what is so damned funny?"

"Grotsky . . . is not a cosmonaut. The Grotskys were Neil Armstrong's next-door neighbors when he was twelve years old."

37

1950/Ft. Lauderdale, Florida

"Oh, no . . ."

Twelve-year-old Neil Armstrong couldn't believe it. Practicing pitching, he had been doing pretty well, firing fastballs through an old tire hung from the grapefruit tree in his backyard with an almost boring accuracy. It was the curve that needed some work. Neil dried his sweaty hands on his T-shirt and changed his grip, felt the stitching of the seam snug up against the side of his middle finger, and stared down at the target. He then rocked from a stretch as if holding a runner on first and let it loose.

"Crap . . ."

As soon as it left his hand, he knew. Sailing high and bouncing off the rim of the worn-out tire, the ball made a dull *thoink* and caromed over the fence into the Grotskys' yard next door.

"Crap on a crutch . . ."

Hoping to simply retrieve his baseball without the embarrassment of bothering the neighbors, Neil climbed over the fence in the direction of the ball's last known trajectory.

Spying a flash of white in the bushes under an open window, he crouched down to get it. But before he could turn back for home he found himself frozen under the window, eavesdropping on a loud argument going on inside the house between Mr. and Mrs. Grotsky.

"Oral sex?"

He listened, rooted to the spot as Mrs. Grotsky's voice rose in outrage.

"You want *oral sex?!*"

Young Neil Armstrong wasn't exactly sure what she was referring to, but Mrs. Grotsky's attitude about it was coming through loud and clear.

"The day you get oral sex is the day that kid next door walks on the Moon!"

Hearing himself being referred to, he felt a shock of self-conscious panic. Crawling out of the bushes on his hands and knees, he then ran as fast as he could across the yard and scrambled back over the fence.

But future Apollo Commander Neil Armstrong would remember that moment and the Grotskys for the rest of his life.

38

"And good luck, Mr. Grotsky, wherever you are." Angela was now laughing as hard as Jake.

Trying to catch her breath, she couldn't help thinking about Augie Blake, wondering why he had shined her on about Grotsky at the Blair House bash. Did he think she was a prude? That didn't make any sense.

"Augie Blake would know that story, wouldn't he?"

Deaver seemed to cool slightly at the mention of his old partner.

"It's an old astronaut story."

Angela refocused her attention on the astronauts in the Moon picture. "All right, then, so this would be Neil Armstrong and . . . ?"

"No, no, this is 18," Jake said. "That's me and Augie at Sinus Medii."

"Oh."

Angela felt an odd sense of portent as Jake laid the print on a scanner bed and copied it to his computer. Once he could enlarge it and play with it on-screen, he gave her a tour, showing various lunar features in isolation.

"Look at our shadows on the ground. This was taken during the day. You see all those stars in the sky behind us?" Jake indicated an area just above the horizon. "The sun washes out the stars during daylight hours, so the sky should be completely black."

"Meaning this picture's been messed with?"

"Nope," Jake said, "that's how it was."

His eyes invited her to solve the contradiction. Angela could feel the fine hair on her arms and on the back of her neck beginning to stand up.

"Jake, anything you want to say here is in complete confidence. Period. Until you say otherwise."

He quit the computer without acknowledging what Angela had said. He looked wound up tight, like the insides of a baseball, and that deep, wounded feeling she had noticed before seemed to surface and then submerge itself. But it was clear they had an understanding. Deaver got up and headed for the door.

"I need some coffee. You want coffee?"

"Sure. Black, with Sweet'n Low. If you got it."

Jake led the way back to the kitchen, passing framed photographs from his Apollo 18 days, samples of calligraphy, and Tibetan artwork.

"How about honey?"

"Fine. It's about those stars, isn't it?" She could feel it coming, whatever it was. Jake glanced back over his shoulder.

"Have you ever wondered why America went to the Moon eight times in four years and then came straight home and never, ever went anywhere again?"

39

1973/Sinus Medii/the Moon

Commander Jake Deaver and Colonel Augie Blake had gone to the Moon wearing the gold-embroidered mission patch of Apollo 18, which depicted their spacecraft rocketing away from Earth beneath the three belt stars of Orion.

There was overt science to do on the surface, months of tedious underwater spacesuit training in the Canaveral tanks finally about to pay off; exhaustive photo documentation, a moonquake monitoring system to set up, a protocol of instrumented readings, surface sample collecting, radiation and micrometer erosion testing, and more. And then there was the covert mission.

"Gentlemen, switch to ALTCOM Two. Do you copy? Over."

"Going to ALTCOM Two. Roger that, Houston."

Having achieved lunar orbit, Blake and Deaver were instructed over the secure channel to open a sealed envelope.

Diagrams and photographs inside showed that their landing site at Sinus Medii had been chosen because it was within rover distance of what was described as "possible anomalous objects" picked up by both Soviet and American lunar satellite cameras.

"Uh, Houston? What are we looking at? Over . . ."

The two astronauts hammered the mission director with more questions than anybody had answers for.

"What you see is what we got, gentlemen."

Most of the answers would have to come from ground truth: Jake and Augie were tasked with photographing and documenting whatever they saw at Sinus Medii and bringing back to Earth up to two hundred kilos of whatever "objects" or "artifacts" could be safely recovered.

This covert mission had to be accomplished in addition to the public science mission, but they were assured that if what the Apollo 18 mission discovered was extraterrestrial in origin, the artifacts would be made public "at the proper time" and the astronauts would be allowed to talk about it publicly "at that time."

For now, however, everything about this was to be considered a state secret and national security concerns would dictate the timing and language of all communications and determine the scheduling and priorities of the mission.

"Nondisclosure. Do you copy?"

"Roger, Houston. Copy that."

Jake and Augie switched back to the normal radio frequency and resumed preparations to set their spacecraft down on the Moon. They'd been told that nothing unusual would be visible from the landing site, so the fixed cameras on the Lunar Excursion Module were considered safe for live network transmission of Apollo 18's Moon landing at Sinus Medii.

But NASA's scheduled, worldwide broadcast soon turned into a nail-biting disaster watch akin to Apollo 13, thanks to an unexpected storm on the Sun.

The first intimations of trouble came moments after beginning their descent.

"Uh, Commander, maintain your present altitude and stand by. We're monitoring some EM coming your way. We may lose you for a bit. Do you copy? Over."

"Maintaining altitude and standing by. Over."

Solar flares were an unpredictable hazard of space travel, wreaking havoc with satellite and spacecraft electronics, not to mention irradiating any astronauts caught in their wake.

This, however, was an M-class solar event, undeflected by the magnetic field of the Earth. As Jake and Augie hovered, burning precious fuel, the EM storm arrived at the Moon in full force, its relentless waves of electromagnetic particles leaving their spacecraft deaf and blind. All voice and data communication with Johnson Space, including Earth-guided telemetry, was lost. Augie took the stick.

"Guidance is now internal."

Standard procedure would be to do nothing until contact could be resumed, using their very limited thruster fuel to maintain a safe altitude: risk the mission, not the men.

"Houston, this is Apollo 18. Do you copy? Over."

Jake and Augie heard nothing but white noise and settled in to sweat out the wait. Going by the book, they faced the real possibility of a scrubbed landing and a failed mission.

"How's our burn minutes, Dog Man?"

"We're at nineteen-point-five minutes of burn."

They were using fuel fast just to maintain position and the margin of safety for the trip home was slipping. But after coming 300,000 miles and knowing how much more than Moon rocks might be awaiting them on the surface, the two men would have sooner augered in than turn back for home.

"Mission Control, this is Apollo 18. Over."

After trying to make contact every ten seconds for two more long, excruciating minutes, Houston remained in blackout. Augie was a hundred percent ready to override the computer and land the spacecraft, but it was Deaver who had to make the call.

"Say the word, Daddy-o."

Jake turned away from the instrumentation and tightened the racing-car harness that held him in his seat.

"Fuck it. Put her down."

"Aye-aye. Manual override is a go. Grab something."

Flying totally without external guidance, Augie fired the lander's little attitude jets, pitching it over so he could eyeball the landing site through one of two tiny porthole windows. Then, righting the spacecraft and sighting on the horizon line, he set it down blind, as if he'd done it a thousand times, with Jake calling out the altimeter reading.

"Ninety meters . . . eighty . . . seventy . . . sixty meters . . ."

At the heart of it was a direct line drawn from the Wright Brothers at Kitty Hawk, North Carolina, to Sinus Medii on the Moon, and the audacious dead-stick landing would pass into NASA legend and the history of human flight.

Whether credited or criticized, Deaver's command decision and pilot Augie Blake's deft handling of the spacecraft would forever be dissected at the Air Force Academy for the benefit of gonzo freshman cadets.

▼

Once radio contact with Houston was restored and all the shouting was over, the astronauts made a concerted effort to keep their heads down and stick to the script, hoping to dissipate unwanted distractions caused by such hotdog heroics.

But the real history being made by Apollo 18 would be made in secret: when Commander Jake Deaver and Colonel Augie Blake became the first human beings to walk among the ruins of an extraterrestrial city on another world.

▼

After securing the spacecraft and completing the public aspect of their first day on the Moon, the two men suited up, switched to the secure channel for communications, and set out from the landing site in an open rover.

"My God," Jake said, gawking as best he could through his gold helmet visor.

"It's awesome." Augie stopped the $20 million little Jeep-like rover with the huge wheels.

Looking up and out from this vantage point, they could now see what satellite photos only hinted at: they had set down inside the remains of a desiccated dome structure. In all directions, the two astronauts were surrounded by a construct of thin, spidery beams eroded to near invisibility and arching high up into the black daytime sky.

Jake lifted his protective visor, accepting the brief UV hit in exchange for a clearer view. It was breathtaking and hugely exciting. Both men were pumped up like Super Bowl athletes taking the field.

"Holy fuck. It's big."

"Houston, y'all should see this damn thing. Wish you were here."

"We copy, Augie Doggie. You are our eyes and ears."

But Augie had already hopped out of the Lunar Excursion Module and begun making a deliberate panoramic sweep of the site with a hand-wound eight-millimeter film camera.

"I'm taking a slow pan now. Looks like a lot of broken glass . . ."

"We copy. Commander, we show your visor in the up position. Over."

"Roger that." Deaver pulled the visor back down as he extracted a large-format seventy-millimeter Hasselblad still camera from its compartment in the rover and used the zoom to get close-ups of the long-abandoned alien biosphere.

"Augie's right. Looks like glass panels on a convex-dome frame . . ."

In a vacuum, glass can be made hard as steel and would be a logical thing for space farers to build with. Jake documented several shattered silicate panels still clinging to lower sections of the dome, refracting and reflecting sunlight into the lens in smeary little flashes.

"How high is this thing, Dog Man?"

"Ten clicks, easy."

The metallic-looking framework was also about twenty-five kilometers across at the base, and grew more and more skeletal as you moved up from the bottom to the top and it gradually became denuded of its glass panels. Jake photographed the biggest openings and noted their locations.

"Jesus, Augie. You see those gaps?"

"Hell, yes, podnah."

The descending orbits of their programmed approach had been more hazardous than they'd imagined. Luckily, gaping sections of the broken dome yawned blackly open in all directions, some a mile in diameter or more. They had to have sailed blindly through one of these huge gaps, probably in their last orbital go-around before the final descent.

"Wouldn't have known what hit us." Augie stared up at the ravaged metal spires reaching out like anguished fingers, some as thin as peanut brittle from millennia of cosmic rain, other sections still sturdy enough to have meant certain death if Augie had crashed into them.

"Houston, do you copy that?" Jake said, suppressing his anger, but adding a task to their already tight schedule: this structure would have to be thoroughly mapped in 3-D for the safety of the next mission. "Houston? We need to take altimeter readings. Over."

After the few seconds of signal delay, the mission director and former Gemini pilot came back sounding strained and apologetic: better satellite reconnaissance would have put them less at risk.

"Uh, loud and clear, Commander. Get everything you can. Over."

Jake secured the Hasselblad, released the altimeter from its cushioned Velcro cubby, and measured every dimension of the lunar architecture until their first day's covert EV time was over and they had to head back.

Jumping lightly into the rover in the Moon's one-sixth gravity, Deaver grabbed Augie's bulky arm and indicated the gaps in the dome above them.

"You're one lucky hotdoggin' son of a bitch, you know that?"

Augie grinned and strapped himself in behind the wheel.

"Stick with me, Daddy-o."

▼

Neither man would be able to sleep much aboard the lunar module, which gave the NASA medical team fits. They used this insomnia to record hours of audio commentary, including observations and speculation about all the things they couldn't talk about except over the scrambled ALTCOM channel.

The Dome, as they came to call it, obsessed them. They presumed that the immense biosphere would have contained some kind of breathable atmosphere. The ETs would've needed to generate a lot of power to maintain such an infrastructure, too, but nothing of that alien technology remained on the surface. At least, they hadn't found it. But their imaginations leaped to fill in the blanks.

Who were they? What were they like? When were they here and why? Where did they go and why? Had the city been abandoned or lost in some kind of catastrophe?

They strained to get a sense of the beings who had walked and breathed and clearly lived here unknown thousands of years ago: intel-

ligent entities capable of space travel and advanced enough to be building arcologies on other worlds when Man was still making tools from
stones and bones and playing with fire.

It was on their final excursion inside the Dome that Jake found the
craterlike depression that was not a crater. Steering the lunar rover to
within ten meters of the hole, the two astronauts checked their air sup-
ply and the battery life on their suits, then marked the time and their
precise position.

"Houston, I think we found something. It's a large hole. Over."

"*Roger. What kind of hole, Commander? Over.*"

Getting used to their bulky suits, Jake and Augie unstrapped, grabbed
up cameras and flashlights, and disembarked in light jumps that were
becoming almost graceful with practice.

"It's like a mine shaft. We're going to take a closer look. Over."

"*Negative, Commander. Spelunking is not on the schedule. Do you
copy?*"

"Copy that, this definitely looks like it could be the entrance to a
habitat or some kind of mining operation. We need to get coverage.
Over."

As they documented the entrance with still cameras, their handheld
lights penetrated only a few unrevealing meters into the tunnel, which
was otherwise occluded by debris. Undaunted, the astronauts argued
vehemently with Mission Control for permission to go inside the shaft.

"*Negatory. No way, gentlemen.*" The Gemini alum wearing the vest in
Houston was firm. "*That is the word and the word is final: document
what you can see from outside, then get back on the rover and back on
sked.*"

▼

Returning to the module, Jake and Augie went a little crazy, conjuring
up what might be found in the ET tunnels underneath the Dome: technology light-years ahead of what the United States had at the time,
logs, journals, corpses of extraterrestrials, which they argued could be
brought back in their backup spacesuits and swapped out in an emergency. But Houston wasn't buying.

"At least let us take the cameras in. Ten minutes," Jake begged. "That's all we want is ten minutes."

But NASA management wasn't going for it on any level.

"That's a negative, Commander. End of discussion. It's a tremendous find, no question. Outstanding. But whatever's down there will still be down there when we come back with the right tools for the right job. Do you copy?"

It was probably wise, but it was a political decision as much as anything. One awkward fall and one spacesuit torn on some unseen jagged piece of alien rebar, and NASA would have one unexplainable American tragedy on their hands: and a scandal that'd rock the program to its foundations.

"Great work, gentlemen. Let's move on."

▼

The remainder of the mission seemed anticlimactic. But on the long coast home, with the blue of Earth getting larger every hour in the port window, Jake did have a consolation prize. Among the two hundred kilos of classified Dome materials they were secretly shipping home was a smooth, flat bladelike piece of indigo-colored silicate he had found that first day under the Dome.

It was almost opaque, like other shard samples taken from the many pools of shattered ET glass. But when held to the light, this one showed six hieroglyphic symbols suspended in the center, somehow etched inside the blade without disturbing its smooth beach-bottle surface.

In the spacecraft, Deaver photographed the symbols backlit by flashlights, uncertain how the pictures would come out, and studied them for hours, copying the glyphs with pen and ink until they were etched into his brain.

Once back on Earth, however, Jake's photos, sketches, and the indigo shard itself, along with all other artifacts from the Dome at Sinus Medii, were whisked off for examination and then archived away from public view.

40

"My God, Jake."

In Deaver's warm high-ceilinged kitchen, what remained of Angela's coffee was cold. Still enraptured by the story, she drank it off.

"Thank you," she said.

Setting fresh candles on the table, Jake had assembled a calligraphy brush, freshly ground black ink, and a pad of art paper. Angela's eyes widened as he drew an elegant hieroglyph from memory, laid it next to the "Grotsky photo" of the Moon, and then continued with the boar's-hair brush and ink.

"Beautiful." Angela stared at the alien rune. "It's beautiful."

"Thanks."

"Any idea what it means?"

"I'm working on it."

Deaver kept drawing as Angela studied the Moon photo with fresh eyes.

"And what about the stars in the daytime sky?"

"Sunlight hitting pieces of glass on the dome."

Once Jake had inked all six lunar glyphs, he arranged them in a careful order on the table. Individually and collectively they seemed to radiate a profound sense of mystery.

Deaver then slipped a graphite rubbing out of his art papers.

"I found this on a wall of the Great Pyramid at Giza."

When the rubbing was set among the lunar glyphs, Angela could see the similarity. It was stunning.

"Oh, Jake, people deserve to see this. The world deserves to see this."

She stood up, taking in all the ancient symbols together and shaking her head in disbelief. "And people think you're crazy."

"Only for the last thirty years."

Angela looked at Jake and then leaned over and kissed him full on the mouth. It was partly a Desdemona kiss for the perils he had passed, partly an expression of appreciation for being entrusted with his secret, all in a moment of spontaneous affection that generated more erotic heat than either of them might have expected. What might be done about it remained to be seen, but it left Deaver surprised and somewhat nonplussed.

Angela tucked her hair behind her ears and leaned back away from his face.

"I suppose that was a lapse in professionalism on my part."

"I'll still respect you in the morning."

Jake's composure was returning, but it wasn't hard for Angela to tell how he was feeling about that kiss. What he might be thinking was another matter.

"You think I kissed you to recruit you?"

Still standing close enough to have easily kissed her back, Jake made a wry face, took her empty cup over to the sink, and rinsed it out, dissipating the sexual tension.

"No, you pretty much had me when I first heard your voice on the phone. But if you're serious about what the world deserves to see, there's some assigned reading. A report made to Congress in 1959 by the Brookings Institute about the risks inherent in exploring space."

Angela gave him a look with her smart green eyes.

"Bring it on."

▼

Ten minutes later, Angela Browning's rented Cavalier blasted past the dark access road across from Jake's property, rattling its way downhill to pick up the interstate back to Denver.

In their nondescript burgundy sedan, the windows half fogged up by body heat, the FBI field agents made dutiful note of it. Markgrin checked the time on his luminous designer watch and entered it in the case log.

"Guess he's not getting lucky after all."

"Hold on."

Stottlemeyer first heard then saw a second car passing by at speed with its headlights off, and his attentiveness was rewarded with a flash of red brake lamps that gave up a little more information.

"Subaru, early '90's, dark green. Colorado plates. Needs a wash."

It was pretty typical: thousands of the little four-wheel-drive wagons with 100,000-plus miles on them could be seen thrashing around the Rocky Mountains all year long. Probably just some local guy in a hurry who forgot to turn his lights on. Stottlemeyer relaxed his vigil.

"Fuck it. Time to drain the snake."

As Stottlemeyer opened the passenger-side door, the domelight flashed, fully revealing their stakeout in the dark road. Markgrin snapped it off.

"Jesus. Put up a billboard, why don't you."

But Stottlemeyer's hard shoes were already stumbling over field rocks and sounding uncertain of their footing until an extended splash and splatter, along with a half-suppressed moan, announced the arrival of relief.

41

The squat, gray Australian relay station had the spilled-beer and moldy laundry charm of a frat house. But for the Aussie grad student it was his kind of frat house: one with $100 million worth of fully automated digital satellite instrumentation and the only direct NASA connection to the *Space Station Alpha* under the Southern Cross.

With lights on, provisions in, and the air-con blasting, Jonathan set fresh water down for Hudson, who was eagerly exploring.

"A yawn, a piss, and a good look 'round?"

After grabbing the chocolate Lab for a quick wrestle, he fed Hudson a doggie cookie. Then he got on the landline to Washington, D.C., and the man who had picked him for the job.

"Colonel Blake? It's John down under. Can you hear me now?"

"*Good. Much better. How's it look, son?*"

"Looking good. No worries. We're moved in and powered up."

"*Let's do a run-through.*"

Working through equipment presets on the station checklist was all they could do before handling a scheduled live feed from the space station.

Launched two days earlier, the Pentagon's *Clementine III* satellite had a last whip-crack flyby today on its way to mapping the dark side of the Moon. From Jonathan's location in Australia, the outback dish would bounce video signals from *Alpha* and the visiting space shuttle *Atlantis* directly to CNN/London. The station was fully automated, but NASA required a live body in situ to monitor, maintain, and provide tech support for station equipment, which is how Jonathan would earn his pay for the next three months.

"Okay, John-boy, there's a VCR and a box of blank cassettes. Find CNN on receiver A. You'll be archiving the Clementine flyby and everything on the event schedule from here on in. Comprende? *And put me on the box, would you, son?"*

"Right."

Jonathan switched over to the speakerphone and found the tape in a black metal rack of relay equipment. Video monitors hanging from the ceiling were already showing test images as *Alpha* cameras zoomed in on the Earth terminus and the exact spot from which *Clementine III* would soon emerge.

"John?"

"Got it. Just gotta whack it in."

Slapping a cassette into the VCR, he hit *record/pause* and surfed through the receiver channels until he found Judy Woodruff reporting from CNN/Atlanta. He then cued the tape up past the leader and hit *record.*

"And next up, on CNN, step on board Space Shuttle Atlantis and the International Space Station Alpha, where the Clementine III satellite will be flying by at eighteen thousand miles per hour on its way to the Moon, coming up live on CNN. Don't go away . . ."

"Colonel Blake? Is that enough level?"

"Loud and clear. You rollin'?"

"Yes, sir. Green light is on."

"Make sure input audio isn't pinning."

The Aussie grad student glanced around to see what Hudson was getting into, checked the record volume, and turned up Augie on the speakerphone.

"Input audio looks good, sir."

"Okay." Augie's disembodied voice filled the cinder block room. *"Now go to receiver B and punch up some numbers I'm going to give you. You should get a PIP window on-screen."*

Jonathan entered the code Augie gave him and a box opened up in the corner of the station monitors showing the view from *Atlantis's* open shuttle bay.

"Whoa. I'll be stuffed."

It was a privileged view: the curvature of the Earth seen live from high orbit. The PIP window then began cycling itself through a network of security cameras on board both *Alpha* and the space shuttle.

"That's the EC, the emergency channel. It's on 24/7 as a safety backup. So, if you get bored, son, you've got all astronauts all the time."

Suddenly the channel switched to show a young *Alpha* astronaut, Lieutenant Heather Charney, floating in zero g at a space-station porthole.

"Whoa!" Jonathan watched the attractive Lieutenant Charney set up a video camera to cover *Clementine*'s approach and final slingshot pass.

The emergency channel then cycled onto another station, CNN came back from commercial, and Augie's voice brought the grad student back down to earth.

"All right. It's show time."

PART
IV

Give your heart and soul
to me, and life will always be
la vie en rose . . .

—Edith Piaf, "La Vie en Rose"

42

Leaning against the doorjamb in Angela's office and watching her partner powering through the on-line database of the *New York Times*, Miriam noted a certain hyperenergized focus that made her wonder if something more had happened in Colorado than Angela had been ready to divulge.

"Don't forget. We've got a meeting on the Hill."

"I didn't forget."

Miriam decided it wasn't so much her energy—she just seemed happier than when she left. Angela waved her on into the room.

"Miriam. Check this out. *New York Times*, December 1959. The Brookings report . . . headline: 'Public Warned to Prepare for Discovery of Extraterrestrial Life.' This is what Jake turned me on to."

Miriam stood behind her and read the subhead over Angela's shoulder.

" 'Blue Ribbon Panel Makes Recommendation to Congress,' blah-blah-blah, 'President Eisenhower requested the yearlong Brookings Institute study'—"

But Angela was already skipping ahead, scrolling down the long document to something else she wanted Miriam to see.

"Sorry, sorry. Just bear with me. It's right near the end."

"Is this the morning-after buzz from a Rocky Mountain high?"

"Wait. This is it." Angela ignored the Miriam mind probe, found the paragraph she wanted, and highlighted it. "Miriam, it all goes back to here. This is where it all got started. It's un-fucking-believable."

Angela read the text aloud.

" 'The government should consider withholding from the public . . . any discovery of alien artifacts on Venus, Mars, or the Moon.' Now, does that sound like a basis for policy, or what?"

"Just hold on, speedo, let me see this." Miriam read it slowly through.

" 'Withholding from the public' . . . they actually say that."

"On the front page of the *New York Times*."

"And who's Eisenhower got making these recommendations?"

"Just wait."

Angela zoomed to the end, highlighting the contributing science folk, etc.

"Voilà: the crème de la postwar crème: Rockefeller, Dr. Werner von Braun, yada-yada-yada, opinion coauthored by Dr. Margaret Mead *and . . .*"

Angela pointed at the name on screen and let her partner read it off.

"Dr. Paula Winnick." Miriam sounded just as shocked as she was.

Angela sat there a moment, letting it sink in before she spoke again.

"Someone of the highest stature. Someone trustable with the nation's darkest secrets for forty years. Somebody with unlimited access and unimpeachable integrity, who just might need to see the truth told before she dies."

"Jesus, Angie." Miriam turned and stared out the window toward the Capitol rotunda and the congressman's office where they were about to go have their meeting. Numerous possibilities for what this Brookings Institute report might mean competed for her attention. One of them won out, hands down.

"Well, I guess there's no reason our Deep Cosmo had to be a man, is there?"

43

Congressional Offices/Capitol Hill

They waited in the anteroom to Chairman Lowe's office, flipping through magazines splayed out on an Early American maple coffee table.

Representative Phillip Lowe, Democratic chairman of the House Committee on Space, was charged with the responsibility of bird-dogging both NASA and, on paper, the Pentagon's growing space program as well.

Back home in his secure North Carolina district, Lowe was well liked but not revered in the same way his father, the late Senator Everett Chambers Lowe, had been. On Capitol Hill as well, the view was that Old Ev's favorite son was certainly bright enough, but: "What's the boy ever done?"

The Space Committee chair was the first leadership position that Phillip Lowe had overtly campaigned for in eight quiet terms in Congress: not a sign of overweaning ambition.

Angela snapped through the normally guilty pleasure of a *People* magazine and checked her watch for the tenth time in as many minutes. By comparison, Miriam was an atoll of calm, perusing the compendium of old news that she was surprised to find was the current *Time* magazine.

"Oh, I reached Dr. Winnick."

"And?"

"Tea on Friday in Georgetown. I didn't say why."

"Good." Angela tossed the *People* back on a pile, her mind racing ahead. "You know, Jake Deaver and Paula Winnick go way back. Maybe he should be in the room."

Angela was finding it very hard keeping Deaver's story a secret, but she was honor-bound. There was one thing, though, that'd simply slipped her mind.

"By the way, and don't get mad because it was the right thing to do, I let Jake scan a copy of the Moon photo into his computer."

Miriam rolled her eyes.

"You fucked him, didn't you."

"I knew you were going to say that."

"Look, all I'm saying is controlling who sees this stuff and who can connect it to us is the only way we have to protect ourselves here."

"Miriam, Jake gave us Brookings, for Christ's sake. He's a good guy and I trust him. Absolutely. And I didn't fuck him."

"You mean not yet."

Angela let that one go and changed the subject.

"So, how is it you know this guy Lowe, anyway?"

Miriam smiled and glanced past a young receptionist fielding the endless onslaught of phone calls, then smoothly got to her feet.

"Later," she said, her smile widening as the Congressman's longtime secretary approached from Lowe's inner office.

"Judith, lovely to see you."

"Miriam, how wonderful." Judith Chen's silver-gray hair was held back from her face by a carved jade piece that looked collectible, lending her the academic air of an Asian-lit professor at Barnard College.

They exchanged brief hugs and Miriam made the introductions.

"Angela, Judith Chen—without whom the Congressman would never be anywhere, know anything, or have any friends left in town."

"A pleasure," Chen said, offering her hand. "I'm just sorry to keep you waiting. Come on back. Angela, we love *Science Horizon,* by the way."

"Thank you. I'm glad."

"We record it every week, standing orders." The diminutive secretary led them toward tall, hardwood double doors with immense brass fittings. "Fair warning, I just reminded the Congressman he has a voice vote on the floor in twenty-five minutes. Anyway—Miriam, you look wonderful."

"Thanks. You, too."

Angela caught her colleague's eye with a questioning look, but Miriam ignored it as she strode into Lowe's office.

▼

"Jesus, Miriam . . ." Lowe said, gathering his thoughts behind an otherwise poker-faced expression. He had examined the whole package: glossy 11" × 14"s of the leaked TOLAS/*Mars Observer* photo of Cydonia, a highlighted copy of the Brookings report, and a three-page brief including Miriam's account of the postshow meeting with Professor Weintraub.

"Well, first off, I want to thank you both for coming in. It's not the kind of thing you want to wake up and read about it in the *Washington Post*."

"Not if you're Space Committee chairman." Miriam noted more gray hair at the congressman's temples than she remembered. "So, what do you think?"

Lowe gave both women an open look, laying his hands flat on the desk.

"Well, if it's true, it's of profound significance. What's your agenda?"

"All we want, Phillip, is for people to know the truth." Miriam turned slightly to include Angela. "We're not interested in any witch-hunts."

"Or the Ringling Brothers/Barnum and Bailey Circus," Angela added.

"The main question is," Miriam continued, "do you think it would precipitate hearings if we did a show on all this?"

The Congressman shrugged. "Not necessarily. It depends."

"Let me put it this way." Miriam shifted her weight and gifted him with her most disarming smartass smile. "Is there a way to present this material on PBS that would be most likely to give Congressman Phillip Lowe the ammo he would need to call for a public hearing, should he so desire?"

Lowe leaned back and retreated behind a more closed expression. Out the window, the Old Senate Office Building could be seen, a site where many a state secret had been revealed and heatedly bargained over behind closed conference-room doors.

"What are you thinking, Phil?"

Miriam asked this as if she had not been asking men the same question all of her adult life.

"I'm thinking about my old friend Admiral Jim Ingraham, late of the NSA. Recently coaxed out of retirement to oversee the unmanned space program at JPL in California. Including the remote satellite exploration of Mars."

"James T. Ingraham. The most decorated intelligence officer in U.S. history." Angela nodded, looking at her partner.

"We didn't know that," Miriam said, getting it: Why would the government put a grand spymaster in charge of data acquisition from NASA's Mars mission satellites if there wasn't something there that they wanted to control?

"I'm also wondering who to trust for a second opinion." Lowe indicated the *Mars Observer* photos. "Satellite experts tend to already be either on the NASA payroll, or working for the Pentagon, or desirous of doing so in the future."

Angela began taking notes: a kind of momentum was building. Lowe seemed sympathetic, cautious but interested in doing something, going forward in some way. It'd make all the difference if he became an ally.

"Congressman, we can work up a short list if you like."

"But let's say you get independent confirmation, Phil," Miriam said. "Beyond a reasonable doubt. How do you feel about the idea of public hearings?"

"With umbrella protection by congressional subpoena for anyone called to testify?" Lowe nodded. "Well, unless something shedding a similar amount of daylight can be worked out with NASA and the Pentagon. Frankly, I'd prefer if all this came out in a more straightforward manner. Though if they thought they might head off a public hearing . . ."

"Could these hypothetical congressional subpoenas cover both current and former NASA employees, military and civilian? And would the hearings be closed door or televised?"

"The people pay for the space program, and by NASA charter, the fruits of the space program belong to the people. They deserve to know the truth."

The U.S. and North Carolina state flags supported by standards to the left and behind his chair lent a sense of authority to Chairman

Lowe's populist position, resonant with overtones of *Mr. Smith Goes to Washington*. Miriam found herself sitting up straighter in her chair.

"That's why I told Angie we had to see you, Phil, before we did anything. Sometimes people just need to be intelligently led."

"Thanks. It's nice to be thought of in those terms." Lowe repackaged the material they had given him and tucked it into a briefcase leaning up against the American flag. "For fifteen minutes, anyway."

He made an un-Capraesque face that communicated an insider's lack of illusions and provoked a good laugh. Then the intercom buzzed with his floor-vote prompt.

"Congressman? It's time."

Rolling down his sleeves and grabbing his suit coat off the back of his chair, Lowe came around from behind the desk.

"Give me a week. And thanks, again, for coming in."

"Thank *you*, Mr. Chairman."

Miriam stood up, offering her hand.

"Oh, please." He waved off the handshake in favor of a hug. "You look great. Sorry to cut it short. Call me if I haven't called you."

"No problem," Miriam grinned, extricating herself from his arms in a graceful bit of choreography. Lowe and Angela shook hands.

"Ms. Browning . . ."

The Congressman then dashed out to be counted.

▼

Once their staccato heels could be heard clacking their way through the marbled corridors-of-power, Angela eyed her partner and decided she had looked about fifteen or twenty years younger back there in the congressional clinch. Miriam leaned toward her, leading the way out of the building.

"Some bombshell about NASA and the spook-meister."

But Angela was not interested in discussing Admiral James T. Ingraham.

"You know what I want to hear about," she said, sounding like Roz Russell flashing her press credentials at a gun moll in a city room deposition. "Spill, sister."

Miriam paused a moment at the top of the Capitol steps and surveyed the famous fountain below before offering up a wholly unregretful confession.

"We were very young, I was very blond, he was very married, it was very brief."

She then descended toward the fountain and the cab stand beyond with as much dignity as she could muster with Angela, giggling like a teenager, in-train behind her.

▼

Behind them, a nondescript man in his mid-to-late thirties carrying an unremarkable leather briefcase followed at a casual distance. In his tailored suit and overcoat, he could have been any number of things: a corporate lobbyist, a congressional investigator, a lawyer for any of a myriad of big-business interests hustling access to lawmakers on behalf of a client.

But like the last choice on a ballot sheet, he was none of the above.

44

Across town, Sandy Sokoff was thinking about his impending meeting with the President and how to say some of the difficult, even disturbing things he believed he now had to say as he steered his black Ford Explorer out of the basement parking in his building and nosed into rush-hour traffic.

The contract operative falling in two cars back in a stealth-bronze Buick LeSabre didn't know what the President's counsel had done to attract the extreme displeasure of his employers and he wasn't paid to guess.

He didn't know Sandy Sokoff *was* counsel to the President of the United States and wouldn't have cared to. Accelerating up a ramp behind Sokoff and merging onto the beltway, the operative had only two things on his mind: getting a positive visual ID on the target and making certain the target was alone in the vehicle. Once satisfied on both counts, he fell back a few lengths for safety before pushing a button on a tiny handheld electronic device that sent a signal to a tiny explosive device hidden in the Explorer's left-front wheel well, blowing the tire and sending Sokoff's truck careening in a shower of sparks until it slammed to a hard stop against the meridian.

Mission accomplished, the operative swerved past the crash and sped away. Relaxing, he loosened his tie and began looking forward to the third thing on his "to do" list: a big pancake breakfast with link sausages and bacon, hot coffee and cold orange juice.

He imagined the crash truck and the busy D.C. cops coming to the accident scene, scratching their heads at the worn-out blown left-front tire. If they were at least half smart they would then check the right-front tire, which the op had also stealthily replaced with another discount Firestone "blem." At which point, it would be game over. Case closed.

Seeing the exit sign for the International House of Pancakes, the contract op carefully looked over his shoulder and changed lanes.

The half-smart cops would conclude that the accident victim had made a bad bet on cheap tires that he should've at least rotated with the rear pair, which looked almost new. It was so simple, it was kind of a shame.

But then again, he thought, happily steering off the beltway toward his IHOP breakfast, *that was kind of the beauty of the thing.*

▼

Sokoff stepped shakily down out of the pranged black Explorer. There was a ringing in his ears, but he could still hear the approaching sirens. Somebody must have called it in right away. He'd been in too much shock to think of doing so.

With looky-loos slowing down to gawk on both sides of the median, he took a quick personal inventory; the air bag had saved him, but it had hurt like hell and his favorite sunglasses had left deep red indentations where they'd broken on his face.

But the shades seemed to be all that was broken. He noticed his hands were shaking and his brain seemed both frozen and way overamped.

"Jesus." He bent at the waist, letting blood flow to his head.

By the time the ambulance pulled up, he wasn't dizzy anymore and he'd had the presence of mind to call Mrs. Travis on his cell phone and reschedule with the President.

Then the paramedics were all over him, checking his eyes for dilation and other signs of shock or concussion and helping him over to their red-and-white van.

"Sir? We didn't see any passengers in the vehicle; were you alone?"

"No passengers."

Submitting to the paramedics' tailgate physical, he learned that his right knee was banged up from smashing into the dash. It'd probably get black and blue.

"Does that hurt, sir?" The medic pressed on the bruise.

"Ow. Fuck, yes. Remind me not to press on it like that."

His scalp also had a swell little knot from smacking into the b-pillar, making the argument for side head air-bag protection. But no nausea meant no concussion: all in all, the President's counsel was a very lucky man.

Once his lucidity returned, Sokoff buzzed the medics with his White House ID and talked them into giving him three Tylenol and a lift to 1600 Pennsylvania Avenue. He'd been prepared to insist that the fate of the republic was in his hands and the President of the United States was waiting to see him, but it hadn't been necessary. Which was probably just as well.

On a gurney inside the ambulance, waiting for his drugs to kick in, Sandy had time to think about the crash and knew in his gut that it had not been an accident.

Of course, his State Farm agent and the D.C. police would investigate, and if he didn't use his clout to make them spend money on serious lab work, et cetera, he'd be very surprised if they called it anything except "tire failure."

But it didn't really matter: he knew. And if *they* were smart, whoever *they* were, *they* would know he knew.

Dead or warned off, he thought, wincing as he stretched out his stiffening leg. *Hey, it's a win-win.*

And for the first time in his life, which was surprising for a Texan, Sandy Sokoff found himself thinking about buying a gun.

45

With the word that a Naval Intelligence team was being dispatched onto their Colorado turf, Stottlemeyer and Markgrin pondered the question of what kind of bullshit politics was going on now.

"Just tell me. Has somebody got a problem?" Stottlemeyer growled into his desk phone in Denver.

All he got, though, was a bored-sounding voice emanating from the hallowed bowels of the Hoover Building in Washington, D.C., reminding them of their obligation to play well with others.

Markgrin watched the red rise in his partner's already florid face as Stottlemeyer hung up. It was like following a child's worsening fever on a thermometer.

"So, what's up?"

Stottlemeyer put together a string of curses in which the words *gay-ass* and *motherfucker* were a recurring theme.

"Let's roll."

"Roll where?"

Stottlemeyer jerked on his Rockies jacket over an air-weight holster and led Markgrin out the field office door, venting as he went.

"Lunch. With some fuckin' gay-ass gym rat NAV/INT motherfuckers. But we're not taking any horseshit, man. You know what I'm saying?"

"And what exactly would that look like?" Markgrin followed in his wake as Stottlemeyer banged his way out into the parking lot.

"Like a bunch of gay-ass gym rats picking up the tab, for openers."

"Oh, yeah," Markgrin said, waving his stocky partner off the wheel side and unlocking their car. "We can put the hurt on 'em there, big guy."

▼

As expected, the meeting with the diffident young Navy creep-team in the bar at the Boulderado Hotel was no love fest. But the two agents gave them what they needed: the rundown on Jake Deaver's daily routine and his teaching schedule at UC–Boulder.

"His afternoon class is from two to four," Stottlemeyer said, making what he thought was a heroic effort not to react to the *beaucoup attitude* radiating toward them from across the table.

"At the college. That'll work." The twenty-nine-year-old team leader did the talking for his hard-muscled crew, who drank bottled water and smirked at the fibbies, hoping to die before they got that old. "How far is the house?"

Markgrin drew a map for them on a restaurant napkin.

"Sometimes he goes for coffee with some of the kids afterward," he added, amused by how the NAV/INT guys kept their shades on to read the menu. It was so MTV. "Travel time from here, figure ten minutes, tops. We can stay with him, if you want. Let you know when he's on the move."

"I don't think that'll be necessary." The team leader signaled the waitress.

Stottlemeyer fumed at the dismissive tone, then ordered the Boulderado rib eye and a bucket of steamers, since he'd decided the Navy was buying. He then leaned across the table after the menus were collected, and bumped up the peaky testosterone level just a touch.

"Do us a favor," he said, addressing the whole crew, using a gravelly Passaic sotto voce which his straight-faced partner thought was pretty funny.

"We live here." Stottlemeyer let the muscle in his clenched jaw jump a couple of times for emphasis. "Don't make us have to apologize for anything."

The G-men needn't have worried: the all-pro Naval Intelligence creepsters executed a meticulous break-in of Jake's cabin and a light toss, leaving little or no trace of their passing. Hacking into the password-secure files in Deaver's computer was a pain, but much easier to accomplish in situ than via the Internet.

In the end, every file and every disk in storage was downloaded onto a portable hard drive, and they were out clean in ninety minutes and off the Denver airport radar three hours later.

The data would then be hand-carried in a secure pouch back to the Office of Naval Intelligence in Washington, D.C. Once there, it would be logged in, put inside a lockbox, and taken by armed detail to the NSA for an eyes-only analysis, which would, in turn, be delivered directly to R. Cabot "Bob" Winston.

46

NASA Station/West Australia

Jonathan Quatraine was starting to feel quite at home in the back-of-beyond station, cooking meals in the rudimentary kitchen and hiking with Hudson around the outback near the dish. What he had come to like most was the thing Colonel Blake had shown him: the *Space Station Alpha* emergency channel with its privileged peek behind the scenes.

Like now, sitting in his chair, drinking a coolie from his lager cache, and watching astronaut Lieutenant Heather Charney floating weightlessly near the sleep sacks, setting out a string of raisins in the air in front of her and snapping them up like Pac-Man.

"The Goddess is in heaven and all's right with the world, mate."

Lieutenant Charney's spiky haircut seemed perfectly designed to look good in microgravity and Jonathan fantasized himself into the scene, the two of them "starkers," bouncing off the walls and making frantic flying love like a porno *Matrix.*

"Bollocks." Jonathan banged down his beer can as the EC cycled to another camera, this one showing two Americans in jumpsuits droning their way down a checklist on a clipboard labeled PROJECT ORION. The Aussie student blinked.

"Orion . . ."

Jonathan didn't remember any Project Orion. With a sinking sensation he rolled his desk chair over to recheck the e-mailed event sked: no Orion.

The screen switched again, to a camera located in the space shuttle's cargo bay. The cargo doors were wide open, revealing a quadrant of space that included a slice of Earth, some twinkly stars above the night terminus, and two suited-up astronauts deploying a large, shiny concave mirror.

"Shite almighty."

Jonathan felt sick. Wasn't he supposed to archive every station event? And deploying a satellite from *Atlantis* had to be a station event, on the sked or not.

Powering up the receiver, he smacked the nearest cassette at hand into the VCR and started recording. Setting sound levels, he could hear the astronauts' chatter with Mission Control and a time code peeping its pulse. Something was definitely happening and he'd almost missed it completely.

"Shite," he shouted, causing Hudson to look up from his water dish.

Jonathan quickly reset the tape counter, scanned his own instrumentation, and double-checked the record light: at least he was getting this much. Then the time-code beep became augmented by a hiss of high-end gain and an audible countdown in Russian, with a shadow count in English.

"Ten . . . nine . . . eight . . ."

Russian? Russian? It was all happening too fast. Glued to the monitor with its beautiful view out the shuttle-bay doors, Jonathan reached for the phone and then stopped himself. What good would that do? He'd just feel like a fool calling Johnson Space Center in the middle of a count just to let them know he'd missed everything up to this point and was a complete and utter wanker.

"Project Orion. Initiate . . ."

Suddenly he saw a bright pulse of light, originating from somewhere below *Alpha* and *Atlantis*, shoot up, forming a powerful standing column of laser light that beamed out past the space station and far into space.

"What the fuck?" Jonathan held his breath. He could hear astronauts and cosmonauts chatting as the mirror SAT he had seen deployed was being remotely maneuvered into position to intercept the laser.

"Oh, God."

Suddenly the space mirror was deflecting the huge, silent beam at an acute angle, redirecting it out past the night terminus of the Earth, where it disappeared thousands of miles downrange. Jonathan was mesmerized.

"This is awesome."

The epic hypotenuse of lockstep photons suspended itself in this sustained manifestation of sheer power for about ninety seconds, underscored by whoops and exclamations in Russian and English on the transmit channel.

And then, as if someone had clicked off a flashlight, the laser was gone. But the Aussie grad student knew what he had witnessed.

"A weapons test. A secret bloody space weapons test."

And the reason it wasn't on the daily sked was that he wasn't supposed to see it, was he?

But he had seen it. He looked down at the video machine: he even had evidence to prove it.

"Project Orion. Krilkey..." Jonathan's fingers were shaky as he punched *rewind*. He noticed, for the first time, that in his haste he had not grabbed a blank cassette and had in fact recorded over a copy of the classic "Cheese Shop" sketch from the *Best of Monty Python* and part of an *Ab Fab*. But he was too busy getting paranoid to mourn the loss.

He replayed the recorded test once more: it was astounding.

"Fuck, fuck, fuckitty."

Jonathan vaulted up out of the chair and paced the room with Hudson at his heels, picking up on his alarm.

He imagined Home Guard helicopters keening and careening overhead and security troopers rappelling down like commandos and arresting him for security violations. He saw himself dragged off and thrown incommunicado into some military/penal hellhole in Canberra and subjected to brutal interrogation.

"Shite!" he shouted, frightening the brown Lab into a barking jag. Jonathan smoothed out the raised ridge of fur on the dog's back.

"There, there, she'll be all right, you mug."

It gradually occurred to him that maybe his fate was entirely in his own hands: erase the tape, destroy the evidence, and Bob's-your-uncle.

But what if there was some way they could know that he'd seen it and archived it? A hidden camera in the station, or a monitoring device in Houston or something.

In that case, not saying anything would be the most suspicious thing he could do. And how could he prove he'd destroyed the evidence, if he destroyed the evidence?

Jonathan wanted to do the right thing, whatever it was, without getting himself shit-canned in disgrace or worse, but he was at a complete loss. Then it came to him: the one person on Earth he might be able to trust.

"Colonel Blake."

Once he realized there might be something arguably appropriate that he could actually do, his fear subsided and he began to think more clearly.

47

February 8/Arlington Country Club/Washington, D.C.

The course at Arlington was a vast swath of wet and soggy turf from the night's rain, and it appeared to be threatening, again. Yellow pin flags snapped horizontal all across the empty course. The cherry trees, fooled into budding early by a series of springlike days, were now getting double-crossed.

With an eye to the sky, Bob Winston, Admiral James T. Ingraham, and NASA Administrator Vernon Pierce elected to take buckets of balls down to the far end of the driving range.

The wind snatched at Pierce's golf jacket, sending a chill down his neck to keep company with the cold sense of dread already lodged in his chest.

"We have a situation, Vern," Winston said, taking practice swings amid the swampy puddles. Pierce slipped the cover off his driver. He knew they had a situation. He'd been up since 5:30 A.M. preparing for this meeting to discuss it.

"Who is it?"

Winston glanced at the Admiral and then bent down to tee up his ball.

"Commander Jake Deaver is in felony possession of above-top-secret material which we believe he's planning to leak or may already have leaked to the media. We'll be consulting with the AG but we want to consider other options."

"Good God." Pierce gaped as Winston mechanically smacked a ball to the one-hundred-yard sign, hardly noticing where it went. "What's Deaver think he's doing?"

"Apparently selling his story to PBS, God knows why. But I think you'll agree the timing is problematic." Winston swung again, slipping slightly in the wet and scowling down at his spikes.

"Jesus Christ," Pierce muttered.

"It gets worse. Admiral?"

Ingraham launched a series of drives that fell in a tight cluster downrange.

"Office of Naval Intelligence and the FBI say Deaver met with Angela Browning in Colorado. And two days ago, Browning and her producer walked a copy of classified material into Congressman Phillip Lowe's office on the Hill. A NAV/INT team subsequently found it on Deaver's computer."

"Goddamn it." Pierce was too upset to swing a club.

"Don't worry, Vern." Winston was finding his rhythm, like the Admiral, driving steadily through a half-dozen balls. "We can still get Deaver back."

"Lowe and Browning will be handled separately," Ingraham said, "but Commander Deaver is *our* shop."

Our shop . . .

Pierce winced at the fresh reminder of Ingraham's end run appointment at NASA's Jet Propulsion Lab.

"Your people looked over the Exposure Act?" Winston said casually.

This was it. Pierce knew what they wanted from him.

"Yes, the ET Exposure Act of 1968. It's a power of quarantine."

Pierce had the authority to have Jake Deaver picked up and placed in isolation. But invoking the Exposure Act to quarantine Deaver could be easily second-guessed and criticized as an abuse of power, even if it was legal.

"Indefinite detention and quarantine." The Admiral ticked off the salient points. "At the sole discretion of the NASA administrator. No judges, no hearings, no appeals. Except to the Chief Executive."

Winston added his two cents.

"The right tool for the right job, Vern."

Pierce imagined how it might play in the media, if it got out: most things eventually did get out. He'd be the one expected to fall on his sword. But Pierce wasn't quite ready to be buffaloed into the scapegoat role. He dug in his heels.

"Absent a public health hazard, we can't arrest and detain Jake Deaver or anybody else. There's no precedent. There's no way in hell it'll ever stand up."

The Admiral watched Winston bag his driver with a disgusted shove. He then faced down Pierce and his constitutional argument with equal disdain.

"It doesn't need to stand up. Just needs to buy us some time. You're not going to get hung out to dry, if that's what you're worried about. You sign off, NSA has Deaver picked up, and it's done. He's their problem after that."

Winston knew that was stretching it, but he let it stand.

"Look, Vern, I'm sure we can get Augie Blake to talk Deaver in. We probably won't even need to use the quarantine. But we need to have it as a last resort."

Augie Blake. Pierce thought about that, grasping at the idea: if that's how it was handled, that'd be fine. He looked up at the darkening sky and thought maybe he was being overanxious. Of course, if Justice did get involved, or if things went bad in any number of ways that they could go bad, all bets would be off. And he'd be out there naked and trussed up for the fall. He shuddered.

"And this is from the President?"

The Admiral faced abruptly away, as if a rude bloom of cat spray had invaded his nose. Winston zipped up his jacket against the cold.

"You haven't had a call from Sandy Sokoff, have you?"

"Sokoff?" Pierce said, puzzled at what seemed a non sequitur. "No. Why?"

But the two men were too busy packing it in to respond. Winston hefted up his golf bag and offered a warning, disguised as a note of personal concern.

"The train is leaving the station, Vern. With or without you."

He and Ingraham then hiked off toward the clubhouse parking lot.

▼

Above, a kettledrum of thunder rumbled deep enough to reverberate in Vernon Pierce's tensed-up stomach. He scowled at the gray clouds crowding together overhead.

"Christ."

Becoming NASA administrator had been the pinnacle of his career in space science and aerospace management, but it was a presidential appointment. If he refused to exercise his authority and invoke the Exposure Act against Commander Deaver, Winston had made it plain he'd be replaced by some Bork who would.

He imagined an ignominious resignation, the look on his wife's face, having to pull his two daughters out of private school and move back to California; damaged goods, his public career over. Maybe he could teach . . .

Big silver-dollar-sized drops of rain began to splat around him.

"Son of a bitch."

Lightning stabbed down from the cumulonimbus coalition now amassed in earnest over the Capitol, and Pierce hustled off the range with his clubs as the first real storm of winter finally broke on top of him like Noah's worst nightmare.

48

Office of the NASA Administrator/Washington, D.C.

Soaked to the skin, Pierce found Congressman Phillip Lowe waiting in the anteroom of his NASA suite and nursing hot Lipton's tea in a ceramic cup. It was a souvenir cup, available on-line with a hundred other NASA souvenir items screened, stamped, or embossed with the agency logo.

"Got a minute, Vern?" Lowe was already on his feet.

"Mr. Chairman . . . of course." Pierce peeled off his wet jacket, noticed the Congressman was holding a large plain manila envelope, and quickly guessed what might be inside. He called to his secretary.

"Stacy? Can you take this?"

"Sure."

The NASA chief handed off his jacket and thought about what Winston had said about Lowe getting together with Angela Browning. He glanced over, looking for a clue about what the thrust of this meeting was going to be, and decided there was nothing in the Congressman's face except the prospect of a bad day getting worse.

Pierce smiled and motioned him into his office.

"Come on in, Phil. Good to see you. Stacy? If there's more hot tea . . . and see if you can track down Bob Winston's whereabouts for me."

Pierce decided he had no choice but to play ball, but he was going to need help in terms of damage control.

49

National Archives Building/Washington, D.C.

Emerging alone from the vaults of the National Archives, Representative Phillip Lowe found himself out in the high-ceilinged lobby feeling very strange: everything had changed. Nothing was physically different from the way it had been when he had walked in. The marble flooring, gilded Doric columns, and temperature-controlled, bank-hush quiet were exactly as they had been an hour ago.

The change was interior to Chairman Lowe.

Behind a mask of severity, he signed out at the security desk with its double bank of TV monitors. Nothing would have suggested to an observer that, for Phillip Lowe, the world was no longer anything like what he had thought it was sixty minutes before.

▼

"Ordinarily, this would require above-top-secret clearance," Bob Winston had said, escorting the Congressman and Vernon Pierce into the repository of the nation's deepest secrets. "But that'd take time we don't have."

Winston stopped at the door to a guarded conference room that might have doubled as a vault for the National Reserve at Ft. Knox.

"If I can just have you sign this." He presented a dense NSA document to each of them along with a gold-tipped pen. "It's a standard nondisclosure."

Pierce scrawled on his copy, but Congressman Lowe declined.

"I don't think so." He sounded pretty firm about it.

Winston blinked: he hadn't imagined that Lowe might demur. Pierce jumped in to mediate.

"Um, I think the Congressman may be concerned that in his role as Chairman of the Space Committee such an agreement might represent a conflict of interest."

Lowe did not disagree, but offered nothing more. He was fully prepared to turn and walk out: it was their dog and pony show. If they wanted to show him something intended to influence him, he had his terms.

Winston disguised his displeasure and folded away the agreements, one signed, one unsigned. Unlike his relationship with Pierce, he had little leverage with the Congressman. And it wasn't smart to make enemies if you weren't sure you could also make them go away.

He nodded to a Marine, who then stepped aside from the bomb-proof door.

"Then the distinguished Chairman's word will have to suffice."

▼

Now, after his hour in the above-top-secret vault, Lowe waited to be buzzed out of the archives building, acutely aware of the security cameras everywhere around him and feeling almost desperately claustrophobic.

God, he thought. *I would kill for a smoke.*

It had been five years since he quit, but at the moment it seemed like five hours. The *brrraaat* of the releasing buzzer startled him, though he knew what it was. A security guard called out from behind his bank of monitors.

"Go ahead, Congressman."

Embarrassed by the prompting, Lowe pushed on the steel-reinforced exit with unnecessary force, swinging the door wide. The electronic locks clapped loudly home behind him.

Out in the street, he was shocked at how naked he felt, how disoriented. By the time he found his three-year-old silver Saturn and was steering toward Capitol Hill on automatic pilot, all the work waiting back at his office seemed trivial.

Snatching up his car phone, he quickly put it back in its cradle. Who was he going to talk to? Who *could* he talk to?

Twenty years ago he had followed his father's footsteps into politics, though without the seemingly requisite fire in the belly that the Carolinian Senator was famous for. Phillip Lowe was a thoughtful, decent, even idealistic man who loathed the mudslinging rhetoric and partisan rancor endemic to the House. True to his nature, he chose a low-profile path: unlike Ways and Means, Judiciary, or the Armed Services Committees, the issues related to Space seldom generated blood-feud party battles. No one could jealously imagine the Space Committee as a springboard to a damn thing.

Had the unimaginable, now, just occurred?

Lowe remembered Miriam's question about a congressional investigation, and knowing what he now knew, he imagined televised House hearings into the violations of NASA's charter, including the suppression of extraterrestrial artifacts discovered on the Moon and Mars. The revelations would be a scandal. The business of the nation would be paralyzed like nothing since Watergate, Clinton's impeachment hearings, or September 11.

And Phillip Lowe, a little-known representative from a tiny district in North Carolina, would be in the white-hot glare of the national media shit storm, presiding over all of it.

Pulling into the members-only parking structure adjacent to the Hill, Lowe realized that this was exactly the kind of leadership role he had been raised and groomed to fulfill, however long he had dodged it.

It would bring unbuyable name recognition. And if he acquitted himself well, in an evenhanded statesmanlike manner, reassuring to the public, who knew? He might just be able to parlay it into a statewide run for the Senate, that more gentlemanly, prestigious, and contemplative Senate Chamber still home to his father's legend. Something often presumed by observers of the Washington scene to be beyond the son's grasp. A presumption he would like very much to prove wrong.

Lowe began to see the scale of the thing, the ducks he'd have to get in a row.

Then he realized who he needed to call first and why.

50

PBS Building/Science Horizon Office

"Congressman Lowe, on line one."

The voice of her assistant on the intercom made Miriam raise a peremptory eyebrow at Angela, who was eating a take-out Cobb salad on the office couch. It was a look that they both knew meant: *Don't laugh or I'll kill you.* After waiting a beat, Miriam picked up the phone.

"Getting a jump on Valentine's Day! You are a shameless man, Phillip Lowe," she said, causing her partner to choke on a bacon bit.

But as Miriam listened to the Congressman, her teasing tone quickly faded.

"Oh . . . no, no, I understand. Believe me. Don't worry about it. You just take care, okay? Phillip? You heard me. Good."

Miriam hung up and swiftly closed the office door, leaning her back against it like the Dutch boy holding back the flood. Angela was all eyes.

"Who died?"

"I think *we* did."

"We lost the Congressman."

Miriam just stood there, looking oddly shaky.

"He sounded scared, Angie. And if the Chairman of the House Committee on Space is scared, what the hell are we doing here, kiddo?"

"Fuck him." Angela tossed her salad in the trash. "And we are not dead."

"Then what's that terrible smell?"

51

February 9/the White House/Residential Wing

From the more public foyer that communicated to the West Wing, the uniformed porter opened a gold leaf and cream enamel door with white-gloved hands, bowed the President and Sandy Sokoff into the residential living room, and then closed the door, remaining discreetly available outside.

A pine-log fire popped and hissed in the Teddy Roosevelt fireplace rebuilt by Coolidge, and Sokoff stared into it as the President crossed to a sideboard bar.

"I've got a ninety-year-old single malt Tony Blair sent over from his private stock. It's like warm peat smoke."

"Sounds good."

Sandy remained standing, but shifted some weight off his bruised right knee. Since the "accident," he had taken a few precautions about which he had chosen not to burden his boss; chief among them was securing a concealed weapons permit and packing his wife, Juana, and the baby off to her mother's place in Austin.

"How d'ya want it?"

"In a glass."

The President fixed their drinks underneath a whimsical portrait of the First Lady with their family dogs, an inaugural gift from David Hockney.

"Here." Quitting the sideboard and handing Sokoff three fingers' worth, he indicated the Band-Aid on Sandy's swollen nose. "So, how is it?"

"It's fine."

"Think you're making somebody nervous out there?"

Sandy made a wry face. The President commandeered eight feet of leather sofa.

"All right, then. Let's hear it," he said, stretching out.

"With one disclaimer." Sokoff gave his back to the fire. "What I am about to say I would never be able to prove in front of a grand jury."

"Understood."

Sandy tasted his drink, nodded once, and began.

"Mr. President, I believe that powers historically reserved for the executive branch and the Office of the President are being clandestinely and systematically usurped. Previous administrations either tacitly permitted it or were too distracted by more pressing issues to deal with it. But there is a cancer on the presidency and I believe it has become a constitutional crisis. You still want to hear this?"

The President took that in, along with a half ounce of single-malt scotch. "You betcha," he said.

52

Reagan National Airport/Washington, D.C.

Jake mumbled to himself, unbuckling the business-class seat belt and wrestling his lone travel bag out of the overhead bin.

"Face it. You're a mess."

Disembarking from the American Airlines 747 at Reagan National, he said his good-byes to the flight attendants and crew who had come back to meet him during the flight and chat about the space program and the Apollo missions.

Deaver then headed out the jetway.

After Jake accepted the invitation to come east at *Science Horizon*'s expense, Angela had said she'd be picking him up at the airport and he was careful not to read anything more into the gesture than logistical convenience. On his end, though, something more had definitely been going on since that kiss in his kitchen: hell, he was talking to himself.

"Yep. You are a definite mess."

He pulled at the cowlick he suspected might be sticking up on the back of his head. It had been a couple of years since he had been romantically involved with anyone outside the rather insular Buddhist community and he felt rusty. The age difference was no small item, either. But Jake didn't really feel all that different than he ever had.

"It's a question of mind over matter," he remembered Satchel Paige once said. "If you don't mind, it don't matter."

Emerging at the gate, he looked around for Angela's face, then remembered that the gate area at Reagan was still for ticketed passengers only. Even so, his posture slumped slightly in disappointment.

"Damn."

He laughed at this evidence of his obvious nervous excitement and continued on out the concourse, past the state-of-the-art baggage X-ray station and a pair of armed National Guardsmen.

And whether it was only about seeing Angela or also about what they seemed to be embarking on, professionally, Deaver was beginning to feel something like liberation. Emerging from the terminal, he saw how, even in mundane things like airport signage and the clothes people were wearing, the colors around him seemed vibrant and fresh.

Jake looked around and realized he'd actually been whistling; something from the Broadway musical *The King and I*, which got him thinking about "whistling past the graveyard" and the time he had driven a car full of Tibetan monks into Boulder from the Denver airport.

Passing the town cemetery, the young Buddhists had gazed out over the field of headstones and cheerfully called out: "Coming . . . coming!"

And then he saw her, double-parked in a red Jeep Grand Cherokee. A rush of joy spread through his chest, and before it could be abbreviated by some attempt at being cool, he had covered the ground to Angela's truck.

"Hey," he said, all too blatantly glad to see her.

"Hey." Angela grinned up at his surprisingly boyish face and unlocked the door. "Is that it?"

She pointed to his solo carry-on.

"That's it." Jake tossed it in back and settled into the shotgun seat.

As Deaver buckled up, he saw how Angela's smile made it all the way to her eyes and then some. He had been thinking a lot about those green eyes. She then deftly launched the big Jeep into an invisible break in the airport traffic and they were gone.

▼

Cocooned in a Cadillac limo wearing diplomatic plates, an elegantly dressed, gray-haired man fell in behind them, kept at a discreet distance by a Russian-embassy driver wearing a chauffeur's cap.

Up front, the race-trained driver was proud of his machine: the glossy black Caddy had been armor-plated, the weight of which necessitated an upgrade in the stock NorthstarV-8, which now put out over 450 bhp, measured at the bench. But all that giddy-up called for some serious whoa, so huge Brembo racing brakes put right-now stopping power at the corners. Finally, grippy new seventeen-inch Pirelli P-zeros and custom suspension bits made sure the bulletproof two-and-a-half-ton cruiser could perform like a Bahn-burner, either in evasion or in pursuit.

But that performance envelope was unlikely to be pushed this evening.

Behind the smoked privacy glass, the only performance in progress was Pavarotti making light work of *Il Trovatore* and the gray-haired man singing along, sipping coffee decanted from a silver samovar in the limo cabinet bar. With the transparency of the Bose sound system as a reference, he could hardly understand why Bocelli's voice spoke so to the popular culture; it was obvious he would never wrest the crown from Luciano.

In the adjacent lane, a yellow taxi displaying an off-duty sign flashed its brights in a brief salute and passed the limo at speed, disappearing several car lengths up ahead in front of Angela's Grand Cherokee.

"Following from in front," the gray-haired man thought, nodding his tradecraft approval.

Then the dapper self-styled entrepreneur, cultural attaché, and FSB agent from Moscow relaxed deeper into the limo's pleated leather upholstery and conducted the alert and sympathetic La Scala orchestra, deftly cuing the great Italian tenor into the chorus reprise.

53

Sandy Sokoff set his empty glass down on the mantel in the residential East Wing living room and summed it up.

"So sometime during the Cold War, as far back as Truman, somebody decided that national security was too important to be left to the politicians. Including the President of the United States."

He took a seat in a worn leather club chair by the fire and waited for questions. The President sat up on the matching couch.

"So, there's a cabal. 'Friends of Bob'?"

He made it sound like a political fund-raising committee. Sandy laughed.

"Yeah. Some are probably FOB, well-placed people in the military, the intelligence services, key players in aerospace/defense. All we can know for sure is: it's big, it's old, it's hugely well funded and all too ready and willing to subvert the Constitution in order to save it. Though I doubt they'd see it that way."

"Patriots."

"Yes, sir. Patriots."

"And at the core, it is all about black budget weapons systems."

"Unacknowledged Special Access Projects."

"Like Project Orion."

"Whoever they are, they decided Orion had gotten too big to hide. Which is probably the only reason we know about it."

"But otherwise, we're out of the loop." The President scowled, looking mad enough to spit. Sandy shrugged.

"I imagine some administrations were brought into the tent and some they didn't trust. I'd bet Nixon was in, Ford I don't know, Carter was definitely out, Reagan was in, and Bush Senior, and Bush/Cheney. Clinton was out."

"So, we're talking about a shadow government. But not a bunch of guys in bombproof bunkers waiting for the next shoe to drop on the Capitol."

"More like an ongoing, secret executive branch."

"Fuck me." The President lurched up, returning to the heirloom side-board below the new Hockney to freshen his drink. Sandy could see that his face was flushed more with anger than with the whiskey from the Court of St. James.

"A secret executive branch, with command and control over the most advanced military weaponry on the planet and billions in public and private moneys, off the radar, with zero oversight."

"And passing itself off to each administration as business as usual." Sokoff nodded, waving off the President's mute offer of more scotch. But he liked seeing the man he helped get elected growing angry. He was angry, too.

"Mr. President, the Republic is in danger."

"Answer me this. Am I or am I not the constitutionally elected President of the United States of America and Commander in Chief?"

Sandy resisted the urge to scratch at the itchy edges of the Band-Aid on his nose. It was a simple enough question. Sokoff answered it.

"Yes, sir. As long as you don't act too much like you're in charge."

The President's brooding expression turned hard, but not at all hard to read. When he spoke, his voice was low and contained.

"What time is it, Sandy? The exact time."

"Nine twenty-four P.M. Eastern Standard Time. Why?"

"Write it down," the Commander in Chief said, with the gravitas of direct order. "Business as usual just stopped here."

PART
V

*Men praise thee in the name of Ra. Thou dost pass over
and pass through untold spaces. Thou steerest thy way
across the watery abyss to the place thou lovest . . . and
then thou dost sink down and make an end of hours.*

—The Egyptian Book of the Dead

54

Three months earlier/The Giza Plateau/Egypt

Former Commander Jake Deaver had left Boulder and flown to Egypt on seventy-two hours' notice. His passport had needed renewing and he had to get Nile-fever and malaria shots, but he wasn't really thinking that much about missing Christmas with his daughter and probably New Year's as well. He was too excited about getting to go inside the Great Pyramid at Giza, which was a measure of Jake's love affair with ancient Egypt and everything about it.

Long before his midlife plunge into the serious study of Sanskrit, Sumerian, and the earliest-known cultures of the Fertile Crescent, he knew he would someday visit the Giza plateau. The circumstances of that visit were important, however: he desired a certain kind of access that mere celebrity would not afford him.

Deaver's space hero cache had at least helped open the door to a cordial e-mail correspondence with Egyptologist Dr. Marcus Mancini which resulted in a dream opportunity: impressed by the scholarship of the astronaut-turned-historian, Mancini invited Jake to Egypt to visit his dig-in-progress at Giza. Deaver promptly accepted.

Blessed with the good timing of winter break, he could grade papers on the long flight to Cairo and back. And after he resolved his holiday plans, neither reports of tourist kidnappings nor the State Department's vocal concerns about his safety could have kept him away.

▼

Shielding his eyes and scanning the desert plateau for signs of his host, Jake directed the armed, embassy-vetted driver to park their Land Rover rental near the base of the Great Pyramid. Gawking up at this Wonder of the World with exuberant pleasure, Deaver abandoned the truck's hardworking air-conditioning for the intense Egyptian sun.

"Commander Deaver!"

Reeling slightly from the initial body slam of Sahara heat, Jake heard the voice calling his name. He surveyed the awesome site overlooking the Valley of the Kings, finally seeing Dr. Mancini descend a four-thousand-year-old sandstone causeway and stride down a sandy incline to greet him.

"Dr. Mancini, I presume." Jake smiled easily as they shook hands.

"Please. My friends call me Marcus, Commander." Mancini beamed at the still lean and fit former space hero who somehow made his sixty years look like forty-nine and holding. "Or should I say *professore?*"

"Jake is good."

"*Molto bene.* I'm so happy you could make the journey. Come."

With Deaver's driver/bodyguard cradling a machine pistol and keeping pace a few steps behind, the seventy-one-year-old Italian archaeologist led the way back up to the Pharaonic causeway from where they could best view the dig.

"Take a look."

Sweating through his T-shirt, Jake caught up with Mancini, only to have his breath taken away by the sight below: within the shadow of the famous Sphinx, three ornate sailing ships were being exhumed from thousands of years of dry dock by a small army of Egyptian laborers.

"*Magico,* eh?" Mancini gestured toward the exotic vessels, which seemed to be emerging from Time itself as much as from the dunes at Giza.

"My God, Marcus. They're beautiful."

Despite the withering stare of Ra, the sun god, and a cloud of tiny black flies that refused to be waved away, Deaver was entranced.

"How big are they?"

Mancini turned to him from beneath the slice of shade afforded him by the brim of a battered Panama hat.

"Oh, somewhat bigger than the *Nina,* the *Pinta,* or the *Santa Maria,*" he said, with a discernible note of mischief. Jake reacted to the implied ocean-crossing range being ascribed to the tall reed ships.

"You tested for saline?"

"*Si, si*. But say nothing, please."

Mancini flicked a glance at Jake's Egyptian bodyguard.

"For the Antiquities Committee," he said, lowering his voice, "they must remain 'ceremonial boats,' at least for now. But I promised myself I would not complain."

The idea that these colorful craft might have once sailed down the north-flowing freshwater Nile to ply the Mediterranean Sea was part of an ongoing conflict that divided Cairo's classicist Egyptologists from many scholars in the West. Long-held basic assumptions about the history of Mankind in the so-called cradle of civilization had come under intense assault from European and American archaeologists for a generation. And the Cairenes were in no mood for further heretical assertions in the scientific literature.

Whether human civilization was dramatically older than modern Egyptians claimed or not, Jake found the debate about it endlessly fascinating.

"I can only imagine, Marcus. Must be quite a tightrope."

"In Egypt, my friend, Egyptology is not just a science. It is also a religion, an ideology, a national obsession, and a blood sport."

As a new student of the ancient world, the Apollo alumnus was aware of the factions and the infighting. Jake had read and closely followed the work of West, Bauval, and other non-Egyptian scientists who'd been given permission to study the Sphinx in the early nineties.

What their university-sponsored testing revealed was that erosion patterns on the oldest portion of the leonine body of the Sphinx had not been caused by eons of scouring desert wind and sand. The evidence in the stone was of water damage: heavy, protracted rainfall and deep pooling water acting on this monumental Egyptian national treasure over hundreds of years.

Problem was, the most recent geological era wet enough to have caused water erosion like that had occurred at the end of the last Ice Age, around 10,500 B.C.E.

This would make the fabled man-faced lion sculpture not simply older than the pharaohs credited with building it; the Sphinx would have to be at least five thousand years older than any known human civilization *capable* of building it. The dilemma this presented amounted to a crisis for the classicists.

"I guess the Egyptians prefer that their Egyptian national monuments stay Egyptian."

"*Preciso.* But what you may be most interested in is up here."

As they hiked together up toward the Pyramid steps, two Jeeps full of heavily armed, black-uniformed paramilitary police zoomed past, kicking up a dust cloud of fine sand. Jake's driver/bodyguard waved them a casual salute.

"Trouble?" Deaver indicated the patrol.

"Radical fundamentalism." Mancini gestured with both hands, as if to keep at bay an invisible army of the night. "They don't know preservation from plundering. Or a Belgian tour bus from invading 'infidel' hordes. But forgive an old man's disappointment over things that cannot be changed in our lifetimes. We go up here."

Without a pause, Mancini proceeded to climb the steep face of the Pyramid like a mountain goat. Already hot and sweaty, Jake and his twentysomething driver exchanged looks, marveling at the older Italian scholar's energy.

Here we go, Deaver thought. Then mindful of the stress on his knees, he made his way up the great sandstone Wonder.

▼

Waiting beneath a frescoed archway, Dr. Mancini seemed unfazed by the climb. He offered Jake a hand up the last step.

"Thanks."

Deaver moved into the shade under the arch, gasping for breath. Looking out from this high vantage point across the plateau, he could see the two principal sister Pyramids, the oldest ones at Giza arrayed in a slightly offset line in relation to where he now stood.

Pulling a large water bottle out of his backpack, Jake offered it around. Mancini accepted, but the young Egyptian waved it off, leaning his shoulder against a shaded wall of two-ton stone blocks and lighting an acrid cigarette.

Jake unashamedly drank down a half liter before tucking the bottle away.

"So, what do you think?" Mancini gestured to the artwork above them.

"Oh, boy."

Wiping sweat from his hands and face with his shirttail, Jake now focused on the fresco and immediately saw what he had come here most wanting to see.

It was a hieroglyph very much like one he had drawn by hand and sent to Mancini for translation: the most Egyptian-looking of the six hieroglyphs he'd brought home from the lunar rubble of Sinus Medii, the provenance of which he'd not shared with the Italian archaeologist.

"It's gorgeous, Marcus."

"A match, or a near match, don't you think?" Mancini said, enjoying Deaver's enthralled reaction.

"Can I take a rubbing?"

"Of course."

Deaver extracted a pad of tracing paper from his backpack, tore out a sheet, and placed it carefully over the glyph. A delicate graphite image emerged as he worked with the edge of a soft pencil.

"God. It's beautiful."

Jake had characterized his original freehand drawing as "an untranslated glyph" he had run across. And the luck of Mancini actually finding a similar one at Giza had made the journey to Egypt feel something like fate.

Securing the rubbing between pristine leaves of vellum and two pieces of cardboard, he slipped it away inside his pack, then took out a small digital camera and began documenting the glyph in situ.

"Does it relate to the Moon?" Jake asked casually, covering the fresco from various angles and distances.

"Well, the context would suggest cosmology. Maybe early Sumer from the clay tablets, but I haven't run a search. I can give you the software we use to sort out glyphs and pictos, Commander, if you like."

"Thanks. That'd be great."

Mancini asked the Egyptian bodyguard a question in his own language. The serious-faced young man unslung his automatic weapon, put out his cigarette, and indicated he would stay where he was.

"All right," Mancini said, leading the way to the Pyramid entrance. "Shall we move on?"

Jake stashed the camera, hitched up his pack, and followed the archaeologist down the dimly lit tunnel that led to the fabled King's Chamber. Mancini stopped a moment as their eyes adjusted to the dark.

"By the way, the word *Cairo* is not Egyptian. It's ancient Sumer."

Jake struggled to place that fact in the context of what he knew or thought he knew about the time line of human civilization.

"So, the name for the Egyptian capitol predates the pharaohs?"

"It's in the clay tablets." Mancini nodded and then continued on in the demi-dark toward the King's Chamber.

"So, what's it mean, Marcus?"

"That's what I'm trying to puzzle out, my friend." Mancini laughed.

"No, I mean what does *Cairo* mean in Sumerian?"

"Oh! Forgive me, Commander." The archeologist laughed again, lighting the way now with a small halogen lamp. "It refers to the planet Mars. *Cairo* means 'Mars.'"

55

February 9/Dr. Paula Winnick's Residence/Georgetown

Dr. Paula Winnick's prewar town house in a posh section of Georgetown was quite some distance from Cairo geographically, culturally, and psychologically. But a jackal-head sculpture in Winnick's art collection was enough to thoroughly transport Deaver back to the Great Pyramid.

"Jake?"

Startled, he turned away from the Egyptian display, hearing tea things rattling and tinkling somewhere off in the kitchen. Angela called out a question.

"Cream or lemon?"

"Neither, thanks."

Inside and out, Dr. Winnick's home had impressed them both as postcard charming, from the ivy-covered fieldstone exterior to the rambling, high-ceilinged rooms crowned with ornate moldings like sculpted cream.

Set off by the deep shine of waxed parquet floors, the exquisite old Persian carpets underfoot seemed too precious to walk on. And adorning every wall were superb pieces reflecting a lifetime of collecting, and not just from Egypt: there were art and artifacts, tools and weaponry from Africa, Asia, Central and South America, and more. It was fabulous and a little intimidating.

Joining Angela and Dr. Winnick around a hand-carved Thai coffee table, Jake sat on the silk-embroidered teak couch and sipped Lapsang souchong tea as Angela gave their hostess the background on her investigative efforts before presenting Winnick with the TOLAS photo of the pyramids at Cydonia.

The Nobelist produced her reading glasses and studied it closely.

"We'd just like to have your reaction, what you think about the possible commandeering of *Mars Observer,* and why NASA might be sitting on this. And if you have any thoughts about who it might have come from . . ."

The intimation was subtle enough to ignore, but Dr. Winnick was not one for ignoring things. She rubbed her eyes and perched her glasses on the top of her head with a decisive stab.

"Well, compelling as this image might be, Ms. Browning, I'm afraid *I'm* not your whistle-blower. Nor, frankly, would I be."

Her voice sounded flinty and patrician. Sipping at her smoky tea, Dr. Winnick gave Deaver a long penetrating look that might have been a reproach or the acknowledgment of an unspoken issue between them that she was not prepared to broach. At least not in front of Angela.

"Was there something else you wanted to talk about?"

Sitting beside the distinguished scientist, Angela could only take her at her word that she was not their Deep Cosmo. She felt a little disappointed, partly at not having been quite as smart as she thought she'd been.

But there was still the hope of making a powerful ally.

"I'd like to ask you about your work at the Brookings Institute, in 1959."

"Ah, Brookings." Winnick glanced at Jake again, seeing where this discussion was going; then she concentrated on Angela.

"I was invited to take part in a congressional study: the Implications and Hazards of Space Exploration. Eisenhower ordered it when NASA was just a high-flying idea that he was crazy about."

"So, you and Dr. Margaret Mead made a recommendation . . ."

"The entire panel spent a year studying and debating the risks of the proposed space program, and in the end we unanimously advised Ike and Congress that 'any discovery of alien artifacts' be kept from the public. Margaret and I wrote the opinion. I suppose that's what you have a problem with."

Angela's face confirmed her assumption.

"I just don't understand it," she said. "You're a scientist. It seems so entirely against everything that you and Dr. Mead would stand for. I just don't understand *why.*"

"Because of the Law of Unintended Consequences, my dear."

Winnick included Jake in her grim, worldly smile and then warmed up their cups from an English fine china teapot.

"The potential for worldwide social, political, and religious destabilization in the face of such a discovery represents the greatest single hazard to mankind inherent in the whole NASA endeavor."

Deaver broke his silence, but with affection and respect.

"Even so, Paula, you must admit the world has moved on in the last forty-odd years. Look at *Star Wars* or *Star Trek.* Polls show at least eighty percent of Americans now believe in the existence of intelligent extraterrestrial beings. The idea of contact is not such high strangeness to people anymore."

"In the first-world countries, perhaps you're right," Winnick allowed. "But what about the billions of people who aren't American or European or Japanese? Who never heard of George Lucas or Captain Picard, who don't know that Americans once walked on the Moon. Half the planet have never even made a phone call! America is not the world, Commander, much as we'd like it to be. Bring us that mask over there, would you?"

Winnick indicated a Polynesian artifact on the wall, lit by a tiny spotlight. Jake took the colorful coconut-husk carving down and passed it to the elderly scientist.

"Impressive," Angela said, hefting the mask.

"It's Turaawe. It always reminds me of Dr. Mead and how she used to carry a Victrola when she went into the bush. She had to stop playing it for the natives, though, because, invariably, when she cranked up the music they'd go pelting off into the forest in fright. It'd take days to lure them back."

"Funny," Jake said, already guessing the impending moral.

"Also kind of heartbreaking," Angela added. Winnick nodded in agreement.

"What's most heartbreaking is that there are no Turaawe masks being made anymore, because the Turaawe, as a people, no longer exist."

She waved an aging hand at the entire Pacific Islands collection.

"Before she died, Margaret gave me all these things because she couldn't bear to look at them anymore. It was her own contact with remote island groups she was studying that ended their isolation and *unintentionally* caused their demise."

"And she blamed herself."

" 'I killed them with curiosity, Polly.' That's what she said. When she went back in the '50's she was just devastated. After being exposed to our metal knives, cooking utensils, and machine-woven cloth, the Turaawe culture was substantially lost in a single generation. Wood carving, boatbuilding, weaving, dancing, singing, most of their language and oral history was almost entirely gone. We can see the same thing replicated again and again from Africa to the Amazon to the hill tribes in Southeast Asia."

Angela saw the connection.

"So, in Brookings, you and Dr. Mead were raising an alarm."

"Loud as bells, my dear. Loud as bells. We had to get people thinking. Even well-intended contact by a technologically superior race can wipe out entire human cultures just as surely as black plague, genocide, or natural catastrophe. And we know that because we've done it ourselves. Who knew what we might find, venturing out into the solar system?" Winnick held up the Mars photo for emphasis and then tossed it back down on the table.

"Even just the confirmed discovery of alien artifacts would irretrievably alter the course of human civilization. Overnight and forever. It is a lesson of history that we ignore at our peril."

Jake felt this last point being directed most sharply at him. He gave Angela a warning glance and then spoke to Winnick with the intimacy of an old friend.

"I told Angela everything, Paula."

"Oh, God."

Winnick slumped back into the couch, the shared secret of Apollo 18 seeming to occupy the room with them now like an undesired guest.

Angela tried to remedy that, leaping into the breach.

"Believe me, Doctor, I have assured Jake and I want to assure you: this goes no further without the Commander's expressed consent."

"Please." Winnick waved her off, visibly upset. But Angela pressed on.

"You know what Jake found on the Moon. And you don't want it disclosed because you still believe we're at risk."

"In ways that we could not even anticipate, much less control." Dr. Winnick set her cup and saucer down with an emphatic clatter. "What you are talking about is imposing a momentous change, by *fiat,* on all of human civilization. An absolute paradigm shift of the first magnitude. Laying the groundwork for momentous change takes time. Unless what you want is to trigger fear-driven demagoguery and violent social chaos that would make Pan-Islamic terrorism and Mao's Cultural Revolution look like walks in the park. People have to be brought along the pathway step-by-step. We found the fossilized Martian microbes in the Antarctic in 1984. And released the fossils for study in '94 just to test the waters, so people could get used to the idea of something alien but nonthreatening: former microbial life on another planet. Next maybe we'll see how they handle microbes or chlorophyll living on Mars today. And if we take it slowly, and gradually roll it out in digestible bites . . ."

Deaver shook his head, making an impatient noise.

"Paula, how can mankind ever grow up as a species if the truth about who we are, the nature of the universe, the nature of reality, for God's sake, is perpetually being held hostage by those in power?"

"It's not being held hostage. It's being unfolded, Jake. Maybe slower than you or Angela would like, but there is such a thing as wise stewardship."

"But isn't this knowledge a birthright?" Angela said, sounding idealistic if not naive. "Don't We the People have any standing here?"

"Oh, please."

"No, really. Our tax dollars do pay for the space program."

"So what?"

Winnick batted down the argument like Agassi slamming home a winner.

"If you paid for a very expensive meal that was going to poison you, and you knew it, would you eat it anyway so as not to have wasted the money?"

The Nobelist pushed herself to her septuagenarian feet.

"Forgive me. But I'm afraid I can't join your crusade to end the world as we know it. However, I can offer you some absolutely wonderful lemon poppy-seed cake."

It was an olive branch of civility putting an end to argument.

"I'll take it," Jake said.

"Let me help." Angela gave Deaver a look, gathering their cups and accompanying Winnick to the kitchen. "By the way, what was it that Dr. Mead used to listen to on her Victrola, out in the jungle?"

Dr. Winnick laughed easily.

"You mean, what music scared the natives off into the trees? Oh! Any strong, disembodied singing voice would do it. Caruso would do it. But there was something about Edith Piaf. 'La Vie en Rose' scared the dickens out of them!"

56

Outside and across the street, the surveillance baton had been passed to a dark blue Dodge van with blackout windows and faux phone-company markings.

Inside, two FBI agents wearing headphones kept vigil, recording everything that was said in Dr. Paula Winnick's living room.

"I don't see why the fuck they don't just swoop on this guy," the younger G-man said.

"Sure," his partner said, sipping flat diet Coke and finishing off the soggy end of a Subway sandwich. "He's just chillin' with some fuckin' TV journalist. Who's she gonna tell?"

"Oh."

The dish antenna on the roof of the mock-Verizon truck did a decent-enough job and they were getting everything on reel-to-reel. They just could've done without the steady stream of folks from the neighborhood wandering over and trying to peer in through the tinted one-way glass.

The two agents knew *why*, but it was still a pain in the ass.

"You'd think a neighborhood like this'd already *have* broadband."

"Shhh."

The junior agent shook his head as a housewife braving the cold in a bathrobe and pajamas began rapping on the blacked-out windows.

"We gotta repaint this truck."

57

Three months earlier/The Great Pyramid/Giza

Urine and bat guano. Deaver imagined the laugh he'd get telling his students about the dominant fragrances to be found inside the Great Pyramid. Breathing in the stale air and bent almost double as he moved down the close corridor, Jake was also aware of an oppressive density that pushed in on him from every direction.

These people were small, he thought, avoiding dusty cobwebs and glad for even the few bare, low-voltage electric bulbs strung haphazardly above them.

But the sense of traveling thousands of years back in time was a palpable thrill, and once they reached the King's Chamber, Jake was able to stand upright under high vaulted ceilings.

Mancini played the light from his halogen lamp across the surrounding walls, which were covered from the floor to a height of fifteen feet with a gorgeous panorama of hieroglyphs.

"Genesis," he said out loud, the word echoing off the hard surfaces.

Jake stared at the epic story etched in stone: the Egyptians' account of the origin of mankind and the birth of civilization. It was a history repeated with small variations in cultures around the world, a celebration of the First Ones, ancient gods who came down from the sky and presided over the artistic and scientific development of human society.

Jake pored over the exquisite carvings, some still holding their vegetable-dye pigments after millennia in the dark.

"My God, Marcus . . ."

"Come, there is something I want to show you."

The Italian archaeologist motioned Deaver over to a low section of the vaulted ceiling. He then reached up and removed a stone facing that covered the entrance to a dark, narrow shaft.

"This leads up to the top of the Pyramid at a very precise angle. Take a look." Mancini moved so Jake could peer up the shaft. Though it was noon outside, he could see a small portion of the sky, black as night, and three stars that were perfectly visible. Deaver recognized them immediately.

"The belt stars of Orion."

"*Si, si,* the shaft totally blocks out the sun. Now the interesting thing is, the three pyramids here on the plateau are aligned in precisely the same geometric relation to one another as the three stars there."

Jake considered the symbolic meaning more than the pure engineering feat.

"Like holding up a mirror to Orion."

" 'As in heaven, so on Earth.' The astronomer priests did real science, tracking the precessional motion of the Earth on its axis."

"Pre-Copernican."

"Oh, *si.* Long before Copernicus. They measured time in epochs of twenty-six-thousand-year cycles, the precessional cycles." Mancini replaced the stone facing. "They wanted very much to know what time it was."

"And you have a theory about why."

"Only a guess at what I cannot yet prove."

"I'd like to hear it."

Mancini took a moment, gathering his thoughts on the hypothesis.

"I believe . . . that part of why the whole complex at Giza was created was to call attention to the recurrence of catastrophic celestial events."

"Extinction events." Jake nodded.

"Not just the K/T event that did in the dinosaurs. There were two Taurid asteroids that ended the last Ice Age, impacting in the ocean off Japan sometime between nine thousand and eleven thousand B.C. and then another mass extinction in the Bronze Age that is just coming to light."

"The underwater ruins off Cuba and Turkey and India." Deaver could envision a cascade of ancient cross-cultural connections. "So, perhaps the Pyramid is predictive. Like a planetary alarm clock."

"*Si, si*. To awaken mankind. To remind us that our solar system passes through dangerous territory in its long journey around the black hole at the center of the Milky Way. To pass down awareness of a cycle of catastrophe, in case we had forgotten."

Jake made a note to himself to revisit the mathematics memorialized in the Cambodian ruins at Angkor Wat, the geometry of the Mayan pyramids in Central America, and the historic myths of Quetzalcoatl and Plato's Atlantis.

"Marcus, does this relate to the Mayan calendar?"

"You mean, does the world run out of time on December twenty-third, 2012? I don't know what to think about that. There is still so much to learn here."

"I understand."

The former astronaut's eyes then fell on a singular object dominating the center of the room: a polished marble sarcophagus. He ran his hands along the coffinlike sides and Mancini moved the light to illuminate the elegant symbols etched all around it. Deaver recognized one picto immediately.

"Horus?"

"Yes, very good, the Great Pyramid was a temple of initiation for The Followers of Horus. One of the spiritual practices of the order, which included the reigning king, was to lie here in meditation for three days."

Deaver traced another glyph in the stone.

"And this means 'sun boat,' right?"

"Yes, sun boat. Or solar boat."

"May I?" Jake indicated the interior of the sarcophagus, where the high priests and kings of Egypt had lain.

"Of course, of course." Mancini helped the former Apollo astronaut climb into a different kind of capsule made for a very different kind of star journey. Once stretched out inside the cool smooth marble, Jake took a few slow deep breaths.

"Can you read to me what it says?"

"Sure."

Mancini's low voice sounded soothing and almost hypnotic as he walked around the sarcophagus and translated the meaning of the glyphs.

You must cross the sky-river in your solar boat . . . The Followers of Horus prepare you for your Journey to the First Time . . . Your Father is waiting for you among the Great Ones whose mouths are equipped . . . You must fly to be with him in the Du-At . . .

"Sirius. The star home of the gods." Jake nodded, closing his eyes.

With his arms across his chest as though lying in state, Deaver began noticing a subtle change in energy, which he experienced as a high-frequency oscillation or hum inside his skull. It seemed to be building in intensity with a rushing, psychotropic quality that was heady but not unpleasant.

It's my nervous system. I'm hearing my nervous system, he thought, the resonance transposing itself, modulating up the scale to a higher frequency.

Within moments, all jet lag and physical weariness had dissolved, dissipating into the marble trough wherever it touched his body, leaving Deaver's mind keen and alert. His essential self seemed lighter, or at least more lightly tethered to his body, and he experienced the locus of his consciousness as if it were floating in the hard casement of his head.

But only because he wished it to be floating there.

The idea occurred to him that if he wished to go somewhere else, anywhere he wanted to go, that he could simply go there. And leave his body behind.

But before he could test this idea, the image of an immense hawk appeared in his mind's eye, rotating slowly and unblinkingly above him.

You must cross the sky-river in your solar boat . . .

He was awed by this vision, so vivid and dreamlike, though he was certain he was awake. And the words he heard in his mind's ear seemed charged with meaning and even a sense of personal mission.

The Followers of Horus prepare you . . .

It was like a mythological riddle was being posed by this supremely intelligent spirit animal; a puzzle for Jake himself to decipher.

Yet Jake was not just himself. He was much more, something profoundly older and more complex, belonging to a noble lineage with sacred duties and tasks that must be performed.

The Followers of Horus prepare you for your Journey . . .

The spirit animal, if that's what it was, was speaking to him now, as if this were the most natural thing in the world. Deaver watched in a kind of rapture as the mythic creature began transforming itself from the form of a hawk into something else: a jackal the size of a man.

No, it's a man wearing the mask of a jackal, he thought.

The creature slowly turned toward him as if angry at being discovered.

Oh, it's not a mask . . .

"Unnhh." Jake opened his eyes, not remembering having closed them.

Dr. Mancini smiled and helped him out of the sarcophagus with an air of ceremony, as if welcoming him back to the dimensional world. He then led the way out of the stone passage toward the light of the sun god, Ra.

"It has a certain power. No?"

"Yes, it does." Deaver checked the luminous dial on his watch and felt a new respect for The Followers of Horus and their seventy-two-hour ritual entombments: all of five minutes had passed since he'd lain down inside the sarcophagus. Then Mancini's voice was echoing off the hard stone walls.

"Commander, stay where you are."

Up ahead he could see the Italian Egyptologist or at least his silhouette at the tunnel entrance. He was in some kind of argument, speaking in rapid-fire Arabic with Jake's bodyguard, who was gesturing emphatically.

Puzzled, Deaver stood still a moment, hunched over in the dim, low shaft.

Listening beyond the voices of Mancini and the agitated driver, he could just make out the chaos of people shouting in excitement or alarm and the sporadic Orville Redenbacher *pop-pop-pop* of what sounded like automatic weapons fire.

Jake then hurried up the tunnel toward his host.

"Marcus, what's happening?"

58

The morning drive-time traffic crossing and recrossing the Potomac was every bit as stop-and-go as Angela had imagined it would be, although ten hours earlier she hadn't expected she'd be dealing with it at all.

Before meeting Jake at Reagan National, she had booked a room for him at the Mayfair Hotel on her *Science Horizon* business Visa. And after saying good night to Dr. Winnick, they'd climbed into Angela's Grand Cherokee and headed back to D.C., fully intending to go straight to the hotel.

Which we almost actually did, Angela thought, deftly applying eyeliner in the truck's rearview mirror as she crept along with the traffic.

Certain images kept coming back from the rest of their night together and she found herself grinning into the mirror uncontrollably. Searching for a word with which to characterize Commander Deaver's generosity as a lover, she settled on *lavish* and almost swooned at the thought.

"Lavish . . ."

Especially the second time.

Science Horizon would be billed for the room at the Mayfair, and she thought about not telling Miriam that Jake had spent the night at her apartment. She could avoid the third degree by just saying that she'd taken him to the airport that morning, and get points for saving the company taxi fare.

Angela touched the brakes, narrowly avoiding a collision with a shirtsleeved man in an E 320 Mercedes who glared back at her blissful face.

Of course, if she was going to continue grinning like a maniac, dissembling was not really going to be an option: her partner-in-crime, Miriam Kresky, was a woman of many talents. One of which was that she could read a smile like Barry Bonds reads the seams on a big-league curveball.

Well, hell, Angela decided, adolescently rebelling at the idea of having to hide how she was feeling. *There're only so many secrets about a man that a person can keep.*

59

The Oval Office/the White House

Shit.

Bob Winston was unhappy, but more because of his own miscalculation than anything else: this was not a level of play with much room for error.

The national security adviser was sitting in a yellow, incongruously cheerful-looking chintz-upholstered chair in the Oval Office, paying close attention to the President of the United States now towering over him from behind the desk built for FDR.

A file containing the findings of Sandy Sokoff's investigation lay open on the President's blotter, including a brief on the *Mars Observer/* TOLAS package that had been given to Congressman Lowe and Lowe's description of his experience with Winston at the National Archives.

Too angry to sit, the Commander in Chief just stood there staring down at the file in excruciating silence and letting Winston sweat.

A few feet away, Sokoff and an uncomfortable-looking Phillip Lowe shared a couch. Sandy observed with satisfaction how Winston ignored them, as if nonacknowledgment was the same as nonexistence.

Sandy, however, felt quite at ease, in a hardball sort of way. Coming when it had, Congressman Lowe's unexpected phone call and subsequent revelations had been providential, if not miraculous. Sandy decided he would have to ask his new friend the Jesuit monsignor what exactly was involved in the Church officially recognizing an event as a miracle. He seemed to remember that the convening of a synod of bishops might be required, but he wasn't sure.

For his part, the President of the United States did not believe much in miracles. He suspected Congressman Lowe's courage in coming forward might have been driven by ambition as much as by the whispering of angels.

But he'd take whatever he could get. The President closed the file.

"Thanks to an independent investigation, conducted at my request, information regarding Unacknowledged Special Access Projects has been brought to my attention, Bob. Information of crucial importance to any sort of informed executive decision concerning Project Orion. The kind I had hoped to find in the briefing paper you provided me two weeks ago."

"Within the constraints of time, Mr. President, I thought that brevity might serve best. I take full responsibility if that was a misreading of what you required, sir."

Sokoff watched Winston coolly taking the heat, like the ceramic tiles on the outside of the Space Shuttle deflecting friction fire during reentry. The President appeared unimpressed.

"In any case, Bob, the issues raised by these Special Access projects will provide the talking points at a National Security Council meeting I'm calling for this afternoon. And I expect your contribution to that meeting to be an unabridged disclosure of all current USAP activities."

"I understand." Winston accepted the presidential reprimand even as his brain raced way out ahead, looking for wiggle room, calculating the extent of damage to his own position, and how to stop further bleeding, and which endangered species of secrets might yet be protected by a more limited disclosure than the President was calling for.

"If I may speak to the gravitas of the situation, as I see it, sir?"

"Go ahead."

"Mr. President," Winston continued, as if they were the only two people in the room, "it cannot be your intention to abandon the preservation of presidential deniability vis-à-vis Special Projects. As your adviser, I urge you in the strongest possible terms to reconsider."

"Bob, that is exactly my intention." The President responded in a deliberate, even tone. "I will not make decisions that affect hundreds of millions of people in self-imposed ignorance. And if it puts this office and my administration in political peril down the road, so be it."

Winston knew that this was his cue to back off, but he persevered.

"Mr. President, I still believe it is a grave mistake. And I must formally protest in the interests of national security."

He had pushed it to the wall with all the dignity he could muster, under the deteriorating circumstances.

"Duly noted," the President said dryly. "And please have your resignation on my desk today before the council convenes. I'll hold my decision on it until after the meeting."

It was the shoe Winston had been waiting to hear drop.

"Mr. President," he said, standing in respect for the Office, if not the man. He then turned on his heel with a certain Teutonic spank and marched out of the room.

Once he was gone, the President snatched up his monogrammed letter opener like a dagger and then drummed it on the dark green blotter.

"He thinks I'm weak because I didn't fire his ass outright."

From the couch, Sandy Sokoff laughed and shook his head.

"No, Mr. President; he just knows he still has leverage."

"Because we need to know what he knows and he knows it."

Lowe shifted his weight and leaned forward, speaking for the first time since Winston had walked in.

"Mr. President, is there a scenario in which you *wouldn't* fire his ass?"

The President gave that some thought.

"I expect our friend Bob is working on that even as we speak."

60

Boulder, Colorado

It was not as if Deaver hadn't been thinking about it. Off and on throughout their drive to Paula Winnick's house and even while they were there, he had found himself fantasizing about Ms. Angela Browning: as he watched her quizzing Dr. Winnick or when their hands touched as they passed things across the coffee table.

He'd sensed that Angela had had some thoughts along those lines, too.

Still, when she had invited him up for a drink at her place, on the way into D.C., there had been mutual astonishment at how combustible they were together.

The urgency and hunger were evident in the trail of their clothing from the hallway (where they'd finally kissed each other) to the bedroom (the bed almost totally symbolic, at this point) to the puddle of clothes on Angela's bedroom floor, where they'd fucked in such a frenzy it was more like jungle-animal sex than making love.

The second time, actually in the bed, had been even better: probing, delicious, funny, intoxicating, languorous, profound.

Pulling into his gravel drive outside Boulder, he still wondered if he had done the right thing by coming home. Jake had anguished all the way out to Reagan that morning, thinking he was insane not to be staying in D.C. for a few more days, but Angela had not suggested it and he wasn't about to presume.

▼

Beat from the flight and the two-hour drive from Denver, Jake dropped his carry-on bag at the door inside his A-frame cabin and surveyed the wreckage.

"Oh, no."

Unlike the meticulous toss courtesy of Naval Intelligence, this time Deaver's artwork and mementos, everything from his shelves and closets, was either missing, broken, or turned out in piles on the floor. The sense of violation did not take long to percolate through the initial shock.

"Son of a bitch . . ."

Angrily kicking through the ankle-deep disaster area of the living room, he righted a toppled bookcase and rescued a sketchpad still intact in the rubble of books and manuscripts. Pocketing the pad, Jake negotiated his way into the spectacularly trashed kitchen and tried the wall phone, but was greeted only by dead air. He slammed it down.

"You rat-fucks!"

A flash of lightning outside drew his attention to the open kitchen door and thunder came right behind the flash like a bang-bang play: close. He could smell the approaching weather.

Jake shoved aside a shattered spice rack and opened the fridge.

"You fuckers better've left me some OJ."

His own scared-stupid bravado cracked Deaver up until he found the juice carton and chugged it, ignoring the trickle down his chin.

When the truck tires crunched into the drive out front, he didn't stand there wondering what it was. He hit the back door and disappeared.

Jake had only one advantage over the younger, faster, and doubtlessly well-armed men who would soon be hard behind him: the home-turf advantage. He'd have to make the most of it.

61

The J. Edgar Hoover Building/Washington, D.C.

Dicks in dick suits, Angela thought.

The two men waiting at her apartment door, after she returned from the airport, clamshelled Bureau IDs at her with a practiced snap and insisted the questions they had would be better answered at the Hoover Building.

Angela cooperated. In a gesture of good faith, she even waived her right to counsel. But three hours later she was still sequestered in a small, plain room with three chairs, a table with a tape recorder on it, and Agents Simmons and Collier.

After she had told it twice, they wanted to hear it again: everything that had transpired between Angela Browning and Commander Jake Deaver; what he said and did, what she said and did, where and when they had said and done it, and who else was in the room at the time.

She was on the cusp of telling them to go stuff it when the questions turned more specific. So he-said/she-said specific it was obvious they had to have been bugging Dr. Winnick's house. When Angela finally asked the agents point-blank, they just shrugged and showed her the transcript.

"Ms. Browning, these are just words on a page, which can be interpreted in different ways. So, if you would please help us out here," Agent Simmons said, with all the casual smoothness of a spider to a fly. "On page ten, about halfway down, Commander Deaver says to Dr. Winnick: 'I told Angela everything.' Can we hear just that portion?"

Agent Collier produced a cassette, cued up to that spot, and played it back.

"I told Angela everything, Paula."

"What did Deaver tell you?"

Hearing Jake's voice, Angela remembered that she hadn't actually seen him board the plane for Denver, which made her wonder if he wasn't right here in the building, in a room just like this himself.

"I'm sorry. What's the question?"

"When Commander Deaver says he told you *everything,* isn't he referring to classified government secrets? Top-secret material which he had leaked to you, in hopes that you'd use it in a PBS exposé?"

Angela saw she couldn't last much longer without perjuring herself.

"Agent Simmons, Commander Deaver never gave me any classified documents whatsoever. And speaking of documents, since I am not a foreign national suspected of terrorist activity, I'd like to see the federal judge's signature authorizing the electronic eavesdropping and privacy violations of which this tape and transcript are physical evidence."

Chief Investigating Agent Simmons looked at his partner with a bleak expression, then spoke to Angela in a low, sincere voice.

"Ms. Browning, I must remind you that even as a citizen of the United States, giving false or misleading testimony to an agent of the FBI is a felony offense for which you may be sentenced to up to five years in a federal facility and fined up to ten thousand dollars."

Angela stared back at them across the table.

"Well, if you're waving fines and prison at me, then I think I *will* need to have my attorney present. And I'm sure he'll also be very interested in seeing that bench warrant, too, if you actually have one."

Angela knew by their reactions that they hadn't bothered with the technical niceties. She grabbed her bag and stood up, her whole body daring them not to let her go.

"By the way, you don't happen to have Jake and me in my bedroom rutting like crazed weasels, do you?" Angela indicated the cassette tape. "I'd sort of like a copy of that."

62

Boulder, Colorado

Lightning was crackling, sending bright white fiber-optic roots to ground all around him, and Jake could feel the hair on his arms levitating. The following thunder was a basso profundo that juddered up the soles of his work boots and deep into the twisted laundry that was his stomach.

There would be a cold squall, and soon.

Jouncing through the brush in his '76 Pathfinder truck, he noticed how his own fight/flight adrenaline made every physical move, every mental action, seem achingly clear and present. It was almost a spiritual experience.

"Scared awake." He laughed, trying to cheer himself on.

Back at the cabin, creeping on foot through a heavy screen of pines that bordered his property, he'd watched the black, unmarked Chevy van unloading its packet of operatives. When the heavily armed team rushed the front door, Jake had made a dash for the garage and his Pathfinder and then roared out the utility road, heading uphill.

With high clearance and four-wheel drive, he now drove as fast as he dared, thinking his best chance of losing them would be off-road. After that, he didn't know what the hell he was going to do, but first things first.

As he took a sharp left into some low scrub, lightning flashed again and the first spatter of rain strafed the windshield. This time of year that should have been good for snow. But whatever was playing havoc with the world's weather systems, it was only freezing above seven thousand feet, so in the foothills of Boulder rain just meant mud.

Good. Jake checked his rearview. *Mud is good.*

Then a wind came up strong enough to buffet the cab, the clouds dropped cargo, and Jake had his wish. Zagging downhill, he slipped and thumped over the rocky terrain and got a first glimpse in the mirror of the black van muscling and banging its way behind him.

"Shit."

The good news was that, so far, the wet had yet to compromise the purchase of the vintage Nissan's all-season tires. He was going to need that grip for all it was worth.

Making a hard off-camber turn that dumped him in a controlled fall onto a rarely used rutted track, Deaver gathered speed and distance for a quarter mile, then jumped back off-road again as the van reappeared far behind him.

▼

Inside the slithering black Suburban that was slamming its bump stops all the way down the hill, FBI agents Stottlemeyer and Markgrin held on to whatever they could, but this was just a courtesy ride-along.

The Defense Intelligence crew running the show had come heavy: cammies, Kevlar vests, flash grenades, machine pistols, and laser-scoped sniper rifles.

"Unhh. Jesus."

Stottlemeyer grunted after a particularly harsh impact as they followed Deaver off-road, and gave Markgrin a look: there was no way this was going to end except badly. He shouted up to the DIA team leader.

"You don't think this might be overkill. Just a wee bit?"

"You were the one who said he wouldn't run. By the way, what kind of weapons would he have in that old rice burner?"

"Weapons?"

"Hunting knives, rifles, shotguns? There was only one in the house."

A cammo'd op produced an unloaded service revolver in a Marine Corps holster. Stottlemeyer rolled his eyes.

"Guess you missed the ceremonial sword. It goes with the dress whites."

"Might not be all he's got," the team leader said, pronouncing this wisdom with a kind of clipped righteousness meant to cut off further discussion.

Then the pounding rain was drumming down so hard on the van's thin roof skin that conversation became impossible anyway.

63

Map Room/the White House

The Secret Service were obliged to wait outside the Map Room in the White House, where the National Security Council was in session: no one guarding the President had the clearance to hear what was being revealed.

Behind those closed doors, Winston led the discussion, standing next to a globe of the Earth that was easily ten feet in circumference. They had already covered antigravitic propulsion technology and high-altitude microwave-beam weapons bouncing death off the upper atmosphere with scaled-down mobile applications for crowd control, and a whole lot more from the dark world of Unacknowledged Projects.

"The next category is weaponization of weather," Winston was saying. "We're playing catch-up with the Russians on Battlefield Weather Modification, but we're making progress. Mainly in forced inducement of drought and flooding, creating earthquakes, tsunamis, and hurricanes. Ongoing testing is, of course, taking place strictly in underpopulated regions."

Winston indicated flagged spots in the Far East, including a few where artificially induced "natural" disasters had regrettably spread beyond isolated test areas, causing widespread destruction and human suffering.

"Battlefield Weather Modification," the President repeated.

"Yes. It's not an exact science, but we can almost put a tornado down on the ground wherever we want to, potentially incapacitating a standing army. When the Northern Alliance was champing at the bit to take Kabul, we stalled them and bought ourselves a couple of days with a sandstorm. Controlling it after it's been generated is something else, but the technology is promising."

"Smart storms," the President said, unsure which was more insane: that this *could* be done or that it *was* being done.

Winston read his reaction.

"If it can be done, Mr. President, how can we afford not to do it?"

Ignoring the rhetoric, Sokoff jumped in.

"Mr. President, you can stop it and we can probably get the Russians to stop it, but we could never go public with it. The liability issue alone . . . every hurricane in Asia would get blamed on American weapons testing. There'd be calls for reparations, business insurance would melt down—"

"Mr. Sokoff, I won't tell FEMA if you won't. Can we move on?" Winston loved hearing the President's counsel making the case for secrecy.

"Unacknowledged R and D is a crucial element of national security, authorized by tacit EOs and funded by Aerospace and Defense monies, congressional allocations, and so-called black budget or off/book discretionary dollars for over fifty years. It's about protecting our security future."

Sokoff coughed into his fist and leaned over to the President.

" 'Tacit' executive orders?"

But the President waved him off.

"How much money are we talking about, Bob? Altogether. Everything."

"Fifty billion annually, Mr. President, give or take."

A shocked murmur among the military men rippled around the room; mostly plain surprise, curdled with jealousy on behalf of their own service's budget constraints.

Winston waited while the hubbub died down. He had decided not to mention the additional billions put to work supplying weapons for every side of every armed conflict, rebellion, or civil war around the globe. Profits sometimes amplified by payment taken in heroin or cocaine and turned into cash by favored drug cartels. He didn't want to muddy the already murky waters for the new Occupant, who seemed understandably out of his depth.

"Fifty billion dollars," the President said. "All right, I want everyone in this room to hear this loud and clear: as Commander in Chief, I can and will impose moratoriums on any or all of these programs, if that is in the best interests of the United States. And I don't give a shit whose bread falls butter-side down."

The President looked around the table, taking in the entire council, including the CIA chief, the chairman of the Joint Chiefs of Staff, the heads of NSA and Defense Intelligence, and others, each of whom had his or her most game face on.

"That is a given, Mr. President," Winston said, "but with all due respect, sir, tarring Project Orion with the same brush as weather mods or these other things would be extremely unfortunate and, I think, shortsighted, given the narrow window."

"We're aware of the timetable," the President said, locking eyes with Winston. "Let's get back to the black budget projects."

64

Everything outside Jake's windshield kept disappearing in the lashing sideways deluge. Steering the spartan Pathfinder by Braille he hoped he was closing on an arroyo where he'd either find disaster or the break he needed.

Squinting between swipes of smeary wiper blades, he got a glimpse of the normally dry creek bed and hit the wet brakes hard. The creek was now a swift and rising river, and he was about to find out exactly how far it had risen.

Jake shifted gears and inched forward, sliding down the collapsing banks and fighting to keep from getting his truck sideways. Grinding through river water up to the engine mounts, he revved the Nissan four-banger furiously until he was out of the water and then gunned it like a crazy man up the other side of the arroyo.

"Whoo-hoo!"

From his new vantage point Jake looked back, swerving parallel with the swollen creek. The pursuing three-ton Suburban could either follow suit or fold.

Through exploding sheets of rain, he could just make out the black truck as it slowly approached the arroyo, tipped itself down the sodden banks at a crazy angle, hit the water, and got bogged down up to the hubs.

"Yes!"

Jake watched the sliding side door open and three DIA men splash out, up to their bulletproof vests in rushing water and battling just to keep their footing.

Then he heard the unambiguous stutter of automatic pistols on rock and roll.

"Shit!"

Deaver threw himself down across the passenger seat, dropping the clutch he forgot he was riding. The vintage Pathfinder lurched and stalled out.

Inside the black van a former Olympic shooting medalist had started getting ready by taking his gloves off and warming his hands like a concert musician. Watching helplessly as the DIA fuckup played itself out, Stottlemeyer and Markgrin found it nightmarish and absurd. It was going bad: lethally, career-endingly bad. When the wallowing Suburban died and the two gym-rat hard-ons jumped out into the water and started emptying their clips, the Fibbies threw themselves past the stunned team leader and out the door.

"Hold your fire! Hold your fire!"

▼

Jake didn't see the G-men or their shouting match and comic wrestling melee with the intel ops in the river or hear what they were shouting. Lying across the hand break and yanking the shifter into neutral, he was too involved with staying low, grinding the starter, and praying for spark.

As lightning lit the scene like a phosphorus flare, he lifted his head and peeked outside. A red dot of laser light flicked across his eyelashes and Jake got a long harrowing look at a man wearing a watch cap and aiming a high-caliber sniper rifle at him from inside the open door of the van.

He knew the truck offered no real protection: a round from a weapon like that had an all-access pass. Even a mediocre shooter could put a bullet through his door faster than you could say, "I'm with the band."

But between the ruby blink of that realization and the impulse to put his hands up in surrender, the situation changed and Jake heard it coming: it was like the hollow sound of the ocean inside a conch shell, amplified and deepened by the concussive rush of rolling rocks and stones that were being swept up into the grainy mix and powering down the arroyo like a runaway train.

Once the flash flood hit, it was over in about five heartbeats. The laser targeting Deaver's face disappeared just as an eight-foot wall of water and highballing stones exploded over the huge black Chevy, skewing it sideways and washing all the former occupants downstream like summer-camp kids white-water rafting.

"Thank you!"

Jake hit the starter again, directing his gratitude up toward any eaves-dropping deities who might have intervened.

"Thank you very much!"

When the damp points caught, he revved the Nissan engine back to life, blessed its 230,000 miles of loyal service, and worked his way down the mountain to the county road.

65

As the two men strode back through the West Wing corridor, Sandy Sokoff thought the President seemed almost jaunty. It was an odd reaction to the recital they'd just heard of horrific new applications of power designed to kill people wholesale.

And he was pretty sure this was probably just the tip of the iceberg. Still, the transcript of the President's council meeting, in the unlikely event that it was ever published, would probably qualify as a new Book of Revelations: the U.S. was secretly decades ahead of the rest of the world in military technology.

Sokoff understood the theoretical upside in terms of defense strength and also how the most compelling new weaponry had become the most tightly guarded secret, kept from even our own conventional armed forces.

But the downside was a complex puzzle: unbeknownst to most of those in the American command structure, the U.S. military was planning and training to defend the nation with hardware that was *generations behind* the capabilities that were being kept secret. The sheer waste in billions of tax dollars and millions of man-hours was staggering.

Even NASA was being crippled, spending a huge portion of their limited budget on incrementally better rocket propulsion systems that had long been surpassed by black projects technology.

For the President, this kind of gaping dysfunction was horrendous enough. What was even more alarming was the realization that any perceived balance of power in the world was an illusion. The bedrock concept upon which international security was reckoned by the world community was false; a confidence game maintained as rigorously as the fiction of a spy's cover story.

On one level, the U.S. appeared to be setting back the Cold War doomsday clock, joining hands with Moscow in reducing our nuclear arsenals and helping the Russians do the same. But it was a symbolic disarmament at best.

The fact was that Mother England's runaway child was only a blink away from possessing the means for world domination on a scale only Deutschland's most infamous housepainter had ever envisioned, burning himself alive with pure methamphetamine crystal and raving in his self-made Bergtesgarden of corpses.

And whether some dark, apocalyptic Pax Americana began here or not depended a great deal on what this new Commander in Chief decided to do at this particular moment in time.

Approaching the Oval Office, the President glanced at Sokoff, who was keeping pace beside him.

"So, how do you feel about Lowe chairing open public hearings on the Hill?"

To Sandy, the President seemed to be animated by an almost perverse enthusiasm.

"Sir, every political bone in my body says bury it where the sun don't shine. But right now I'm more concerned about the Friends of Bob."

"How do you mean?"

Sokoff peered around at the Secret Service agents, who were leading the way in front and trailing behind. He lowered his voice.

"Mr. President, the first use of power is to retain power," he said. "I'd double your personal guard. And I mean now."

"Have faith, Sandy. The system is going to work," the President said, waving off the idea. "Besides, we don't want them thinking they've got us running scared, do we?"

As they reached the outer office, his secretary flagged them down.

"Mr. President."

"Yes, Mrs. Travis."

"You have the 4-H Club from Des Moines for a photo op on the lawn in ten minutes and then the Russian ambassador's credentials presentation in the Blue Room, but—"

"Thank you, Mrs. Travis. Buzz me in five minutes."

"Yes, Mr. President," she said, deciding that telling him about the Brahman bull that was currently fertilizing the Kentucky bluegrass off the portico could wait.

Sokoff was pulling on a freckled earlobe and staring out the Oval Office's bay window as the President closed the door. He still didn't know what the putatively most powerful man in the world was being so cheerful about. As far as Sandy could see, Bob Winston had them with their pants down over a barrel of moonshine and he could hear banjo music.

"You know, you have that look, sir."

"What look?"

The lanky President grinned and joined his much shorter counsel in a Mutt-and-Jeff tableau at the window. Outside, a gathering of outsized but extremely healthy-looking farm animals seemed to be attaining critical mass.

"The I'm-the-smartest-man-in-the-room look."

"I'll try to work on that. In the meantime, give me the three-minute version of what's in the Vatican Archives that President Carter wanted to see and why I should ask His Holiness for permission to see it myself."

66

After prying cold, clenched fingers off the steering wheel, Jake shook out his hands and felt them trembling. He forced himself to slow the truck down, take several deep, deliberate breaths, and he was just getting calm enough to be worrying about what to do next when a helicopter made a pass about a hundred feet above him and sharply wheeled back around.

"Aw, fuck." Deaver pumped the brakes, but they still locked up, sending him slaloming toward the little blue-painted Bell now setting down on the road in front of him behind a curtain of gray rain.

"Jake!" The treble edge of a bullhorn cut through the helicopter whine, but he ignored it, desperately trying to turn around in the mud-pie track.

"Jake! Hold up, there, podnah!"

Deaver stopped: he knew that voice. And then, between the slapping wiper blades, he saw a stocky body jump out of the chopper wearing a hooded sky-blue slicker and matching NASA baseball cap. It could not have been anybody else.

"Son of a bitch." Jake yanked on the brake handle and splashed down into the road, looking like he just might kill Augie Blake with his bare hands.

"You! You son of a bitch!"

Jake stalked toward him, yelling over the whine of helicopter rotors and repeatedly losing his footing in the slop.

"You son of a bitch!"

"Hold on now, goddamn it."

Augie shouted into the loud-hailer, standing his ground.

"This is not my show, podnah!"

But Jake slogged furiously toward him, getting soaked to the bone.

"Not your show? Not your show! What the fuck does that mean?! You were just in the neighborhood?"

Augie clicked on the bullhorn again.

"It's a long story," he said. "Wanna take a ride?"

Speechless, Jake just stopped and gawked. With the prop wash whipping rain into his face, he squinted past Augie at the little two-place Bell: it was empty.

"It's a rental!" Augie grinned wetly and waved him closer. "Come on, Daddy-o, let me buy you a drink."

Jake stood in the pelting downpour for a moment, then splashed back and yanked the keys out of the Pathfinder's ignition, cursing to himself all the way.

67

Augie took them up over the aspens, banking radically and pushing the performance envelope of the whirlybird to about ten-tenths. Though strapped in tight, Jake was still plastered to the Plexiglas door by the g-squash.

It reminded him of late-'60's flight-simulator hell: he and Augie in astronaut training and Augie's hotshot "Hey, is that all you got?" test-pilot swagger. Not a fond memory.

When he could sit upright again, Deaver was still hot.

"So, what the fuck is going on? And don't tell me those aren't the same pond scum you threw in with."

Augie eyed him with a mix of affection and weary irritation.

"Jesus God Almighty. You know a shitload has happened since you hit your dinger and hung 'em up, son."

"Just tell me how come your asshole buddies back there are out trashing my place and chasing me down, like *America's Most Wanted!*"

"Aw shit, now, don't play dumb. Your little tête-à-têtes with Ms. Angela Browning? They think you're poppin' up in the toaster, podnah."

"Oh, God." Jake swiped rainwater off his face. "Fuck me . . ."

Augie made a slow sweeping turn and pulled a hand towel and a sweatshirt out of a sports bag under the seat.

"Here."

Jake rubbed his hair and face with the towel, then stripped off his jacket and sopping T-shirt and pulled the dry sweatshirt over his head.

"Augie, I swear to God, if they hurt her . . ."

But he was unable to finish the thought.

Tilting over sharply, Augie pointed down at an old cinderblock pilots' bar near the rental helicopter hangars.

"You remember the Condor."

"Oh, God."

Jake saw the painting of the huge endangered bird, faded and peeling on the bar's rustic tin roof. He braced himself with both arms and legs.

Getting clearance from the Denver tower, Augie swooped around and made a roaring hotdog approach, free-falling the last five hundred feet before catching it like a baby and setting the chopper down on its skids with masterful aplomb. It was vivid in Jake's mind, as he fumbled with his seat belt, exactly why he really hated flying with Augie Blake.

68

The Condor Bar/Denver Airport

"So, we went back," Jake said, a shot of *cuervo anjo* beginning to warm his body from the inside out. Across the Formica table, Augie hunkered down over the Condor Bar's scalding black coffee.

"Hell, yes," he said, "with the Soviets."

Cocooned in the privacy of their corner booth, Deaver made no effort to disguise his astonishment.

"You have it on good authority or you know for a fact?"

"I wore the vest."

A mission director's sartorial choice back in the Mercury program had become both a tradition and an emblem of the job itself, a player-coach kind of job often taken up by former astronauts.

Jake tried to imagine hot-shoe Augie Blake riding herd on a clandestine Moon return from a chair at Star City Mission Control in Soviet Georgia. Then again, who, besides he himself, would know better what a crew putting down at Sinus Medii should look out for?

Unlike Deaver, Augie had been trusted. He had stayed with the NASA team after Apollo 18, moving on to other challenges within the space program as if not at all burdened by the weight of keeping the nation's darkest secrets.

"Incredible . . ." Jake said, around a forkful of eggs and salsa. He knew the true price of bearing that burden. Deaver looked away, tasting a bitterness in his mouth not put there by the Condor's grill chef but by his own ego roiling with a sudden, poisonous envy.

Yeah, the team player gets the rewards. Go along and get along. Follow orders, keep your nose clean, and put "doing the right thing" aside, along with your conscience.

Jake knew he could never have taken Augie's path: he had been much too righteously angry back in 1973. Mad at NASA and at the Navy when they wouldn't back him up. Mad at his ex-wife and others he'd counted as friends when they made it clear that he was on his own if he refused to go along. Mad most of all at Augie Blake, for what had felt like the most personal possible betrayal.

But now, thirty-some years later, looking at his old partner, Deaver was already becoming bored with watching his own rampaging ego grasping at all the old-news victim fury welling up from decades past.

So *what?* Jake thought, addressing that fading, reptilian part of his brain as it slowly loosened its grip. *So fucking what?*

"Tell me about it," he said out loud.

Augie warmed his aging pilot's hands around the house coffee cup. "Shit, sure."

And fueled with shooters and Tecate, Jake listened as Augie ate *huevos rancheros* and told it.

▼

After the Apollo 18 voyage was declared the last of the Moon missions, the U.S. ambassador to Moscow showed his Russian counterpart some color stills of what had been confirmed at Sinus Medii, and proposed a collaboration. Of the two nations, only the Soviets had both the technological base and the social control necessary to mount and support a Moon mission in guaranteed secrecy.

Thus, under the umbrella of back-channel protocols, the two nations set aside their antagonisms so that astronauts and cosmonauts might begin training together at the Cosmodrome for a covert return to the Moon.

Ultimately launched from Star City, using a Russian Titan-class rocket for the heavy lifting, the adapted Apollo spacecraft was manned by a joint Russian/American three-man crew.

Landing at Sinus Medii on Christmas morning, 1974, the crew had a clear-cut mission: to find and enter the alien habitat and document everything they could see underground. High on the science agenda was the collection of any artifacts that would shed light on the nature of the extraterrestrials: what they were like, why they had been there, what kind of technology they had, where they were from, and why they were gone.

Analysis of the extensive film photography from inside the multilevel habitat resolved certain key questions: a catastrophic decompression caused by a breaching of the aliens' protective dome had blasted out everything near the entrances that was not bolted down. Whether it was caused by an asteroid hit, a large-scale industrial accident, sabotage, or an act of war was unknown.

Artifacts from inside the tunnels were recovered, secured in the return module, and later pored over by a cadre of U.S. and Soviet scientists. And from the study of film and photographs and five hundred kilos of recovered material, a picture of the former extraterrestrial colony on the Moon gradually took shape.

It had been a mining operation, built in six levels below the surface. Alien machinery, electronics, and hardware had remained intact, preserved for millennia in the super-cold airless tunnels and chambers, shielded from meteoritic erosion and solar radiation as if waiting to be found. And many intriguing pieces of this ancient advanced technology had been brought back to Earth.

What was at first bizarre and indecipherable, in 1974, became recognizable under high-powered microscopes as microminiaturized electronic circuitry and fiber-optic filaments for carrying digital information. These were among the most promising discoveries yielded by the artifacts that had been retrieved from the Moon. Replication or back-engineering from the ET samples would take a decade or so, but the jump start those samples had provided in advancing U.S. computers and communication was profound. And that was just the beginning.

▼

Outside the windows of the Condor Bar, private jets and little four-place Cessnas taxied by; and commercial aircraft flying overhead rattled the rafters inside, where Tex-Mex was getting a big play on the jukebox. Jake and Augie hardly noticed any of it.

"So, tell me," Deaver said, lucidly drunk. "What were they like?"

"Like us, only smaller: two arms, two legs, two eyes, six fingers, six toes."

"Humanoid."

"Yeah, humanoid."

"And they were extracting minerals?"

"You remember when we dropped that hammer and all the moon-quake sensors went ape-shit?"

"Yeah, I remember they said the ground kept on ringing for hours."

"That's because it's damn near hollow. ET had mined the shit out of it, podnah." Augie chuckled and swiped a corn tortilla through a puddle of egg yolk. "You know what the Russians did when they got back?"

"Stopped building big boosters, I imagine."

"Confiscated every copy of Titan-class plans, cut up the ones they'd already built into scrap, and melted 'em down. Every goddamned one of them."

"Scared shitless."

"Hell, so were we. At one point, they asked this KGB guy Douchenko, the guy in charge of the SR-21 program at Baikonur: if these folks came back today, did the Russians have something we didn't know about, something we could defend ourselves with, if necessary? He just laughed and said, 'Nyet.' That's when the idea of collaborating on planetary defense started getting kicked around. What eventually became the Strategic Defense Initiative."

"Was that Reagan's idea or Gorbachev's?"

Augie looked out at a helicopter setting down on the tarmac.

"Bush. Bush the Elder. The old spymaster sold the space-shield concept to Reagan as a strategy for winning the Cold War. But it was a smoke screen for a two-track deal. Reagan tripled the national debt and fast-tracked SDI knowing the Soviets'd go bankrupt trying to match it. That gave the black budget program a head start and gave Gorbachev the internal argument he needed to outflank the hard line anti-perestroika, anti-glasnost factions at home and initiate real talks."

"But Star Wars was a bluff. We couldn't have built it."

"Hell no, not then. But we needed a way to end the Cold War and get Project Orion, the real-deal space shield, started. Now we've got supercomputers on a chip and science and resources from France, England, Japan, Germany, Brazil. And it's finally going up even as we speak, podnah. Thanks to what you and I found up there, in 1973."

Jake thought about his trashed cabin and the intel ops trying to pick him up.

"So, that's why . . ."

"That's why."

Deaver took that in along with everything else, brooding over it.

"Was there any guess on how old that habitat is up there?"

"Micrometeor abrasion says ten to twelve thousand years, give or take."

"God. And if they had all that ten thousand years ago . . ."

"Can't even imagine what they'd have at this point. Can you?"

Jake just shook his head, unable to wrap his mind around it.

"So, what happens now?" he said.

"Well, I've been thinking about that." Augie looked Jake directly in the eyes. "And I say it's time."

He spread his hands like a blackjack dealer showing he wasn't palming any chips. Deaver leaned back away from the table.

"Why now?" he said, looking as wary as he felt.

Augie grinned across the breakfast plates and empty shot glasses.

" 'Cause if we wait till we're dead, Daddy-o, the bad guys win," he said, and then laughed. "Look, we're sitting here because push has come to shove. And I don't see another way out except by means of extreme daylight."

"For me, maybe. I thought you still had something to lose."

Looking honestly contrite, Augie finished his coffee, taking a couple of beats to think about what he had to say before he said it.

"Look, podnah, we're joined at the hip, you and me, like it or not. But the main thing is, I owe you. You were right and I was wrong. I should have backed you when you wanted to say no to NASA and Nixon and that whole sorry-ass crowd. But I didn't do it. I stood up and lied like a man for duty-honor-country instead of having the guts to tell the truth and damn the torpedoes. The only satisfaction I ever got was seeing that lying ski-nosed bastard chased out in disgrace. Even now I look around and I see why people distrust and despise the leaders they vote for. It's because they expect to be lied to when the chips are down, and that's serious long-term damage. But fuck it. Point is: I'm sorry. I'm sorry for my part in the bullshit. I'm sorry I hated you and your righteous integrity. I'm sorry I watched you quit and walk away and sneered at you behind your back: 'Flaky Jake, what a shame.' But then, I guess you never do forgive the man you have wronged. So let's just say I want a chance to make it right. You swabby-ass, lime-sucking pothead son of a bitch."

Augie offered his hand across the table.

Jake looked at it and then took it. It was starting to feel a little like the old days, the good old days. Augie grinned and flagged down their waitress.

"Darlin'? We need a pot of coffee, high-test, and another cup. And tell me, you ever been up in a helicopter?"

Deaver left Augie flirting with the waitress.

"Extreme daylight," he mused, not really sure what that would be like, but starting to get an idea. Unsteady on his feet thanks to the shooters, Jake made his way toward a door marked CABALLEROS and the pay phone next to it. He badly needed to talk to Angela, but she was going to have to call him back from another pay phone.

PART
VI

When you come to a fork in the road, take it.

—Yogi Berra

69

Angela was feeling both scared for Jake and personally responsible for the spot he was in. She was elated to know that he was safe, for the moment, but he was by no means out of the woods. And Angela didn't feel better about the situation until they had worked out a plausible way forward, a way, though, that involved both of them taking a risk.

Now that she was free to tell her partner everything, the two women had strategized together after Miriam's initial shock wore off. They honed their pitch until they were ready to walk into the offices at PBS legal and get what they needed.

▼

"That's some story," Arthur Maclewain said, giving his knack for laconic understatement some exercise. Marvin Epstein, the attorney's young associate, spoke without looking up from their tightly crafted two-page proposal.

"So, you're saying you want to offer *Science Horizon* as a forum for Colonel Blake and Commander Deaver to make a public statement about discovering an extraterrestrial city on the Moon."

Angela turned toward the junior attorney.

"It will be the science story of the decade. Like getting the first Apollo Moon landing exclusive to PBS."

"But we won't just be scooping the networks. We'll make 'em bid to share our feed," Miriam added. "No reason not to make it good business as well as landmark television."

"That's not the issue." Maclewain fiddled with a gold Cross pen.

"You mean, is it covered speech? You tell us."

The senior attorney looked extremely uncomfortable.

"Whether it's protected under the Constitution or not, you're putting your careers, *Science Horizon,* the station license, and the corporation at risk."

"Like Edward R. Murrow taking on McCarthy. Or Dan Schorr and Vietnam." Angela sounded as tough and defiant as she felt.

She and Miriam looked back and forth between the two lawyers.

"So, is it constitutional free speech and free press or not?" Miriam repeated.

"I don't know," Epstein said, turning to the senior counsel with an odd light in his eyes. "But I want the ball."

70

Returning from Denver on Air Force transport, Colonel Augie Blake had a car pick him up at Andrews AFB and drop him at the NASA building in D.C. Stopping in his own office, he checked messages and e-mail, including a cryptic note and a small video file from Jonathan Quatraine, the grad student in Australia.

Huh . . . Augie looked at the time, then opened the file.

Since he was already aware of Project Orion, the short quick-time sequence of the secret weapons test was surprising only because the Aussie grad student had picked up on it and, impressively, even gotten it on tape.

"Well, good on ya, mate," Augie said, in a Dundee drawl.

He was playing the file back and wondering how to reassure Jonathan about what he had done when something caught his eye. Augie played the Orion test again. And then again, until he was sure of what he was seeing.

"Those cowboy sons of bitches."

He then hustled upstairs to join the crisis management meeting already in progress in the office of the NASA Administrator.

71

Office of the NASA Administrator

"I talked to Deaver. After you folks's little fiasco."

Augie was splitting his attention between Vern Pierce behind his desk and Bob Winston, who was sharing the office couch with Admiral Ingraham. Winston wasn't giving away much, but Pierce seemed anguished.

"I hope you told him it wasn't supposed to have been like that."

"Yeah, those stuntmen did pretty well screw the pooch." Augie laughed lightly. "I don't know whose dick was in whose hand out there in Colorado."

The attitude alone was almost enough to make Winston walk out, but the dour presence of the Admiral beside him quashed any such impulse: Ingraham hated prima donnas.

Augie turned to the two Intelligence heavyweights, who seemed to be competing for the grim face award.

"I'm afraid y'all've got one pissed-off Apollo astronaut on your hands, outside the tent and ready to start pissing in."

"Where is he?" Ingraham said. Augie shook his head.

"Someplace safe, I'm sure. And ready to face the media with a hundred-percent hangout, whether we like it or not."

Pierce looked pale.

"He wouldn't dare! Justice would be forced to indict."

"Validating Jake's story," Augie pointed out. "Not to mention bringing it all crashing down on our collective heads. Unless . . ."

Augie paused, as if reconsidering his own suggestion.

"Unless what, Colonel?" Ingraham said.

But the National Security Adviser was already there.

"Unless the one man, the one and only eyewitness who could cast doubt on Deaver's testimony, contradicts his story," Winston said, letting it hang out there.

Ingraham studied the idea from different angles. Pierce was slack-jawed.

"You can't be serious."

"Maybe it's a bad risk." Augie shrugged, as if having second thoughts or feeling reluctant at being fitted for the Judas role. But the Admiral was warming to it.

"Better a live fool than a dead martyr."

"What exactly are you imagining here?" Pierce said.

Augie explained.

"What if Jake and I go on Angela Browning's PBS show together, the both of us, and we let Commander Deaver flat-out tell his story . . . ?"

"But that's insane. It's out of the question."

"Wait, Vern, this is just a backup." Winston held up his hand like a traffic cop. "Let's play it out."

Augie leaned heavily forward, resting his forearms on his knees.

"Just so we have no illusions here, gentlemen: unless you find him first and take him off the street, former Apollo Commander Jake Deaver is gonna say what he's gonna say in one public forum or another, like it or not, or grits ain't groceries. All I'm saying is, if I'm at least *there* when he does it, I can set it up so that Jake says his piece first, and then when it's my turn, I can reluctantly and compassionately decline to confirm the Commander's version of events."

"Jesus . . ." Pierce said, weighing the potential PR nightmare.

"Then you, Vern, have your spin-flacks all geared up with tabloid handouts about Flaky Jake's psychotherapy, Flaky Jake's Buddhist-cult practices, Flaky Jake and his psilocybin adventures, 'Drug Bust Astronaut Sez: "Alien City on the Moon!"' Shit, who the hell's gonna run it as a straight news story?"

"While you and Colonel Blake take the high road." Winston nodded. "'Commander Jake Deaver was a courageous, respected member of the

Apollo family and always will be, regardless of any unfortunate personal circumstances,' blah-blah-blah."

"So, Deaver tells all and becomes the latest Jay Leno joke," Ingraham said, savoring it. Augie made a face, but did not disagree.

"After which he can say absolutely anything, folks, and nobody who matters will give a good goddamn."

But Pierce appeared unconvinced.

"Look, I just don't think . . ."

Ingraham silenced him with a look, then focused his intelligent black eyes on Augie like the arch-spook interrogator he'd once been.

"Colonel, I know there isn't that much love lost between you and Deaver." The Admiral's voice was an intimate rasp. "I just want to be sure you could do this."

Augie understood and took his time before responding.

"Admiral, I know Jake Deaver. And I know that when he's mad, he's one stubborn son of a bitch. Well, right now he's as pissed off as I have ever seen him, drunk or sober. That old boy is ready to walk, head high, through hellfire, draggin' yours truly right along with him. And he's not askin' anybody's opinion or permission, least of all mine. What his old podnah might want, or how what he does affects me and the rest of my life, is totally off his fuckin' radar. Now, I may know him like my idiot brother and I may understand why, but forgive me if I say fuck that noise to the bone. And if I have to save his sorry butt to save mine, so be it. That said, Admiral, there is one thing . . ."

Augie leaned in close, his voice sinking to a quasi-confessional register.

"Jake's made some bad choices, all right? So, the way I see it, he is forcing my hand. And I can and will consign my old podnah to permanent public irrelevancy. But make no mistake."

Augie turned to include Winston.

"If an *unidentified assailant* robs him and leaves him dead in the street, or there is some tragic, fatal *hit-and-run* accident? Or CNN reports he was found *overdosed on heroin,* or some other shit he does not use, in his cabin in Colorado? You know what I'm saying. If Jake Deaver so much as chokes on a goddamn chicken sandwich, instead of dying in his sleep a very old man, I will know who did it. And I will track you down and put each one of you down like rabid, feral dogs."

Winston was afraid to look over and see what Ingraham's reaction might be. But the stern-faced Admiral was actually rather amused, although he believed Augie Blake meant exactly what he said, 100 percent. They all ignored the NASA chief, who was too busy eating his tie to say anything.

"I don't suppose he'll thank you," Winston said.

"No." Augie relaxed back into his chair, looking oddly pensive. "I don't suppose he will."

72

February 15/PBS Studios/Washington, D.C.

A phone bank was set up at the PBS station and staffed, just like pledge week, with volunteers poised to handle the expected tidal wave of calls. Additional security was laid on, both inside and out, with instructions that nobody go in or out without a verbal okay from Miriam.

Once the *Science Horizon* staff understood that the show was going "live" and why, everyone was too excited to complain about the restrictions, which extended to e-mail and phone calls: a full lid was down.

A video team was dispatched to cover Augie on location at his NASA office, the PBS soundstage was set up and lit, and a Chinese take-out feast was making the table groan in the greenroom. Jake's whereabouts, however, remained a mystery to everyone for safety's sake: he'd be calling in his interview from an undisclosed location.

Leading Marvin Epstein, the junior attorney, into the greenroom, Angela and Miriam looked at the clock and then addressed the buzzing staff and crew, who were busy loading plates full of Kung Pao chicken and vegetable chow mein.

"As you know, this may be a little like Orson Welles's *War of the Worlds* tonight," Angela said, "except we're dealing in fact not fiction."

Miriam then introduced Epstein.

"So, everybody say hi to Marvin, from the PBS legal department, who is here to provide his counsel and support for the duration, just in case."

The greenroom crowd shouted, "Hi, Marvin!" The slightly abashed young attorney waved hello back, and then got in line with Angela for the dim sum.

▼

Across town at the Mayfair Hotel, Richard Eklund and a cadre of Mars Underground comrades had taken over a high-floor suite. A green felt poker table with fresh decks of cards and a rack of clay chips was already set up.

Overtipping the exiting room service waiters, who'd laid out a small buffet with sandwiches, soft drinks, and coffee, Eklund put the "Do Not Disturb" sign out and locked the door.

"Okay, no outgoing calls, nobody leaves the room until it's over. And anybody hungry better eat now."

He retrieved several laptops hidden in the bedroom closet and his colleagues began networking them off the business suite's DSL connection.

"Richard?"

"Yep." Eklund tuned in PBS on the hotel TV.

"Are you gonna tell us what's up now?"

"First, give me a hand here."

Eklund and another Underground techno-god opened and shuffled the decks, dealing out hands of stud and setting stacks of chips in front of each empty chair.

"So, we're not gonna play cards?"

Once the poker table looked more like a game-in-progress, Eklund abandoned it and put the hotel TV on mute.

"All right. We're tuned to PBS and wired into *Science Horizon* because they are airing a very important special tonight, a program that's going out *live*, for reasons you will understand when you see it. Our job is to protect the show's Web site and all the mirror sites, and believe me, we're gonna see a huge number of hits. Huge. You're gonna need to work fast to manage volume and at the same time be ready to react quickly to serious signal jamming. I mean, cyberspook, heavyweight hack attacks, so get your game on."

"Must be a helluva special."

"You could say that."

"What kind of jamming?"

"Won't know till it happens. But expect the full Monty."

"What about *Science Horizon*? Is that all we get to know?"

Eklund took a roast beef sandwich from the room-service buffet and began to make quick work of it. He'd been too busy to eat since Miriam Kresky had taken him to lunch and asked him for help.

"I can't tell you what we're going to see before we see it."

He paused and chased a mouthful of sandwich with some diet Coke.

"But if this thing goes on as planned and we can *keep* it on, I can promise you we will remember where we were, who we were with, and what we did tonight for the rest of our lives."

73

In his office at NASA, Augie Blake stood stiffly in a beribboned Marine colonel's uniform and massaged the keys on his computer, revisiting his e-mail.

Across the room, the remote-camera operator was tweaking the shadows, and a sound engineer, who'd fitted Augie with a clip-on mike, was setting levels.

"Say something, Colonel. In your normal speaking voice."

"Testing, testing, one-two-three . . ."

▼

A few blocks away, Augie's plush Lincoln Navigator was parked somewhere near the Jefferson Memorial. Inside, Commander Jake Deaver shuffled through some three-by-five cards with his prepared statement, tuned in the public-radio simulcast, and talked to Miriam on the hands-free phone.

"Can you hear me now?"

"Loud and clear, Commander. But turn down your radio."

"Jake? You ready?" Angela said, and heard Deaver's disembodied laugh.

"Ready or not. Will Augie be able to hear me?"

"Yo, Daddy-o. We are good to go . . ."

▼

In her booth above the PBS soundstage, Miriam orchestrated the elements: Angela down on the floor, Augie's on-camera remote, and a still picture of Jake and the phone-patch audio from his still-undisclosed location. She glanced at the clock: time to call CNN, which had won the live feed in secret bidding.

"Wolf? Miriam Kresky. We're live in five . . . no, so far so good . . . thanks, you, too . . . and buckle up."

Miriam put on her headset and looked down through the double-paned glass, seeing Angela on her mark, with the red light up on Camera One. She glanced at the monitors, turned to Marvin Epstein, who was sitting nervously behind her, and gave him a conspiratorial wink. Then she got on the talk-back.

"Okay, everybody. We are *live,* no jive, so if you screw up just keep on going, there's no going back. Angie? This is it, kiddo. In thirty . . . break one."

She acquired eye contact with Angela and raised her right hand, the way she had done a thousand times before. But this would not be like any time before.

"I'll count you in . . . five . . . four . . . three . . . two . . . *and* . . . go!"

The monitors in the booth and televisions all across America that were tuned to *Science Horizon* now showed Angela Browning standing in a tight pool of light on a dark soundstage, speaking to the camera.

"This is Angela Browning. And tonight, this special edition of Science Horizon *is coming to you live in order to offer a forum for two very special guests, Apollo astronauts Commander Jake Deaver and Colonel Augie Blake . . ."*

▼

Across the street, a plainclothes snatch team had taken over Flowers Not to Reason Why, a florist shop with a view of the PBS Building entrance. Hiding behind a "Closed" sign and a large spray of yellow spider mums, they'd been hoping to catch Deaver going in or out. So far, no luck.

Still with nothing to report, they checked in with Bob Winston.

▼

The President's adviser for national security was taking his calls in the NASA Administrator's office, where he and Vern Pierce were watching Angela Browning on a bookshelf TV.

"Commander Jake Deaver, who is on the phone with us, and Colonel Augie Blake, speaking from his office at NASA, have asked to make personal statements for the first time concerning their Apollo 18 mission to the Moon in 1973, and Science Horizon *has agreed to provide a platform for them tonight."*

"Jesus . . ." Vernon Pierce said, pacing behind his desk.

A damning government psych profile and press kit on Deaver had been printed up and was already in the hands of the NASA PR staff, along with Pierce's own carefully crafted official statement. Pierce was still nervous.

"Anyone interested can also access supporting materials and streaming video on our Web site at www.ScienceHorizon.org/TOLAS."

Winston, sitting alertly on the couch, was confident that he had assets in place for every contingency. Taking down the *Science Horizon* Web site would be easy; they'd make it look like it got swamped by hits. For the show itself, blocking the satellite feed, if necessary, meant taking the whole satellite off-line: messy, but doable. Ingraham was in charge of that.

"Commander, are you there?"

"I'm here, Angela."

"Commander Deaver will speak first, reading a prepared statement."

The screen was divided into windows: Angela at PBS, Augie in his NASA office with the remote crew, and a third window with a still picture of Jake.

"Go ahead, Commander . . ."

Deaver's window was enlarged as he began reading his statement.

"Thank you, Angela. In 1973, Colonel Augie Blake and I had the extraordinary privilege of undertaking for NASA, and for the United States of America, the Apollo 18 mission. Four years earlier, Neil Armstrong had been the first among mankind to take that historic step . . ."

▼

At home in her Georgetown town house, Dr. Paula Winnick watched Jake's image fill the screen, and listened to his speech with equal parts fear and fascination.

"But what the Apollo 18 mission discovered, which we are now confirm-

ing publicly, is that Man was not the first intelligent being to set foot on the Moon."

"We shall reap the whirlwind," Winnick said out loud to the empty room. Then the phone began ringing, the first of a dozen people calling to tell her to turn on the TV. She ignored it.

▼

Inside the Mayfair Hotel room, Eklund and his Mars Underground colleagues had been distracted from their work. They were shouting in astonishment and staring at the Moon photo of Jake and Augie now being posted on the Web site.

"Oh, my god!"

"Hoo-yah!"

Eklund turned up the volume on the TV and cracked the whip.

"KEEP THOSE SITES UP!"

▼

The video lights had heated up the NASA office and Augie was sweating in his uniform. He fiddled with his earpiece: Jake's cell phone was going in and out of phasing static. Angela's voice interrupted as the connection got bad.

"Commander Deaver? We're starting to lose you."

"Sorry . . . maybe I should move."

"Yes, go ahead and see if you can find a spot with a stronger signal. We'll talk to Colonel Blake for a bit. Uh, Colonel?"

"Yes, Angela."

▼

Across town, Jake started the Navigator, turned up the radio so he could hear what Augie was saying, and slowly drove off toward the Washington Mall.

"You're not saying that you saw extraterrestrials up there . . ."

"No, no. At least I certainly didn't. And if I may, I'd like to confine my own remarks to what I personally witnessed."

"Fine, Colonel. Why don't you go ahead."

▼

Nine floors upstairs from Augie, Winston smiled a vaguely reassuring smile in Vernon Pierce's direction.

"Here it comes."

The TV screen filled with the live image of Colonel Augie Blake in his office, standing in front of the NASA logo. Augie's voice was loud and clear.

"On the ground at Sinus Medii, the principal thing which I saw with my own eyes and was able to document on eight-millimeter film was the ruins of a large, degraded, domelike structure of unknown age and origin which was clearly the product of an advanced intelligence."

"That son of a bitch." Winston was transfixed with shock.

"Oh, my God. Oh, my God."

"Where is he, Vern? What floor is he on? That motherfucking son of a bitch!" Winston snatched up his phone and attacked the keypad. Pierce gasped out the suite number as he hovered, hors de combat, over the office trash can.

▼

In the Black Chamber at the heart of the NSA facility in Maryland, Admiral James T. Ingraham listened and hung up the phone.

Looking over a tech officer's shoulder at a translucent tracking screen, Ingraham studied the grid map of Washington and the GPS-style flashing dot that represented Deaver's current position.

"We've got him. He's moving, sir. Between Twelfth and G . . ."

Once Jake had started to speak, his cell connection to the PBS station in D.C. had been quickly traced and jammed, and his location triangulated.

Ingraham looked up from the tracking screen at a waiting Defense Intelligence crew in black jumpsuit uniforms.

"Good luck, gentlemen."

"Aye-aye, sir." They saluted in ragged unison and hustled out the door.

"All right. Next . . ."

Moving over in front of an emerald laser holographic display of the Earth, the Admiral was able to see the orbital position in real time of every satellite—commercial, scientific, or military—of every nation to within one-hundredth of an arc second.

"Admiral? When you are ready." A civilian tech op under NSA contract made some adjustments on a large panel and indicated a red flashing icon in the hologram: the satellite carrying *Science Horizon* among hundreds of other programs.

"How's the weather on the sun today?"

"Plasma eruptions every hour, sir. It's sunspot season."

"Plays hell with our magnetosphere, doesn't it?"

"And with our satellites, sir."

"On my mark."

The Admiral then made a brief phone call on a scrambled line as the tech op sat at the ready.

74

From three TVs in the Oval Office at the White House, Angela's voice projected out into the room as the President and Sandy Sokoff, surrounded by late-shift staffers, watched both PBS's and CNN's live feed of *Science Horizon.*

"Colonel Blake, both you and Commander Deaver have been bound by oath not to publicly speak about this, under pain of federal prosecution— isn't that correct? Why have you decided to break your silence now, Colonel?"

"There's a good question," Sandy said, to no one in particular.

The President made a guttural noise in his throat.

"How many people are seeing this?"

"PBS? A few hundred thousand. CNN? Well . . . that's CNN."

"Get me Winston on a landline, Sandy. I want the council here. Now. And I mean everybody."

75

NASA Station/West Australia

At the downlink station, the Aussie grad student was tuned to CNN and practically bouncing off the ceiling.

"My God! It's like Galileo! It's just like fucking Galileo!"

Colonel Augie Blake's Moon revelations were the most exciting thing he'd seen since The Thorpedo took home all that swimming gold at Sidney in 2000.

"Augie, Augie, Augie!"

Jonathan pumped his fist and shouted, pacing up and down as if tethered to the TV screen, his dog Hudson barking and trailing on his heels.

"Angela, we were assured that the truth would be told, that the American people would ultimately be told 'when the time was right.' And frankly, neither one of us has another quarter of a century to wait . . ."

"Augie, Augie, Augie! Oi, Oi, Oi!"

76

NASA Building/Washington, D.C.

"Security! Colonel Blake! Open up! Colonel Blake!"

The soundman looked at the camera operator and shrugged, shaking his head. He'd already boosted Augie's levels until the mike started feeding back, but the shouting and pounding outside the bolted door was still bleeding in. Augie raised his voice under the hot lights and carried on.

"The thing is, Angela, under the NASA charter, we all have a fundamental right as Americans to whatever knowledge is gained by the American space program. All of us. And if suppressing certain discoveries was justified, in the context of the Cold War . . . that justification is long over."

A chaos of nightsticks and flashlights began beating on the door, melding into the angry male voices shouting in the outer office.

"*Colonel Blake? You obviously have some pretty insistent folks outside your door, there. Can you make out who it is?*"

"No, ma'am . . ." Augie glanced away toward the noise. "But listen, if you lose me? Check the bulletin board. There's an e-mail there . . . Jake? You copy?"

"*Bulletin board? Copy that.*"

"*Augie? I've just been told that Wolf Blitzer at CNN is asking if that's NASA security or the FBI . . .*"

"Can't really say . . ."

"*Augie? Marvin Epstein from PBS legal is here and he's now advising us that you probably need to find out who they are, and if it is the FBI or the D.C. police, we'll have to continue this under different circumstances. Okay?"*

"Well, all right, then, hold on."

The camera operator pulled focus as Augie stepped to the door and got a great shot of NASA security guards bolstered by FBI agents exploding into the room flying-wedge–style, like crackhouse raiders.

"GET DOWN, DOWN, DOWN! EVERYBODY DOWN ON THE FLOOR!"

"Hey! Whoa! Hold on there . . ."

Wrestled to the carpet, Augie was quickly handcuffed by the FBI: a scene shown mostly from a low angle, once the camera was knocked to the ground.

"Hey! We're cooperating here!"

▼

In the booth at PBS, Miriam had not anticipated this. She looked at Marvin Epstein, who was standing up now, his eyes getting big.

"And the whole world is watching."

"No kidding."

Then it was over. The shouting and the anarchy of equipment being trashed and Augie and the video crew being dragged out were the last sounds and images broadcast, before one of the Fibbies had the presence of mind to pull the power plug.

Of course that TV minute would be rebroadcast on CNN news every half hour as part of their lead-story coverage for the next three news cycles, which meant maybe a billion people would see it.

▼

With a small crowd around him in the Oval Office, the President watched the fiasco and cursed under his breath.

"Was that the FBI?"

"I believe so, Mr. President."

"Jesus fucking Christ. Has everybody gone insane?"

On-screen now, a visibly angry Angela Browning was giving the federal agents' performance a scathing review.

"*Well, folks, there it is. Something more reminiscent of the former Soviet Union and the KGB. What appear to be agents of the FBI and we're presuming security guards at NASA, placing Colonel Augie Blake and the Science Horizon video crew under arrest after confirming Apollo Commander Jake Deaver's statement about seeing an alien habitat, an extraterrestrial structure or arcology on the Moon. Our American tax dollars hard at work. Unbelievable. Miriam? Do we have Commander Deaver back?*"

▼

Miriam spoke through her headphone mike.

"Angie, sorry, no Jake yet. But we're getting Wolf Blitzer; he's got some questions for you. Give me thirty."

Angela then filled thirty seconds with a recap as Miriam called cameras and fielded a flood of urgent incoming calls. Behind her, Marvin Epstein burned up a phone line trying to track down the whereabouts of Augie and the video crew.

"Angie? We have a still on Wolf. And . . . go."

Miriam brought up a photo of Blitzer picture in picture along with his live audio.

"*Angela, this is Wolf Blitzer at CNN in Atlanta . . .*"

Then all the monitors went blue.

Through the glass they could see Angela and the crew staring in disbelief at the prerecorded "technical difficulties" station announcement that had automatically blipped up and started broadcasting itself.

"Shit! We're off the air," Miriam said. "They can't do that, can they?"

Epstein looked up from his conversation with the D.C. police.

"Not without shredding the First Amendment."

"*Miriam?*" The intercom buzzed from up front. "*There are some gentlemen out here who say they are from the Federal Bureau of Investigation . . .*"

Miriam raised a cool eyebrow at the junior attorney.

"You wanted the ball . . . ?"

▼

In the suite at the Mayfair, Eklund was working furiously, but he immediately recognized Miriam's voice on the room phone.

"*Richard, what's happening?*"

"It's the satellite. We're on it. Can't talk."

Eklund hung up. The hotel TV glowed blue in the background as he and the other Mars Underground geeksters smacked frantically at their laptops.

Suddenly their key-clacking and cursing was interrupted by a firm, hard knock at the door that might have been room service with a fresh pot of coffee.

But it wasn't.

77

NASA Building/Tower One Elevator

The shooting pains down Augie's arms and up the side of his neck were what he felt first, not anything in his chest. It seemed like one minute he was standing, handcuffed, and going down in the crowded NASA elevator with an FBI agent on each side, and the next moment he was down on the floor hearing a lot of shouting and oddly not giving a damn what it was all about.

78

Kinko's/Washington Mall

On the west side of the Washington Mall, Jake had stopped trying to revive the phone connection and had driven like a madman to a Kinko's down the street, where all the available rent-a-computers were already in use.

"I'll pay twenty bucks for five minutes," he said, brandishing a crisp twenty-dollar bill. "It's an emergency. Who wants twenty bucks?"

"Me!" A fourteen-year-old black kid jumped up from a computer and started collecting his schoolbooks.

"Thanks." Jake handed him the bill and sat down. Accessing the *Science Horizon* bulletin board, he saw a file labeled ORION and opened it. After reading Augie's attached note, he played the sixty-second video file.

"Good God in heaven."

Jake dug out his wallet again and stood up.

"Anybody have a clean Zip disk? Twenty bucks for a disk!"

Four hands with blank Zips shot into the air.

▼

Outside on the street, a black GM sedan had double-parked next to the Navigator. Four men swarmed the truck.

Peering out Kinko's storefront glass, Jake could see them. But all he was thinking about was where he had to go now, and the one stop he had to make before he went there. Salvation appeared in the form of an on-duty D.C. cab stopping right at the corner, less than a ten-yard sprint away.

▼

On the PBS soundstage, Angela and Marvin Epstein were hip-deep in a flood of Fibbies fanning aggressively out through the studio. The brown-shoe bio-invasion was led by a graying, beefy agent-in-charge named Stansfield, waving an official-looking document.

"We have a federal warrant to search the premises for a Commander Jake Deaver," Stansfield said, confronting Angela. "And I expect everyone here to cooperate fully or you will be subject to arrest. Turn off these cameras."

"No!" Epstein pointed at the camera crew. "Keep going."

Marvin thought it curious that the agents didn't know they'd been knocked off the air. It was going to tape, but that was irrelevant: this was a pissing contest.

"Keep rolling, keep rolling!" Angela gestured vigorously as Epstein got right in Stansfield's face.

"A search warrant does not convey the authority to interfere with or abridge lawful activities. And Agent, uh, Stansfield, here, either knows the law or should know the law."

The agent-in-charge looked ready to drop Marvin with the butt end of his gun. Instead, Stansfield just glared, turning away in disgust and raising his voice to include everyone on the soundstage.

"All right. I'm only going to say this one time. Obstructing justice, harboring a fugitive, or interfering with a federal agent in the exercise of his duty—these are all federal offenses. If anyone here knows the whereabouts of Commander Deaver and does not come forward now, I assure you, you can and will be subject to felony prosecution . . ."

The staff and crew remained silent, documenting everything on tape as Stansfield's team of agents straggled back from their search empty-handed.

"Thank you, Agent Stansfield," Epstein said. "Now, if your unproductive search of my client's premises is complete, not to mention your willful attempt to disrupt a public broadcast . . ."

Stansfield glanced at the red light on top of an RCA camera moving closer toward him. Up on the in-house monitor he could see his own mottled complexion growing unflatteringly larger and larger. Epstein grinned.

"Lovely. And for twenty-nine ninety-five you can order a copy of this program, along with a transcript, if you like. Just go to ScienceHorizon.org—"

"Save it for your licensing hearing, jerk-off."

Stansfield and his men retreated as swiftly as they had crashed in. Crew and staff broke into cheers and applause.

"Marvin Epstein . . . Studley Do-Right!" Miriam exclaimed, rushing down from the booth to give him a hug. Angela joined the love-in.

"Good work!" she said, kissing him on the cheek.

"Thanks."

Epstein looked both pumped and a bit embarrassed as the camera crew huddled around to shake his hand. Miriam's assistant handed her a phone.

"Wolf Blitzer and Larry King . . ."

"Gentlemen!" Miriam was exuberant, almost shouting into the mouthpiece. "We expected a reaction, but shit-canning the Constitution?! What? Oh, no. Oh, shit. Hold on a second. Angie . . . ?"

"What?" Angela heard the bad news in her partner's voice.

"Augie's at Bethesda Naval Hospital in the ICU."

"Oh, no."

"What else, guys?" Miriam grimaced, locking eyes with her partner, and repeated the news as she was hearing it. "Emergency bypass . . . It's not on-air yet . . . How about the crew?"

"Oh, God. People . . . everybody? Quiet, please." Angela gestured for everybody to settle down so Miriam could hear.

"D.C. cops, okay. Do you know which station? Thanks. Who? Yes. Jesus! For what? Okay, thanks, guys. You got it."

Miriam hung up.

"Marvin?!" She called it out at the top of her voice, not realizing he was standing right next to her.

"Yo."

"Sorry. Jimmy and Danny . . ."

"The video crew?"

"Right. They're with the D.C. cops. We don't know what the charges are, probably resisting or interfering. Try and get it dropped, would ya?"

"Got it. What about Colonel Blake?"

"Augie's in surgery at Bethesda, emergency bypass. We'll know more in a few hours. Also, Eklund and his buds have been arrested by the FBI for gambling at the Mayfair Hotel. I want to bail them out, too, okay?"

"Gambling?" Marvin looked puzzled and then hurried out.

"Angie? CNN wants a stand-up, live, they're sending a crew—"

"What else about Augie?"

"He's under the knife, kiddo. That's all we know."

"Angie?"

Angela turned as her secretary began whispering urgently and gesturing toward the back entrance to the studio.

▼

Jake was waiting at the top level of the parking garage with the taxi running as Angela dashed out the back door and threw herself into the cab, where they held on to each other like reunited refugees. Angela broke it off first.

"Augie had a heart attack."

"Oh, God. How bad is it?"

"Don't know. He's in surgery. And the FBI just left, looking for you. It's like we hit a beehive with a baseball bat."

"Well, hang on, it's not over. And it's not just about us."

Above them, a helicopter was sweeping past, whipping its harsh white light around. The cabdriver craned his neck up in curiosity and then looked at Jake in his rearview mirror.

"You got an address for me?" he said, chewing and cracking Nicorette gum in a nervous mechanical rhythm.

"Sixteen hundred Pennsylvania Avenue." Deaver looked at Angela and held her hand hard as the taxi took off.

79

By the time they arrived at the White House with a black helicopter in pursuit and two cars full of DIA operatives closing from behind, there was only one decision to make: to whom should Deaver surrender.

Directing the petrified taxi driver to the Marines manning the guard-post entrance, they decided Jake's best chance was with the Secret Service and Angela insisted on staying with him. Without looking back, they jumped out of the cab and ran as hard as they could past the cement antivehicle barricades and out toward the White House lawn.

"Hey! Stop!" Triggering a deafening alarm, the Marines at the gate shouted after them and hit the high-powered area floods, turning night into day.

"Stop! Stop right there!"

The Defense Intelligence sedans careened up to the post, but were quickly blocked by a Jeep full of heavily armed Marines who didn't seem all that impressed with their identification.

Jake and Angela were too occupied with flat-out running to see any of it. After twenty yards there were Secret Service appearing from all directions and more Marines sprinting toward them as the insectoid chopper hovered overhead, rotating around the axis of the searchlight it was painting them with.

Within sight of the colonnade just off the West Wing offices, Jake wheeled directly toward the Secret Service and grabbed for Angela's arm.

"Now!"

They threw themselves down onto the White House lawn, where they were handcuffed, searched, and then led away laughing like idiots and trying to get their breath as the Treasury agents established their authority.

80

The conference room down the hall from the Oval Office was crowded with National Security Council members: the Joint Chiefs represented by the chairman, the secretaries of state and defense, the heads of NSA, CIA, and DIA, Sandy Sokoff, and Bob Winston, whose resignation still lay on the President's desk. Plus special invitees not usually part of the mix: the Attorney General, the Russian ambassador, and Dr. Paula Winnick.

People talked in small groups, watching muted news coverage on monitors around the room, and the President huddled with Sokoff, letting his chief of staff handle the flood of calls and messages.

"We've had a hundred thousand e-mails," Sandy said, "and about twenty thousand phone messages. I think people are a bit anxious."

"Who's working on a response? I want a draft."

The chief of staff had already put the President's communications A-team to work.

"Excuse me, Mr. President." An aide appeared with a phone. "It's the Cape."

"That'll be about the long count, sir," Sandy said.

At Cape Canaveral the space shuttle that would deliver the last satellite needed to fully deploy Project Orion was being held in launch delay mode on the President's orders. He cupped his hand over the mouthpiece.

"Sandy? I need more time."

Sokoff looked at his Baume & Mercier chrono, new this Christmas.

"We have ninety minutes before we start to lose the window."

The President nodded, spoke briefly into the phone, and hung up.

"All right, can we please begin?"

A White House aide handed him a note and stepped back, waiting for a response. The President used his reading glasses and then looked up.

"Deaver and Browning?"

"The Secret Service has them outside, sir."

"Good." The President looked at Attorney General Sorens.

"We have Deaver."

He watched the AG's face harden. Then the President instructed his aide.

"Send them in."

81

Discussion dissipated and people turned away from the TV news crawl as the two were brought in, flanked by Treasury agents. Jake and Angela looked sober-faced now, and a bit disheveled.

Jake saw Dr. Paula Winnick seated at the table, her disapproval palpable. Bob Winston murmured something about Deaver being persona non grata to the AG, who seemed to be mentally consigning Jake and Angela to a purgatory of civil and criminal hells.

All eyes were on the new arrivals. The President broke the silence.

"Commander Deaver, Ms. Browning? Please sit down. Attorney General Sorens and I have decided you should see what happens when breaking a story means breaking the law. In your case, the Official Secrets Act."

"Mr. President—"

"Commander, take a seat. Ms. Browning? Please."

Chairs were pulled out for them, but Jake remained standing.

"Mr. President, unprovoked acts of military aggression are being carried out without your knowledge or approval . . ."

Bob Winston made a nasty noise in his throat.

"God, haven't you dishonored yourself enough for one night, Commander? Get this goddamned wacko out of here." He hitched his chin at a Treasury agent, who took a step forward. Jake stood his ground.

"This is about Project Orion, Mr. President."

"Wait." The President held a hand up. "What about Orion?"

"It's not a defense shield—it's a strategic space weapons system that is already being tested against nonbelligerent targets. And we can prove it."

"Any strategic capability of Orion technology violates the joint-development pact, as Madam Secretary and your government surely know." The Russian ambassador glowered at Secretary of State Wyman. She shook her head.

"All testing has been done in strict compliance with our agreements, Alexei. And in concord with the Orion Protocol."

"I'm afraid that's not the case," Jake said.

The President studied Deaver for signs of mental imbalance.

"Prove it, Commander."

Jake turned to one of the Secret Service agents, who, with a nod from the President, handed Deaver his confiscated copy of the Orion weapons test.

"Mr. President, this is completely absurd. It's ridiculous." Winston stood and raised his voice, pointing over at Jake. "This man is a known head case, not to mention a fugitive from justice. Deaver belongs in prison or a mental health facility—"

The President cut him off.

"Please sit down, Bob. Sandy? Give Commander Deaver a hand."

Winston sat. The room then broke up into knots of rumbling, hushed conversations as Jake loaded the disk into Sandy Sokoff's laptop.

With the military men conferring and the Russian ambassador joined in close colloquy with Secretary Wyman, Angela had a chance to glance over at Paula Winnick. The Nobel laureate's patrician features seemed to be a study in judgment, her eyes communicating only that irreparable damage had been done and that Angela shared responsibility for the consequences.

Angela sighed and looked at a monitor above Winnick's head, where CNN was rerunning Augie's dramatic on-camera arrest, and streaming updates at the bottom of the screen reported his medical status at Bethesda Naval Hospital. No news yet.

Then Jake had the Orion test cued up and everyone gathered around the little computer screen. But the whole of his attention was focused on one person.

"Mr. President, Colonel Blake has authenticated this video, which was taken a few days ago by a camera on board the space shuttle Atlantis. I believe it shows two things: the first thing is the Orion technology being demonstrated as a strategic weapon."

"Go ahead, Commander, let's see it."

On-screen, the photon laser could be seen shooting up from Earth and then being deflected by an orbiting mirror satellite toward a handful of bright star-like lights thousands of miles downrange.

The capability of the deflected beam was clear: it could be directed not just out into space, but anywhere, in all directions.

"The range in minutes of arc, in other words, how much the orbiting mirror SAT can rotate, demonstrates that incoming missiles are not the only things that Orion can target." Jake pointed at the screen and replayed the sequence. "With this kind of flexibility, Mr. President, any city on the planet can be held hostage."

Moscow's most senior man in Washington had seen enough.

"The Commander is right. This is not a software glitch. The capability of the mirror satellite has been all too clearly engineered. Overengineered. It is plainly flexible by design. We did not agree to this! I am conversant with every paragraph of our agreement. We agreed to build together a defense shield with strict, negotiated limitations. What can we conclude now, except that the American leadership and its partners at TRW have conspired to violate our trust? On behalf of my government and my President, I must formally protest—"

"Alexei Alexandre," the Secretary began, but the President took charge.

"Mr. Ambassador, whatever the technical issues may be, I assure you that Orion will be brought into strict compliance and your concerns will be fully addressed and resolved. In the meantime, I hope that your continuing presence here in the Security Council will be taken as evidence of our good faith."

The ambassador seemed hardly mollified, but Jake seized the chance to intervene.

"Mr. President, there is something else."

"Commander?"

"The targets, sir."

Rerunning the digitized video of the Orion test in slow motion, Jake now indicated what looked like a cluster of stars visible just above the horizon line.

"See these little stars out here? If you watch closely you can see they *react* to the laser pulse."

The President and everyone focused on the star-like lights. In extreme slo-mo replay, they could now see the laser bounce off the mirror satellite and the little lights begin streaking away, disappearing out into space as the pulse was directed toward them.

"These can only be one of two things," Jake said. "Experimental vehicles of Earth origin. Or intelligently guided extraterrestrial spacecraft."

The silence in the room was total.

"I can assure you *we* have no such vehicles," the Russian ambassador said, challenging the Americans to be equally forthcoming. The President was already fairly confident about what the Russians did and didn't have, but saw no reason to embarrass the proud Muscovite by saying so.

"Well, that's a relief." He turned toward the rest of the table. "At least an act of war has not been committed against the Russian Federation. Well, what about it, gentlemen? Assuming Commander Deaver is not perpetrating a hoax, are we shooting at our own targets?"

Bob Winston's furiously impassive expression seemed to be holding both his comments and any further military secrets in abeyance. The NSA and CIA directors shook their heads. The Secretary of Defense cleared his throat.

"To my knowledge, Mr. President, we have no manned or unmanned spacecraft, even in prototype, with that kind of performance capability."

"General Thornton?"

The President turned to the Defense Intelligence chief.

"Not at this point in time, sir."

"General Henderson?" He turned to the chairman of the Joint Chiefs. "Any relevant projects the Secretary might not be aware of?"

The chairman, representing all the military services, looked at Bob Winston for a long moment and then responded with simple candor.

"Even if we had some kind of robotic experimental spacecraft like that, sir, they'd be hugely expensive per unit. We wouldn't waste them as targets in a weapons test. And for the record, sir, I was not informed of any targeting exercises being part of the Project Orion demonstration."

"So, what are we looking at, Bob?"

The attention in the room shifted almost entirely to Winston. He didn't flinch.

"Mr. President, we're looking at extraterrestrial spacecraft and the first successful human attempt at space-based planetary defense."

The note of triumph in Winston's unhesitating voice mixed oddly with the surreal sense of disbelief reverberating around the table.

"These things violate our airspace and the security of our defense facilities at will and have for decades. Everyone knows we've had no real countermeasures. Entire fighter wings are scrambled and maybe we pick them up on our gun cameras, but that's about it. All they have to do is show up at our ICBM sites in Wyoming or the Dakotas and the electronics just shut down, compromising our launch codes and leaving us helpless. It's totally unacceptable. Ask Alexandre about Russian air defenses."

The ambassador shrugged, unsure of his ground.

"I've been told by reliable general officers of similar incidents."

"Which is more than I can say, Alexandre." The President drummed his pencil on the table. Looking stung, General Henderson reacted.

"Mr. President, I supported the deployment of the Orion platform as a national security measure. But incursions by unidentifieds was never prioritized and planetary defense strategies were never discussed among the general staff, much less the initiating of hostilities."

"This is completely insane," Dr. Winnick said flatly. "From beginning to end, Mr. President."

"Absent any real provocation, using the Orion test like this amounts to initiation of hostilities. A willful act of war," State Secretary Wyman added.

"Not to mention extra-constitutional." The Attorney General nodded. "On whose authority was the laser weapon used to target these, um, unidentifieds?"

The President and everyone else in the room waited silently for Winston to respond. He would not go gentle.

"Mr. President, we should be glad for America and glad for the human race, and we should thank God for Project Orion. The President approved a scheduled test of the space weapon prior to deployment. And, yes, it was directed against a target of opportunity. But that's not an act of war! At the very most, it was a shot across the bow: we knew their capabilities, we knew they were observing and could easily evade the laser. But seeing the response to the weapons system is as critical to designing a planetary defense as building the weapon itself. How the hell else do you assess a military threat? What you're seeing here is all of mankind standing on its own two hind feet for the first time in history and saying: 'Thus far and no farther!' And God help us if that's *extra-constitutional*."

Winston aimed a contemptuous glare at the AG.

"No, God help you, Bob," the President said, and then gestured at the Secret Service.

"I am accepting your resignation, Bob. And what I thank God for today is that there are laws in this country against usurpation and conspiracy to usurp the constitutional powers of the President of the United States. Mr. Sorens?"

The Attorney General stood up as two of the President's Secret Service bodyguards each took one of Winston's elbows and drew him to his feet.

"So, I'm the traitor and Deaver and Blake are heroes." Winston sneered, without looking at Jake. "You have no idea what's going on, do you? None of you have any fucking idea. You will not be forgiven for getting this one wrong."

Accompanied by Sorens, he was led out of the room.

Angela took Jake's hand and glanced again at Dr. Winnick. The Nobelist seemed speechless, as if surveying the landscape of a looming but undeniably brave new world.

Aides and staffers took advantage of Winston's exit to hurry in with urgent messages. The President took a call from Cape Canaveral and gave an order over the phone. He looked over at Sokoff for a moment and then raised his voice to quiet the rising volume of conversations blooming in every corner.

"All right, ladies and gentlemen, here are the rules." He looked around, making eye contact. "No one speaks publicly about what is said in this room without written authorization from me. Understood? Mr.

Ambassador, please inform your president we will complete the testing of Project Orion. Tell him I've decided it's better to have it and not need it than vice versa. After that, I intend to unilaterally place a moratorium on all U.S. space weapons development pending multilateral consultations at the highest levels."

The Russian diplomat bowed slightly in acknowledgment, already mentally preparing for that conversation with his boss. The President then turned to Jake.

"Commander Deaver, I hardly know where to begin. One reason I chose Kenny Sorens as my attorney general is that I know he doesn't give two shits about public opinion polls when it comes to enforcing the law. And if that means I'll be obliged to award you the Medal of Freedom in the Leavenworth stockade, then so be it. However, right now there's a lot of frightened people tying up the White House switchboard and I'm going to have to go out there in a few hours and tell them something. Something I hope will make them feel a little better about their government and maybe even have a passing resemblance to the truth. So, if you'll excuse me . . ."

The meeting was over. Everyone got to their feet.

"Mr. President . . . ?" Sokoff pointed to a TV monitor.

Overhead, a screen tuned to CNN was now showing live coverage of the successful NASA launch of space shuttle *Endeavor* from Cape Canaveral in Florida, after a final eighty-nine-minute hold on countdown that the anchor person was saying had raised fears of a postponed mission.

82

Bethesda Naval Hospital/Maryland

In the ICU at Bethesda, Augie was still benefiting from the anesthetic arts that are a paradoxical part of major surgery: saving one's life requires taking a chemical walk to the doors of death. On a certain level it was no biggie. He had watched the surgical team from outside his body, floating above the table in the operating theater and observing the actual bypass procedure. From his vantage point near the ceiling, Augie had felt no pain and very little anxiety about the outcome. He had heard the doctors and nurses chatting and joking. He could have recounted most of their comments and gossip, even the music that was playing as the chief surgeon inserted the stents.

If he lived, he thought, maybe he would tell them he had liked the Miles Davis more than the Archangelo Corelli, just to see their expressions. But at the moment it was all Augie could do merely to wake himself up. His eyes were at half-mast when he could finally focus them enough to recognize Jake and Angela sitting in chairs beside the bed.

"Hey." Jake moved the tubes from the IV tree and took Augie's hand.

"Hey," Augie whispered, his throat dry. "Are we in jail yet?"

Angela laughed and helped him sip some bottled water through a straw.

"Bethesda, podnah," Jake said. "And I think we're gonna be okay."

Augie focused on his former partner. Deaver held his hand and nodded.

"We did good, Dog Man."

Angela flashed Jake a look and leaned down close to Augie, pitching her voice in a conspirator's whisper.

"Listen . . . you know that Mars photo you sent me? And the Moon picture with 'Grotsky' on it? That was you, wasn't it . . . ?"

Augie settled back into his pillow with an enigmatic smile.

"That's classified information, darlin'."

He laughed with them at his own joke, but sounded tired and hoarse. Angela helped Augie drink some more water and eyed Jake: they'd better go.

Deaver then took a fax with a White House header out of his pocket.

"One more thing and then we'll let you get some sleep."

He held the faxed document so Augie could see it up close: it was a petition.

"This was sent to the White House, Dog Man. It's everybody, all the guys from Mercury to Apollo, supporting our statements. Gordo Cooper, Ed Mitchell, Buzz Aldrin, even Neil and John . . ."

Augie grasped what it was and what it meant. He gave a small thumbs-up without lifting his arm, but the drugs were kicking in and he was fading. In a few seconds he was fast asleep.

A Navy nurse came in to signal that time was up. Angela kissed Augie on the cheek and covered his cold, bare hands with the blanket. Jake laid the astronaut petition on the night table and they both slipped out the door.

▼

"Commander Deaver? I'm Augie's sister, Emily."

"I remember."

Jake recognized the uniformed, middle-aged nurse-practitioner as she got up from a chair in the corridor. It had been over ten years since they'd seen each other, but he was still surprised at her gray hair.

They hugged for a moment.

"Emily, this is Angela."

The two women shook hands. Angela indicated the Bethesda facility.

"Are you working here?"

Emily laughed lightly, recalling her hectic twenties as a Navy nurse.

"No, no. I'm in private practice. Was he still out?"

Deaver shook his head.

"He opened his eyes and stayed with us for four or five minutes and then fell asleep. They said it went well, but didn't tell us much more."

Emily made a face that apologized for the harried staff.

"Well, he's had a mild arrhythmia for some time and kept putting off a cardio exam, like a stubborn mule. So, finally there was a ventricle fib. I understand the crash crew had their hands full getting him into surgery."

"What's the prognosis?"

"Too early, still. But this is a high-percentage procedure these days. He's got a couple of stents in there, keeping things open, but there was muscle damage and damage to the surrounding tissue. I like the chief surgeon here, Dr. Hagar—he's excellent, he's the one I wanted Augie to see, but we're not out of the woods . . . I authorized an implant, a defibrillator as they did with Cheney, so if we can get him through these next few days . . ."

But Angela had stopped listening: two flat-faced men with Treasury Department written all over them were stepping out of the hospital elevator.

"Jake?" She indicated the agents with her eyes.

Deaver turned and felt weary to the soles of his feet.

"What now?"

83

Situation Room/the White House

It was nicer going in the front door at 1600 Pennsylvania Avenue, without the handcuffs and under their own power, but things were moving too fast to allow any musing about their shift in status.

In the crowded, buzzing, high-tech Situation Room, Jake and Angela sat elbow to elbow with Dr. Paula Winnick, drinking coffee served by a uniformed Marine and observing the proceedings.

A wall-sized high-definition screen dominated the room, showing the real-time positions of *Space Station Alpha*, the newly launched space shuttle *Endeavor*, and all the Project Orion mirror satellites in orbit above the Earth.

Winnick glanced at Deaver and saw that he was keeping his feelings close to his vest, but she had a question for him.

"So, do you assume there is a connection between what's on the Moon and the artifacts on Mars?"

"And what's here on Earth." Jake nodded.

"Meaning *us*," Angela said, staring straight ahead and sipping some coffee from the presidential china.

Winnick took that in, and a loudspeaker boomed to life as the final Orion mirror SAT was positioned in orbit by *Endeavor* astronauts.

"This is Houston Control . . . Project Orion, Primary Activation Alpha. We are good and holding the count at T-minus-ten to activation."

Monitors around the room showed the giant photon cannon at the

Little Cosmodrome in the Ukraine, plus various camera views from the Alpha space station and the *Endeavor,* to which the astronauts were slowly returning.

Winnick sat, enthralled by the spectacle. Jake and Angela held hands and watched: this was it. Like it or not.

The President had asked their opinions about activating Project Orion as a planetary defense. Each one, including Deaver, had said his or her piece and then had been invited to stay and witness the testing of the fully deployed system.

Both Dr. Winnick and Angela had thought Jake's argument the most passionate, if not the most persuasive.

"Mr. President, I believe these beings have been here and had contact with humans for thousands, maybe tens of thousands of years. We may even be genetically related. Whatever the truth is, I absolutely do not believe we are being militarily threatened. And if we put up the Shield, I think we send exactly the wrong signal. Not just to 'them,' but to ourselves: we are demonstrating our fear, we are telling the world to be afraid. And at the very least we could actually be helping to trigger the kind of negative mass reaction Dr. Winnick and others have been most concerned about."

▼

But the bedrock military argument had prevailed. Across the room now, they could see the President chatting with Sandy Sokoff, Generals Thornton and Henderson, the defense secretary, and the intelligence chiefs. Off to one side, the hard-pressed Secretary of State, Beth Wyman, was whispering to the Russian ambassador, whose expression phased from stoic to skeptical and back again.

A DOD/Space Command controller sat at a console wearing a headset and coordinating communications between NASA and Pentagon satellite teams.

"Houston. This is Sit Room. We show all stations standing by, over."

"*Copy that. Endeavor and Space Station Alpha standing by . . .*"

"Cosmodrome, this is Sit Room. Report your current status."

"*Cosmodrome. We are good. Standing by for primary activation . . .*"

"Mr. President?" The controller indicated they were ready for him to give the command to initiate activation of the system. "On your mark, sir."

The Commander in Chief took his place at the console and was just being fitted with a headset mike when the wall screen lit up and a cacophony of excited voices began erupting around the room. Looking up, the President understood why: beams of bright light could already be seen connecting each of the orbiting Orion mirrors.

"What's happening?"

"I'm not sure, sir." The Space Command controller stabbed at a panel of touch pads, and tech engineers at similar stations scrambled to determine the problem.

"Uh, Houston Control, this is Sit Room, we are showing activation or a false activation, can you confirm, over?"

The loudspeaker blared the response from the Johnson Space Center.

"Roger that. We're seeing it, Sit Room, but we do not show the photon laser being lit. Repeat, negatory on laser activation. We show T-minus-ten-and-hold. You're not running a simulation, are you? Over."

"Copy that. Negative on the simulation. Over."

"Cosmodrome? This is Houston. We're indicating a false positive on activate. Can you confirm? Over . . ."

"Roger, Houston. We are still at standby. Repeat, holding at standby."

The Space Command controller hit another touch key.

"Alpha Station? This is Sit Room. We may have a malfunction. Do you have direct visual contact? Over . . ."

"Uh, copy that, Sit Room." The station commander's voice was slightly delayed, but loud and clear. *"I'm looking out the window, we have direct visual. The Shield appears to be activated,"*

▼

"What's going on?" the President asked as Generals Thornton and Henderson joined him at the console.

"We don't know yet, sir." Thornton pointed to the screen. "What's the Alpha commander's name?"

"Colonel Lawton, sir," the controller said. The President got on the mic.

"Colonel Lawton? This is the President. What we see down here onscreen is what looks like a laser beam connecting all our satellites. But the photon cannon in the Ukraine has not been activated. What exactly are you seeing up there?"

"Mr. President, I have direct visual and the mirror SATs appear to be connected by laser transmission, but the source of the laser is not apparent, at least from our position, perhaps the shuttle commander—wait. They're moving . . ."

▼

All those sitting rose to their feet as the high-def plasma monitor showed the Orion mirror satellites, each still connected by a brilliant beam of light, slowly repositioning themselves like dancers in a zero-g ballet.

"Jesus . . . what's happening?"

"Good God . . ."

"We're not making this happen, are we?" the President asked, staring in awe at the display. The generals could only shake their heads.

"No, sir."

"Definitely not, Mr. President."

"*They're* making it happen . . ." Jake said as the mirrors were gradually arranged in a series of primary geometric shapes: a pyramid, a cube, and then a sphere, with laser light playing connect-the-dots.

"Can't we stop it?" The President looked around as a wave of fear washed through the room and the general officers gave a series of commands in a frantic effort to override the commandeering of the satellites. Nothing worked.

"The satellites are not responding, sir."

"Mr. President," Jake said, "this is not aggression, this is communication."

The Situation Room filled with awed, anxious exclamations as each shape resolved itself, almost like picnickers at a Fourth of July fireworks show. Nobody could imagine the technology needed to produce such a demonstration. It was both impressive and frightening, making a mockery of the martial intent of the weapons system. Whoever was doing it was very advanced, indeed.

"My God, look . . ." Angela pointed as the satellites finally re-formed into something new and more abstract: a constellation. Deaver recognized it, too.

"The Archer: it's the constellation Orion."

Fear gave way to wonder as the President saw that Jake was correct.

"Orion. That's exactly what it is." The President gave his generals a look.

Then one by one the mirror satellites returned to their former positions in orbit and the laser light connecting them winked out. The show was over.

"Uh, Mr. President?" The controller's voice broke the silence with as much matter-of-fact professionalism as he could summon. But his hands were trembling.

"Yes."

"The mirror SATs have returned to initial geosynchronous positions, sir, and all systems appear back on-line."

All eyes turned to the President. Everyone understood what had just occurred: a formal trans-species communication at the highest level, the fact of it being even more profound than the almost playful technological mastery that had been demonstrated in the process.

"Mr. President, do you wish to resume activation of the Shield?"

The President turned to Jake, Angela and Dr. Winnick, then glanced around at his cabinet, his generals, the Russian ambassador, and finally Sandy Sokoff.

"Only if we can figure out what the hell we want to say."

84

February 16/Miriam's Condo

Miriam Kresky, wearing nothing but a man's white dress shirt and a yellow silk bow tie, found herself unconsciously humming "Hail to the Chief" as she ground the beans for coffee. There were sixty-eight new messages on her voice mail, but she wasn't ready to power through them quite yet.

Once the dark-roast Italian blend was dripping into a carafe, she surfed the network morning shows and cable news programs on the kitchen TV, but there was only one topic of discussion: Commander Deaver and Colonel Blake, the historic *Science Horizon* revelations, and the worldwide, overnight political, social, scientific, and religious fallout.

And, of course, there was avid speculation about what the President would say at the press conference scheduled in the Rose Garden at 10:00 A.M., Eastern.

Miriam zoomed through the channels.

Hardball with Chris Matthews on MSNBC had a panel discussion called "Heroes or Traitors" and guests Oliver North, John McCain, and a Justice Department lawyer debated the ethics issues in relation to Deaver and Blake.

Larry King Live had Catholic, Muslim, Jewish, and Buddhist leaders discussing the religious implications of what the astronauts had revealed.

Geraldo Rivera was taking instant polls and man-in-the-street interviews, getting public reaction to the news of an "Alien City on the

Moon" and whether this might validate the decades of UFO sightings around the world that the government had long denied and dismissed.

BBC World News showed clips of international leaders buttonholed for their reaction as they emerged from top-level meetings and took questions at their own hastily called press conferences.

Good Morning America featured a Vatican Statement of Reassurance from the Pope with guest Monsignor Michael Joseph Kilgerry. The brief missive declared that God had created all life throughout the universe and that the glory of His Creation was not limited to life on this world alone. The Jesuit monsignor noted that the papal statement had been translated into twenty-nine languages and posted on every Church Web site on every continent around the globe.

On a special edition of *World News Tonight*, Peter Jennings was interviewing several astronauts who had seen UFOs on their missions into space or during high-altitude aircraft testing and were calling for open, public congressional hearings on ET-related government activities.

And on PBS, Daniel Schorr editorialized in support of *Science Horizon* and then moderated a panel of journalists debating the free-press and free-speech issues raised by the government shutdown of a PBS program.

▼

"God bless you, Mr. Schorr," Miriam said, filling two bowl-sized ceramic coffee cups that she had bought *en Provence* and carrying them back to her bedroom on a wicker tray.

A certain recently bailed-out NASA scientist was still sprawled across the queen-sized bed next to an unplugged phone, two stale champagne glasses, and a dead soldier named Moët.

"Hey . . . wake up and join the party." Miriam leaned close to his ear, pitching her voice in the low-and-sultry range.

"Mmmff," Eklund said, without opening his eyes.

She set a steamy bowl of coffee on the nightstand nearest his nose and turned on the bedroom TV.

"Come on, you're gonna want to see this. Emmy is lap-dancing with Mr. Pulitzer, that slut!"

85

The Rose Garden/the White House

The normally sticklike rosebushes had been tricked into leafing out by anomalously springlike weather, but few were noticing the greenery. Pushing through the print- and broadcast-media journalists assembled in the White House Rose Garden (a press corps swollen to accommodate over a hundred credentials) Jake and Angela were much more the focus of attention and celebration as they pressed toward reserved chairs near the podium. The hubbub around them was hyped up almost to the point of hysteria.

Like a sudden course shift by a school of fish, that media attention turned to Sandy Sokoff and Representative Phillip Lowe as they emerged from the Oval Office, and took places on a raised platform with an assemblage of cabinet heads, service-branch chiefs, astronauts, and National Science Academy guiding lights, including Nobelist Dr. Paula Winnick.

▼

Things quieted down only when the White House press secretary appeared, stepping to the lectern decorated with the presidential seal and adjusting the microphone. Looking gamely out and around, he then willed everyone to a respectful silence, holding the event hostage until he got it.

"The President will make a short statement and then take your questions. Ladies and gentlemen, the President of the United States."

Reaching their assigned seats as the French doors opened off the

West Wing, Jake and Angela stayed standing with the other journalists and dignitaries now rising to their feet as the first notes of "Hail to the Chief," played with nineteenth-century vigor by the Marine Corps Band.

And then he was there, striding up to the presidential podium, the smiling leader of the greatest nation on Earth, seeming to enjoy the inexplicably warm February sun and the wash of camera flashes before hurtling into his speech without preamble.

Republican and Democratic presidents alike have wrestled over the years with the duty and responsibility of protecting this nation, oftentimes at the expense of a more perfect candor with the American people. During the Second World War, Franklin Delano Roosevelt and Harry S. Truman both bore the terrible burden of their knowledge of the top-secret Manhattan Project, developing the first atomic weapons, something that could not have been shared openly with the public during wartime, for obvious reasons. Governments must be able to keep defense-related secrets. It is a legitimate and crucial element of a nation's overall security.

A few miles away, the President's speech was being heard on a portable boom box in a morguelike medical lab at the CIA's compound in Langley, Virginia. On a stainless steel table in the chilly room, a cadaver identified only as Dunsinane Man was having nail samples taken from its six-fingered hands.

During the long Cold War period, every administration faced a similarly difficult national security problem as a result of the Space Race with the Soviets and discoveries made by both Russian and American satellites and confirmed by Apollo astronauts on the Moon . . .

The CIA nurse/technician placed genetic samples into tiny glass vials for testing and sealed each one with a label marked DUNSINANE.

On another metal table a few feet away, another body waited its turn. This one, however, was smaller, less than four feet in length, and encased in a Lucite chamber in which a precisely controlled environment was maintained. Through the thick plastic casing she could just make out the texture of its tough, gray skin and hairless limbs and torso: so different from the robust quasisimian quality of Dunsinane Man, but the finger-count of six digits on its hands was the same.

As most of you now know, what was discovered on the Moon were arti-facts left behind or abandoned by another intelligent species, a space-faring species like ourselves, who visited the Moon thousands of years ago. How-ever, who they were, where they were from, why they left, and where they went—these are questions that remain a mystery.

At an enclave in Maryland horse country, every nuance of the President's speech was being weighed and dissected by Admiral James T. Ingraham and a den full of key intelligence officers, Pentagon officials, and others from the private sector.

This has been one of our nation's most closely guarded secrets for many reasons: one reason, frankly, was our pursuit of strategic advantage against America's Communist adversaries during the Cold War decades. Our lead-ers wanted, understandably, to turn any technological discoveries made by the space program into a defense advantage for the free world. I personally believe it was a well-intentioned policy, a justified response during a diffi-cult era in our history, but it was a policy that evolved beyond its useful-ness. Unfortunately, the almost obsessive secrecy that come to surround it ultimately caused the government, our democratically elected government, to break faith with the governed: with us, the American people.

"We can work with this."

Admiral Ingraham's commanding voice seemed to resonate with confidence. But exactly how reassured his grim-faced guests were was hard to determine at the moment.

From somewhere in the direction of the guarded front entrance to the compound, Ingraham's two well-trained German shepherds began to bark and then went silent in a way that made the Admiral turn away from the President's words.

Listening intently, he heard shouting from the direction of the heavy, electronic back gate. And then hard-to-identify scuffling sounds.

"Christ," he said, when he was certain what it meant.

Then the den was awash in armed FBI and ATF agents taking both Admiral Ingraham and his outraged guests into custody and reading them their rights.

▼

Into the homestretch of what would thereafter be referred to as "The Rose Garden Speech," the President looked out at the assemblage of leaders, scientists, astronauts, and journalists and then turn his gaze straight into the TV cameras.

We share a different world now, a world of uncertainties beyond even those of the Cold War. In the face of the challenge of international terrorism, the great Russian and Chinese peoples are counted among America's friends and allies. Many of you may wonder why, then, the profound truth that we are not the only intelligent life-form in God's universe continued to be kept a secret by your government. The simple and most basic answer is: Your leaders were afraid. They were afraid that you would be afraid. But I believe that the American people prefer to know the truth and deserve to be told the truth.

Stopped by cheers and standing applause from everyone, including the press, the President waited for the reaction to die down.

Eyeing Jake's more reserved reaction, Angela pulled him close.

"What?"

"Nothing about Orion," he said. "Nothing about hearings."

Angela squeezed his arm, refusing to be unhappy.

"It's a beginning. A huge, important beginning."

▼

At Bethesda, Augie's sister Emily opened the curtains to the sunlight and watched with a professional eye as the Navy nurses deftly changed the linens underneath the former astronaut's unconscious body.

The veteran ICU nurses were proud to be attending the Space Hero as they changed the bags on his IV, took a blood pressure reading, and listened along with Emily to the President's speech on the hospital-room TV.

Today, this administration intends to forge a new path of peaceful, international manned exploration of space and a new era of trust between the American people and their government. But before we talk about the future, I'd like to commend Commander Jake Deaver and Colonel Augie Blake for their public statements and for their moral integrity. In particular, I want to send our heartfelt best wishes for a speedy recovery to Colonel Blake, who underwent heart surgery at Bethesda Naval Hospital last night . . .

▼

When the loud alarm on the heart monitor went off, Emily jumped up to help the attending nurses in their heroic effort to revive her brother. Despite their ministrations and those of the attending physician, Augie had suffered a severe stroke, and twenty-three minutes and eighteen seconds later, he was officially pronounced.

86

In high Earth orbit, the Orion array of mirror satellites had been computer-tweaked into perfect alignment.

With a sharp stab of white igniting it from below, the Shield was silently illuminated in the awful, perfect deafness of space, encircling the world for sixty seconds in a Fulleresque soccer ball pattern of laser light.

And then, by executive order of the President of United States, the test activation of the planetary defense system was over.

87

February 21/West Texas

It wasn't bitter cold, but the temperature was low enough that they could see their breath. They had parked the rented Subaru Outback on a dark rural road miles from the highway, but big-rig headlights could still be seen navigating toward the diffuse glow in the distance that was Houston.

Clamping two mesh cables on the terminals of the SUV's battery, Jake followed the shielded lines with his little halogen flashlight to a black electronic device that had been set up between two camp chairs. He checked the settings.

In one of the chairs, wrapped in a thick wool Navajo blanket, Angela sat holding a cigar box and looking up at the stars.

"You know what?"

"What?" Jake wiped his hands on his jeans.

"Sometimes I feel this odd little rush of panic. You know? And then these waves of longing for I don't know what that just haven't made any sense to me. But I think I just figured it out . . ."

"Is it about innocence?" Jake held the flashlight so he could see her face.

"Or maybe just simpler times." Angela shielded her eyes with the back of her hand. "Or the illusion of simpler times. Y'know what I mean?"

"Yes, I do."

Jake kissed her impulsively, then aimed the flash back down on the black box device. He could feel her smile without having to see it.

"You ready?"

"Good to go."

Deaver then tripped a toggle switch, triggering six pencil-thin red lasers that shot up into the desert sky, forming a three-sided pyramid.

Out beyond the laser geometry, the belt stars of Orion and the winking yellow light of Mars seemed to swing above them in the small wind that had come up, a breeze carrying the smell of sage and mesquite.

A gibbous moon waxed huge on the horizon.

Augie had been cremated and buried with ceremonial honors at the Arlington National Cemetery. But when Jake asked as a favor that his sister allow part of his ashes to be brought back to West Texas, she had agreed that Augie would probably like that.

Angela looked at the moon, imagining the young Colonel Blake in his spacesuit at Sinus Medii with Earthrise reflected in his gold visor. She then opened the cigar box she'd been holding.

Inside, a small amount of ashes kept company with a few tiny pieces of bone that had refused to burn. Then, standing together, she and Jake each took a handful and looked out through the ruby laser projection now etching new geometries in the night air: pentagons, tetrahedrons, rhombuses.

"Well, hell." Angela tossed the ashes into the lines of light and Deaver followed suit, transforming the gritty remains into the whirling carbon glitter of star dust, which is the beginning of all things.

"And good luck, Mr. Grotsky . . ."

"Wherever you are."

A NOTE FROM THE AUTHOR

Although this book is a work of fiction, readers often ask how much of the story is true. And basically the answer is: "as much as possible" and "more than could be included." Here are a few of the more intriguing facts I uncovered in my research.

1. *The Brookings Report.* Commissioned by President Eisenhower in 1958, it was submitted to Congress a year later. The purpose of this blue-ribbon study was to identify the potential consequences and dangers to mankind inherent in NASA's proposed exploration of our solar system. In regard to the issue of revealing evidence of extraterrestrial intelligence to the public, the report cited a potential for unprecedented social, religious, and political chaos. Authored by Margaret Meade, among others, the report recommended that the government consider not disclosing such information.

2. *The Authority of the Department of Defense.* All exploration of space is officially considered by the U.S. government to be under the jurisdiction of the Department of Defense, regardless of the NASA charter establishing the Space Agency as civilian. The Defense Department is also the primary client of the Space Shuttle program.

3. *The ET Exposure Act.* In 1968, the year before the Apollo program succeeded in putting a man on the Moon, Congress passed a little-known piece of legislation called the Extraterrestrial Exposure Act. It gave the head of NASA the right to indefinitely "quarantine" anyone exposed to extraterrestrial life or alien artifacts.

Only the President could overrule the NASA administrator's judgment, and anyone quarantined had no right to a judicial hearing and no recourse beyond appealing to the President of the United States.

4. *The USA and the Moon, 1969–1975.* After six manned trips to the Moon, the Americans came home and never set foot there again.

5. *The Face on Mars.* It was first photographed by the Viking mission in 1976. The Face and "pyramidlike objects" found in the Cydonia region on Mars are aligned with planetary primes similar to the alignments of the oldest Pyramids found on the Giza Plateau in Egypt and at Teotihuacan in Mexico. Sir Arthur C. Clarke has called attention to striking symmetries in many monumental objects on the Martian surface, which suggest "manmade" rather than natural creation. NASA's official position remains that these are all natural formations, that the symmetries suggesting the work of intelligent beings are coincidental, and that the Face and the "pyramids" are tricks of light and shadow.

6. *President Carter and the Vatican.* During his 1976 presidential campaign, Jimmy Carter revealed to a reporter from *Rolling Stone* magazine that he had twice seen UFOs when he was in the Navy and vowed to find out what the government knew about them if he was elected to office. Once President, Carter asked his inherited CIA chief, George Herbert Walker Bush, for the intelligence files on UFO phenomena. Bush declined, referring the new President to an obscure Select House subcommittee. A report was compiled and given to Carter by a woman working for that committee who had also attempted to obtain documents from the Vatican Archives in Rome concerning UFOs and extraterrestrial encounters going back hundreds of years. The Vatican declined to make this information available.

A senior counsel to the Jesuits who had been the White House's unsuccessful go-between with the Vatican has since publicly acknowledged his effort and the subject matter.

7. *Space Weapons Technology.* During the 1980s, President Ronald Reagan publicly offered Mikhail Gorbachev the U.S. research and technology for the Space Defense Initiative, a.k.a. Star Wars, as a gift to the Russian people, and made public remarks about the future need for planetary defense. The Soviets declined the offer, proceeding to develop a photon laser cannon capable of striking targets in space. This work continues under various names in both countries, along with the development of so-called scalar weapons and other microwave beams adapted for military purposes and capable of intercepting targets at high altitude.

In a speech at the University of Georgia in 1997, Secretary of Defense William Cohen expressed concerns about terrorists having access to newly developed electromagnetic scalar beams capable of weaponizing weather and causing earthquakes, volcanic eruptions, and even hurricanes.

In 1998, the Russians offered to put out a raging forest fire in Indonesia by creating an artificial hurricane, which they announced could be done from space. The Indonesians declined. Though this was reported in such major newspapers as the *Los Angeles Times,* there was no comment offered by the U.S. government.

8. *The Great Pyramid at Giza.* The Great Pyramid is aligned with Sirius, the brightest star in the Southern Hemisphere, and with the constellation Orion in a way that makes it a "planetary clock," capable of measuring the precessional movement of the Earth. The three oldest Pyramids at Giza are geometrically aligned on the ground in the same precise relationship to one another as the three stars that make up the "belt" in the constellation we call Orion. These pyramids are no more than five thousand years old, but their orientation and alignments appear to reference an earlier time: 10,500 B.C.E.

9. *The Sphinx.* In 1995, American and British university scientists studied water damage on the monument that had been previously assumed to be caused by wind and sand. Their confirmation that the damage had been caused by water places the building of the

Sphinx at approximately 10,500 B.C.E., thousands of years before the existence of any known civilization considered capable of such a feat. This break with the theories of classical Egyptology has created an ongoing controversy. The Sphinx is oriented to the rising of the planet Mars and the word *Cairo does* mean "Mars" in ancient Sumerian.

10. *The Billion-Dollar* Mars Observer *Mission, 1991–1993.* From the moment it was launched, the *Mars Observer* mission was dogged by controversy over the issue of reimaging the Cydonia region. It carried cameras with a fifty-times greater resolution capability than those of the Viking mission in 1976 and would easily have been able to settle the question of whether the Face or the so-called pyramids in the Cydonia region were natural rock formations or products of intelligence. NASA promised that the pictures would be taken. The entire imaging contract, however, had been taken away from the famous Jet Propulsion Lab, in Pasadena, and subbed out for the first time in NASA history to a private contractor. NASA was then no longer responsible for imaging priorities, no longer committed to any live broadcast of images from Mars, and the private contractor could delay the release of any photographs for up to eighteen months.

    Mars Observer performed flawlessly until forty-eight hours before it arrived at Mars, at which point it inexplicably "went dark" before any images could be transmitted back to Earth. It was officially declared lost. For years, NASA offered no explanation, and only recently confirmed rumors that the crucial radio link to the satellite had, against all established protocols, been accidentally turned off.

11. *The Red Planet.* The *Mars Global Surveyor* and *Mars Odyssey* satellites have confirmed that Mars did at one time have abundant water, a dense atmosphere, and a much warmer overall temperature, similar to Earth's. According to NASA, the fossils present in the Martian asteroid ALH 84000 strongly suggest microbial life on

the planet appeared 3.5 billion years ago: 1 billion years before life is known to have appeared on Earth. This presents a potential time frame for the development of life, possibly intelligent life, on Mars that would give it a considerable head start on the Earth.

12. *The Last Ice Age.* Civilization is something that occurs between periods of glaciation. And the most recent such period ended abruptly about 12,500 years ago. The end of the Ice Age was marked by vast flooding, earthquakes, volcanic eruptions, and extreme temperature swings, which had devastating effects on life all over the planet, including mankind.

Ice-core samplings in Greenland and the Antarctic taken in the 1990s confirm rapid, catastrophic climate changes during this pre-historic time, resulting in the extinction of thousands of plant and animal species.

The impact of two huge Leonid meteors capable of causing crustal dislocation and continental shifting are among the prime suspects in the triggering of this extinction event. The Leonid group is a collection of asteroids and cometary bodies that follow a long but calculable Earth-crossing orbit around the sun. Egyptian astronomers were keenly aware of the danger this cyclical phenomenon posed to mankind over periods of thousands of years and followed it closely.

After just such an event, God-like beings called the Old Ones are said to have helped the indigenous people to rebuild, and gave them new arts, science, and architectural knowledge. And then they either "flew away across the water" or were chased away or killed. The same origin legend in different forms also appears in the oral traditions of the pyramid-building cultures of pre-Mayan Mexico, Central America, and Egypt.

13. *The USA and the Moon, 1995.* In 1995, the Defense Department sent an unmanned satellite to photograph the Moon with the latest imaging technology. This lunar mapping mission, dubbed Clementine, was the first known all-military planetary surveillance mission. Though aided by scientists borrowed from NASA, the

military acted outside the NASA charter, and the American public has no inherent rights to access the Clementine images.

Also in 1995, despite military security restrictions, a composite of leaked images from Clementine were posted on the World Wide Web. Within twenty-four hours these classified photos disappeared. Selected photographs have been subsequently published, but research-quality copies of all collected Clementine imaging are not available to the public.